THE
DEAD END
BOYS

THE
DEAD END
BOYS

S. T. LAMB

iUniverse LLC
Bloomington

The Dead End Boys

iUniverse books may be ordered through booksellers or by contacting:

iUniverse LLC
1663 Liberty Drive
Bloomington, IN 47403
www.iuniverse.com
1-800-Authors (1-800-288-4677)

ISBN: 978-1-4759-9411-7 (sc)
ISBN: 978-1-4759-9412-4 (e)

Printed in the United States of America

iUniverse rev. date: 10/26/2013

1

HOBOKEN

It's one of those winters that seems like it's never going to end, and this day is no different. A Canadian Clipper is whisking through the area, providing a cold, brisk wind and some light, floating flurries. The wind travels down one of the main avenues, Washington Street, which leads through this small city, past its shops and cafes, and to the Port Authority Path Train that joins into the main arteries of transportation, underground and above.

This February is extremely cold. Chunks of ice are visible in the river and along the shoreline. The Newark *Star-Ledger* dated February 1, 2001, sits on the sidewalk of a grocery store. The front page lifts with each gust of wind and reads, "Another Cold Snap!" It's one of the chilliest winters in recent history and has taken its toll on the residents all across the tristate area.

Thickly clothed bodies emerge from the underground Path station. Ben Jones is walking against the cold breeze that's unavoidable; at least that is what the skin on his reddened face is telling him. The soles of his work boots try to find stability as he crosses another cobblestone-layered side street. The light from the traffic signal displays "Walk." The seconds on the display count down until that status changes. Ben's navy peacoat and faded work jeans provide him some protection, but the damp cold passes through his clothes nonetheless. The buildings on the sides of Washington Avenue act as a wind tunnel, only intensifying the cold wind on this gunpowder sky day. As he steps on the sidewalk, his blue eyes connect with a pretty brunette. He sends a half smile as she returns the favor. He continues to walk, only now with an extra swagger in his step, as a horn from the traffic blows. His just-above-six-foot frame suddenly feels taller. His athletic shape feels a little lighter, even though it's not exactly the first time he's shared a smile with a complete stranger.

Ben's almost a full year older than his friends, twenty-four years old to be exact. He was a casualty of missing the cutoff date when entering grade school. His friends are college educated and work in and around the city. Ben never cared too much for the so-called higher learning, but he did give community college a shot. He lasted two semesters before dropping out.

Ben had a job at a deli in South Jersey when one of the customers, a truck driver from a company in Hoboken, told Ben he was leaving his position. Ben decided to get his class commercial driver's license and applied for the position. He landed the job a few months ago. So life has just become a little easier. He now drives a truck for his employer, delivering and selling meats to delicatessens in the North Jersey area—some that are thriving businesses, some that would make the health departments cringe. Ben has finished his rounds and is heading to his apartment.

Ben's from South Jersey, a town called Absecon right off of the Garden State Parkway just outside Atlantic City. He moved to Hoboken a year ago to be close to his three friends who he grew up with. Hoboken, at least to them, is a different world. Although it's less than sixty geographical miles away from their hometown, it feels like another country. It's another world, moving at a different pace.

Hoboken is the birthplace of Frank Sinatra and its country's national pastime, baseball. It's a place where the after-college, twenty-something professionals settle down. They work in New York City and come to Hoboken at night.

Anyone unfamiliar with the area might believe it be just another borough of the Big Apple. Cobblestone streets line up between the early nineteenth-century buildings. Steps lead residents out of their apartments into the cement city that has forty-eight streets laid out in a grid. Numbered streets run east to west, and most of the north-south streets are named for US presidents. Fresh produce flows onto the sidewalks outside of the grocery stores. Hoboken's residents and New Yorkers are similar types of people, speaking with similar accents and rooting for the same sports teams. The exception being the vast skyscrapers lining the streets, giving you neck pain from looking up, and, of course, the notoriety.

The residents here are of the bridge and tunnel crowd. Those who pay rent here truly know the difference between Hoboken and the more famous city next door. For a cheap, dollar-and-change ticket on the Path Train that travels underneath the Hudson, they're in the Big Apple in a matter of minutes.

Ben moved here knowing that, if things didn't work out, he could always move back. He and his friends feared being stuck in a small town the rest of their lives, having dead-end jobs, ending up like other kids they went to school with living out the remainder of their lives in a place where everyone, like Ben's mother, who works at the casinos in Atlantic City as a blackjack dealer, is always trying to squeeze a nickel out of a dime.

Ben doesn't talk about his father at all anymore. He doesn't even consider the man to be his father. He's just a man who left his mother a single woman years ago. This is the reason he's stated numerous times that he has no urge to ever get married.

Ben's always been hard on himself, probably due the expectations placed on him because of his athletic prowess in his younger days. During his grammar and high school years, people within his community put him on a pedestal. He thought at the time their adoration was normal. Now when he looks back, he sees the naïveté in himself as the kid who thought the days when everything came easily would last forever. Eventually, the admiration he'd basked in without even realizing it would come to an end. Near the tail end of his senior season, with college scouts looking on, he tore his anterior crucible ligament. The injury had ended his chances for a scholarship. Ben knew once sports was over, work was going to be something he never could love. He was looking forward to a life of meaningless employment to make ends meet, just like his mother. Nothing would ever beat out sports, or his first crush in grade school, Janet.

He would be reminded at certain times, by kids he'd run into, just how great they thought he was when they were growing up. He'd run into younger kids who'd gone to a different high school, drinking at some random place—maybe in the woods or a rundown hotel—and hear the same thing: "I thought you'd be playing football somewhere now, like Rutgers or something. What are you doing now?" He'd have to explain that it was all over and that he could be found working around town and feel the disappointment of their own hopes and dreams for him in their tone. He doesn't miss that now that he's in Hoboken.

As he walks up Washington, smoke from the grills of the restaurants permeate the air. He notices some people heading to happy hour in a town that was once known for having the most bars per square mile in the world. He stops at a door numbered 304 and turns the key. The front window of a sushi bar is right next door. He feels the eyes of the customers on him as he quickly steps into the foyer. The apartment Ben shares with his friend Rob is on the third floor. He treks his way up the stairs as his thighs start to burn. The extra steps up to his residence are worth it, and the higher rent shows it.

The upper unit has perks, like higher ceilings, skylights, and a better view of the street below, over the other two apartments in the building. A metal ladder that opens to the roof allows its tenants to climb into another existence. They can see the Manhattan skyline staring down at the river, Lady Liberty at Ellis Island holding her torch. It's their outdoor escape when those rough weather months have most people living inside. During the warmer months, the water-swept breeze can really cool things off.

Last summer, Ben would spend time up there when he and his friends weren't down at the shore having a cold beer and laying out while listening to the Yankee games or catching the Macy's fireworks show exploding over the Hudson on the Fourth of July.

Lunging up the last set of stairs and through his apartment door, Ben throws his bag on the floor and kicks off his boots. He heads to the back of the apartment to the kitchen, grabs a cold beer from the refrigerator, pops it open, and begins to gulp it down. It's been a long week, and after all, today is Friday.

He sits down to turn on the TV, opens his roommate's laptop, and rubs his hands through his short-cropped, dirty blond hair. Their couch, which Rob had during his college years, has seen better days. A flimsy plastic coffee table displays two empty beer bottles, a recently ashed roach in the ashtray, and a *Playboy* magazine. He logs into his e-mail and checks his messages. He sees that an acquaintance of he and Rob has sent both of them pictures from a recent trip he took to Miami, Florida. The title of Josh's e-mail states, "Greetings from Miami."

Ben hasn't been on vacation in years. As a matter of fact, he only went once in his life. His mother won a trip from a casino—a door prize from Harrah's—when a friend convinced her she needed a night out. Ben has never forgotten the trip that he took with his mom and younger sister to South Carolina.

He checks flight and hotel prices on a discount website and realizes that a trip to Miami is something he could probably afford right now. He starts to think about a getaway, the parties, the beach, and the girls.

Rob opens the door and enters the apartment.

"Josh e-mailed us some pictures from his Miami trip. You've been to Florida. How was it?" Ben asks him.

"Had a great time. You know"—he pauses—"I'm a stud." Rob's tone is matter-of-fact, and he lets out a sigh. "I met tons of chicks, partied my ass off. What else is new?" He chuckles.

Ben looks at him, deciding to keep his mouth shut for now and let Rob revel in his ego for the moment.

"You thinkin' about going?" Rob asks.

"This winter feels like it's gonna last forever. I need a break."

"Tell me about it." Rob sighs loudly. "Looks like you're ready for happy hour. I'm gonna get dressed and grab a beer. I'm glad we can stay close tonight."

Mike and Brian are at bachelor party of an acquaintance from college who Rob had a falling out with a few years back.

Rob does a lot of driving at his job as a pharmaceutical sales rep. It takes him all over the state of New Jersey and the tristate area. As a result, he normally stays in Hoboken on the weekends, with the very occasional night out in the big city. He's sometimes aloof. His friends kid each other about how he holds down a successful job. Rob's a jokester, even though sometimes he doesn't mean to be. A happy-go-lucky guy, Rob is one of Ben's crew from South Jersey, where they were known as "The Dead-End Boys." They grew up on the wrong side of town on a dead-end street. None of them liked that nickname at first, but over time, it stuck. Even though life has tried to take them in separate directions, the boys have never drifted apart.

Rob and Ben finish their beer and head out of the apartment, down the steps, and onto the electric sidewalk traffic and the unknown future of the night.

A few hours later, the morning light sneaks its way through the curtains on Rob's window. He opens his crusted eyes on this Saturday to feel the effects of another morning hangover. His mouth feels like one of those pictures from *National Geographic* of a dried-out riverbed turned desert. Growing tired of this weekly aftereffect but still feeling it's just part of having fun, he tries to go back to sleep. It's no use. He's awake for now, if you can call it that. He stumbles out of his room and sees Ben sitting on the couch. "What happened last night?" he asks as Ben turns around. "I was talking with this girl one minute; then we did some shots, and after that I can't remember anything."

"I turned around one minute, and you were gone. I figured you went home," Ben tells him.

Rob looks up at that moment and sees they have a visitor. It's a girl they met last night. She walks out of Ben's room.

"Cindy, meet Rob O'Sullivan. Rob meet Cindy," Ben introduces them.

Rob mutters, "Oh, hi."

Cindy searches the floor for her shoe, leans toward the ground once she's spotted it, and gently coaxes it onto her left foot.

"Can I get your number before you go?" Ben politely asks her.

She grabs his phone and enters her number. He opens the door like a gentleman as they say their good-byes. His night is officially over at noon.

Rob and Ben peer out of their front apartment window to the street below, watching her do the walk of shame out of the building and down the sidewalk—her high heels clicking every step of the way like a loud clock hand. They see her move her chin toward the ground as she passes a couple, hiding behind her hair. Rob turns to Ben with a smirk. "You dirty dog."

"Go get yourself cleaned up," Ben says, digging at him.

Rob steps back into his room and sees his shirt from last night on the floor. He picks it up and, unwrapping it, exposes a red stain from a shot that didn't quite make it down the hatch. He looks into the mirror to get a look at himself. His green eyes are surrounded by red. His memory is slowly coming back into focus, like seeing a live video from the night. He sees himself getting hammered and starting to dance, his frayed-bottom jeans sapping up barroom floor party fouls, his introduction to Cindy and her friends.

Rob sees his six-foot body lead him out of the bar and up the bar—and café-lined avenue in a daze of streetlights. A car rolls by, and the glowing headlights momentarily blind his eyes. The car hits a pothole, and water splashes against his jeans. He's oblivious to the squeaky brakes of light trucks and buses as he crosses the street. He fumbles for his keys and is able to remember his building code that he has entered a thousand times. He makes his way up to the apartment and lays his weary, alcohol-logged head to rest.

Rob steps out of the room after his flashback and downs some Tylenol to relieve the pressure from his headache. He takes a seat with Ben in front of the TV to watch the pregames talk on this college football game day.

"You hear anything from Mike or Brian?" he asks Ben.

"They texted me about going to the Black Bear to watch the Rutgers game," Ben replies.

"Any stories about last night?" Rob asks.

"They said we would talk later. But that it was crazy."

"Can't wait to hear what those animals got into last night."

Ben nods in agreement. "Are you ready to meet them?" Ben asks.

"Give me one minute. This headache is killing me."

"Nothing a beer can't take care of," Ben says, trying to motivate his friend.

Ben dresses for comfort, not fashion or to look good, even though he does look good most of the time. Jeans and a T-shirt is the normal attire. Not trying to look good has always suited him well and is a style he could always afford.

He and Rob head into their rooms to bundle up for the short walk across the street to meet the other half of their foursome. Out of all the Dead-End Boys, Brian is Ben's closest friend. The two grew up two houses away from each other and have no secrets when it comes to each other's family life, which for both of them was dysfunctional to say the least. Ben knew Brian's older brother, who was hit by a car and passed away—a tragic victim of a hit-and-run accident; and the person responsible was never found. Brian was eight at the time.

Brian is the clean-cut looking one of the crew. He's always dressed with a preppy style even though his family didn't have any money. As a result, Ben tagged him with the nickname "college boy." He always did well in school too and stayed out of trouble for the most part. Sporting a baby face never hurt when it came to helping him get out of trouble.

Ben has played the older brother role to Brian ever since they were kids. Even now, Brian tends to follow and go along with Ben. It's expected and predictable at this point. The choir boy looks are a facade, covering some of the problems his family faced growing up. Brian's still close with his sister and mom, but his father left home a long time ago, another thing he and Ben have in common.

Ben sees his buddies crossing the street, heading in their direction. The short walk is nearly unbearable, with the wind whipping in their face. It's a wet, damp air running underneath another slate sky. "Let's make this quick," Ben says. "I hate the cold!"

They enter the bar and find a round top table with a view of one of the flat screen TVs. As they peel off their layers of jackets and sweaters, placing them on the back of their chair, Ben notices Rob's thick, white belt.

"Nice belt! Where did you get it? At one of those shops in Greenwich Village?" Ben prods him, gathering some laughs from the boys.

Rob shoots back, "Yeah? What about your new Diesel sneakers?"

"They're not bad," Mike says after he and Brian check them out.

"Thanks. Too bad I already got a stain on them from the bar we were in last night. I just got these on Wednesday," Ben informs them.

Rob plays off Ben's teasing and asks about the bachelor party. "So"—he pauses—"how was it?"

"It was fun. We stayed at the Borgata with three other guys and Ronnie. God, I can't believe he's getting married. We went to a couple of shitty strip clubs. Overall, it was a good time. But there weren't a lot of people in at the casinos last night. Probably because it's been too cold," Mike informs them.

"Yeah I hear that," Rob says.

Ben lights up a cigarette as the boys scan the menus right before Rutgers kicks off against West Virginia. The waitress comes over and starts to take their order. The front door blows open from a wind gust. Ben always sits facing the door. He's done this ever since he was a kid. Some would call it paranoia, others street smarts. Mike doesn't even notice, as he's on his cell phone.

"You're *always* on that thing," Ben tells him.

"Yeah, I could do this with my eyes closed. Just watch," Mike tells him as he shoots out an e-mail.

Ben loses his patience. "Anyway. This weather has got me down. It's too cold out here. There's no relief." He looks around the table.

"So what are ya gonna do about it? It's like this every miserable winter. This is Jersey," Mike replies.

"I tell you what I'm gonna do about it. Florida." He pauses to see their reaction. "Aren't you sick of this shitty, cold North Jersey winter weather?"

"I don't know. I kind of like it," Rob says.

The boys all look at him like he's crazy.

"Anyway," Ben says pretending not to hear Rob's response. "Let's take a trip. Warm weather. I checked it. It's like eighty degrees," he adds, enticing them.

"You haven't made any trips with us," Mike states.

"Yeah. I was always looking after my family. I've never had any time to get away. I'm not living down there anymore. Now things are going okay with this new job, I send money home, and I got some time coming up that I can take," Ben tells them.

"I agree," Brian says. "Sounds like a great idea! Whaddya think, Mike?"

"If you're in, then I'm in too!" Mike responds.

"All right, all right," Rob reluctantly agrees.

"South Beach it is, boys!" Ben excitedly exclaims, smacking the table with gusto.

They all slap each other high five and toast their drinks. The future stories echo off the glass as they toast.

Mike gets up from the table and heads to the back of the bar to use the restroom. He swings the bathroom door open and checks his dark, slicked-back hair in the dirty mirror. He looks like Budd Fox recently off the set of the movie *Wall Street*. Stepping up to the urinal, he notices the Newark *Star-Ledger*'s sports section on the wall in front of him and decides to catch up on some of the scores from last night that he missed while partying. He finishes reading, along with the other duty at hand; makes his way over to the sink; washes his hands; and throws the paper towel in the wastebasket. Something catches his eye.

He reaches into the basket and pulls out the paper's front page. The headline at the top of the Newark *Star-Ledger*, Saturday February 2, 2001 reads, "Gangster Slim Jimmy's Body Found." His heart pounds as his eyes race across the words. He tries to digest them.

Mike rushes out of the bathroom to the front of the bar. He throws the paper down in front of the boys. "You guys gotta have a look at this!" Mike tells them.

They all lean in to the table and read the headline.

"Slim Jimmy is dead?" Brian looks at the boys with astonishment.

Ben picks up the paper and reads the story. "The Jersey gangster known as Slim Jimmy has been found dead. Authorities had to use DNA evidence to identify badly decomposed body parts that were found in the woods in a remote area in South Jersey. Jimmy Martino, a.k.a. Slim Jimmy, has been found dead. The Jersey gangster's remains were recently discovered in the woods in a remote area in South Jersey. Authorities had to use DNA evidence to identify badly decomposed body parts and confirm them as Martino's. Slim Jimmy was a hit man and had recently been brought in by the FBI for questioning about missing cases. He was figured to be a suspect in over twenty missing persons cases." Ben pauses. "Wow!" he says, dumbfounded. "I guess we don't have to worry about him anymore."

2

SOUTH JERSEY

It all happened one autumn day. It was October 28, and Ben was ten years old. He and his mother were just getting back from a trip to get him a Halloween costume.

The street sign reads "Mockingbird Lane." A 1978 Ford Country Esquire—the one with the "woodie" panels on the side—turns the corner. The wheels barely even clunk over the curb before Ben is manually unlocking the doors and bolting out of the car like a flash of lightning. The woodie runs over a couple of oil stains that cover the surface of the driveway, resembling an ink blot.

Ben was always embarrassed riding in that car. He would slide down as far as he could in those pleather seats, but his attempt to hide was of no use. Everyone in his neighborhood knew his mom drove that car. People from other towns looked at him and his friends as subclass. The first time he realized this was in grade school when he and his teammates would play sports at other schools. He and his friends noticed how other people looked at them. Ben and his teammates were treated differently. Nothing needed to be said;

he could feel it. They were out of place. The other parents had new cars and dressed well. The kids they played against had the newest sneakers. The schools were nicer and more modern. His mom's car was a constant reminder of their status.

"Could you grab the paper, honey?"

"Aw, come on, Ma!" he pleads and is quickly overruled by his mother's eyes. He moves toward the porch and picks up the *Atlantic City Times*, which is resting on a pile of multicolored leaves that have fallen from the neighborhood trees. "I'm going to play ball with Bri," he tells her, sensing that only a few moments remain on this fall day.

He runs through his backyard and jumps over the fence to the front of his friend's house. "The Robertson's mailbox hangs next to the door. He rings the doorbell, and Brian answers.

"Wanna play?" Ben asks, lifting up a bat with a glove wrapped around the handle.

A born competitor and athlete, Ben had talent and natural ability at most athletic endeavors. Ben loved playing against Brian, even though it wasn't much of a challenge. Brian always pushed himself hard despite not having Ben's natural gifts. It was something Ben admired in his friend.

The difference was that Ben had great expectations for himself from the very beginning of his childhood. They started with his family and his friends, but the community newspaper soon joined in. Ben had always been his own greatest critic whenever he believed himself to have not met those expectations.

Brian's angelic face lights up. Ever the squeaky-clean boy, Brian looks, as usual, like the altar boy that he is at the local church. He doesn't even answer. He disappears from the door for a moment and then runs out of the house with a hooded sweatshirt.

The two boys are off in an instant, in a race against the fading sunlight, running through Brian's backyard, through Ben's, and then down the street, where it meets its dead end at the edge of the woods. It's where they've earned the nickname around town as the Dead-End Boys. Ben discards his thick coat. Brian takes a minute to catch his breath. He's smaller and frailer in stature. Ben sees Brian frustratingly throw his bat down on the ground.

"Everything okay?" Ben asks.

"I guess. They were fighting again. I don't really feel like talking about it."

Brian's parent's fights could get nasty. Sometimes during the summer, when things got heated, the boiling would spill out of the open windows. The neighborhood could hear everything. Brian was always embarrassed and would walk around with his head down for days after. Ben was his crutch in those times. He watched out for Brian. The two boys leaned on each other, and hearing about Brian's family issues made Ben realize his wasn't the only family with problems.

Ben's father was a prison guard. He had a thing where he'd come home from work, leave the lights off, and sit there alone, drinking in the dark. It was something that Ben would think about for years to come. Ben's father was tough on him. He'd lecture him on how he would amount to nothing. He was barely ever home, even when he lived there. The problem was that the family was always stressed awaiting his arrival, which could come at any moment. When he did arrive, he was a weed in a flower garden, not fitting in and out of place. Even when he left, his presence was always hanging, hovering around for years to come, like a shadow. He was a dark cloud gathering, and you never knew when it was going to rain. Ben had to be the man of the house and look after his mom, brother, and sister at an early age. It made Ben grow up a lot faster than anyone else he knew. At this point in time, his father hadn't been living at home for nearly six months. Ben and his mom were going to keep it this way.

"You know you can talk to me about anything," Ben says to Brian, looking directly into his eyes and putting a hand on his shoulder.

"Yeah. I know." Brian starts to walk with the ball to pitch. "Thanks," he responds as an afterthought. "Now let's get started."

Brian must be feeling lucky this day because he decides to throw one right down the middle as hard as he can. "Ding!"

The sound of the aluminum bat echoes when Ben connects with the ball on the sweet spot. Brian looks disgusted, as he knows too well what that sound means. He's heard it too many times before. Turning around to see the ball flying over the pine treetops into the woods, he throws his hands down and turns to see Ben smiling.

"Now look what you did!" Brian says.

"I know! I think that's the farthest I've ever hit any ball!" Ben tells him.

"Not that! Now we gotta find it! It's the only ball we've got! We've been losing so many in there," a dejected Brian tells him.

"Come on. I'll help." Ben persuades him.

They step into the woods and wander back to look for the ball. "It should be around here somewhere," Brian says.

"I think I hit it further back," Ben says, trying to rub it in.

After a few minutes, they forget about the ball and start discussing their costumes. Ben tells Brian about the cape and accessories he just got, expecting Brian to be impressed.

"Well I'm gonna be Jason," Brian retorts. "Ya know, from *Friday the 13th*? I got this hockey mask I'm borrowing from my older brother and this awesome fake knife. When you stab someone with it, the blade disappears into where you hold it. It's awesome!"

Ben knows that he's been outdone and shrugs his shoulders. "It's okay," he answers, sounding unimpressed to conceal his disappointment.

At that moment, the boys hear the sound of voices from farther back in the woods and turn to each other with bewildered eyes. Their mothers have always warned them about wandering in the woods. They've been in trouble many times for getting caught disobeying orders. Sometimes though, the risk is worth the fun. With over a million acres of pine trees in a region known as the Pine Barrens, there are plenty of places to play.

"Let's move closer," Ben whispers and points toward the ground.

They get on all fours and slowly crawl forward. Settling in behind some brush, they peer out into the woods, lying among the dead pine needles, dried up leaves, and dirt. Ben rests the weight of his body on his forearms. The leaves crackle and crumble with each movement. The dirt is damp underneath the dry leaves. His skin feels colder as his body shivers.

It's hard to make out what's going on, but they're able to push aside the branches and thorn bushes to get a look as they crawl even closer. They see a white van and three men standing outside it. One of the larger men slides the side door open. One at a time, he pulls three men out. Each of them falls to the ground immediately upon being removed from the vehicle. The boys see they have something wrapped around their heads.

"They have blindfolds on," Ben mouths.

"Are their hands tied behind their backs?" Brian asks him as they're confused gazes connect.

"I think so," Ben mouths back with wide opened eyes, his head filled with running thoughts as he tries to make sense of what he's seeing.

Two of the blindfolded men are now picked up and set in a kneeling position with their hands behind their backs in front of the van. The third man has been lying motionless on the ground since being pulled out.

"What's going on?" Brian mouths.

"I don't know yet. Just stay down," Ben hisses through clenched teeth.

An abnormally thin man is smoking a cigarette. Flicking the butt, he steps closer to one of the blindfolded men. The thin man now leans down to say something to his prisoner, grabs him by his hair and punches him. The boys see the man fall down to the ground. The skinny man spits on him and turns to the next one.

"Looks like it's the next guy's turn," an intrigued Ben relays to Brian.

The skinny man now grabs the other blindfolded man by his hair and gives him a violent backhand. *Crack!* The sound disperses into the woods.

The thin man then motions to his crew to lift both of the blindfolded men back onto their knees. The skinny one paces back and forth, continuing to speak, but the boys are just out of earshot. Ben is able to make out the man's sunken face. Behind a long, skinny nose and protruding cheekbones, the rest of his features sink back, and his dark, beady eyes are nearly hidden. He continues to punch and slap the blindfolded men while his two thugs keep them upright. He stops talking, puts on a pair of gloves, and reaches into his gray blazer. He pulls something out and walks over to the van. The boys' sight is blocked by the other men, but they hear it. A muffled shot from a silencer buzzes in the damp October night.

Brian's shaking and begins to breathe heavily.

"You need to stay quiet!" Ben pleads with him just above a whisper.

"What was that noise? Did he just do what I think he did?" Brian silently asks him.

"We didn't see anything yet! He might be just trying to scare them!" Ben hisses back.

"Well, they're scaring me! Let's get out of here!"

"We can't! They'll see us! Just sit tight, and when it's all over, we'll get out of here," Ben demands in a hushed tone.

Through the brush, Ben continues to look at this situation, which is getting even more desperate by the second. Brian can't bear to look.

The boys hear one of the blindfolded men scream, "Please! I beg you! I have a wife! Don't do it! I'll do anything!"

Another muffled shot, and Ben sees the blindfolded man fall to the ground.

"What happened?" Brian asks.

"You don't wanna know," Ben answers with a pale white face. "Just stay down, and we'll get out of here." Seeing his friend's back rise up and down off the ground from his ferocious breathing, Ben knows he has to keep Brian calm.

The menacing trio takes the blindfold off the last man as he too starts to beg for his life. He turns around to make eye contact with all of his captors, but it's too late. The slim man takes another step toward him from behind as the hostage turns his head forward. He looks up into the brush looking for some miracle. He catches Ben's eyes. Ben is frozen. The man yells, "Help me!" as he looks directly at Ben. But these are his final words, as the last bullet ends his life.

Ben sees the skinny man wipe down his gun and take off his gloves, putting the gun back in a holster on the inside of his blazer.

He takes out a white handkerchief and dabs some of the scattered blood off his clothes. He takes a second to light up another cigarette and then motions to his two thugs. One of the thugs walks around to the back of the van, pulls out two shovels, and starts digging in the area the slim man pointed too. Ben can hear the two men talking as the sound of the shovels slice through the dirt. The slim man continues to pace as the cigarette smoke slowly billows in the air. He makes a turn and is headed in the direction of the boys.

"Stay down," Ben whispers, pushing his hand against Brian's back. He lays as flat as he can.

The slim man continues to walk toward them. Ben can hear his footsteps getting closer but does not look.

Ben's body is shaking. The slim man is twenty feet away. Ben's mind races, wondering if the slim man knows he's lying here. Ben holds his breath. The man could probably smell the boys if he tried, but the sound of cracking dry leaves under his footsteps stop. Ben sees the orange glow of the cigarette land next to his face. Ben can make out the word Marlboro around the wrapper. The smoke billows up as the smell flows into Ben's nostrils. The sound of the cracking leaves start again. Ben peeks up to see the man walking back to where his thugs are still digging in the dimming light. They emerge from behind the tree and start dragging the bodies of the man into their shallow graves.

After a few minutes the three men make their way into the van as if nothing has happened. The van disappears into the twilight. The woods are silent again. Ben and Brian are frozen for a few more moments.

"Are they gone?" Brian asks him.

Ben picks his face up from the dirt and wipes it clean of leaf fragments.

"Yeah, they're gone," he states, his tone emotionless. The shock has consumed him as he tries to process these events he has just witnessed.

The leaves rustle under their shoes as they get up to their feet. They hear nothing but the sounds of the dry leaves cracking from their movement.

"We have to tell someone! Should we call the cops?" Brian asks as he grasps for air.

"What? Are you crazy or somethin'? Those guys are dead! And if we tell anyone, we will be too!" Ben responds emphatically.

"Our parents won't be mad if they find out we were here. They'll be happy that we're alive!"

"No, stupid. Did you see the guy who killed them? You don't think he will try to kill us if we start to tell people what we saw—if we tell people that he was the one who did it?"

"I don't know," Brian answers. "He didn't see us. He doesn't know who we are."

"Yeah. But he'll find out from somebody. Did you hear that thing with Johnny Brown's cousin who was a witness in a trial? He was gonna rat on a guy who killed someone during a robbery. Well, before it went to trial, they killed him. Then there was no witness to the robbery. Case closed. The cops were supposed to have him in protective custody and everything. A lot of people think the cops were in on it," he tells Brian.

"Well, what do we do then?" Brian asks his friend.

"We don't do anything. We don't say anything. We don't tell anyone. Ever. This is our secret forever. Swear to me on your grandmother's grave."

"I swear." Brian holds out his pinkie to meet Ben's, and they pinkie swear.

They walk out of the woods and don't say a word. Brian turns to look at Ben as they change direction to make their way home. Ben's already looking at him and has his finger over his lips as if to say, *Remember. Don't tell anyone.*

The darkness is setting in on the day as they both make their way home. It feels like it will stay.

3

THE BODIES

The bodies were found the next day. A dirt bike rider barreling down one of the trails was thrown from his bike. He staggered back to his feet to mount his vehicle, but it was stuck. He pulled the throttle and jerked the bike back and forth as it kicked up dirt and leaves, digging out a few inches of sand. That's when he saw the pale white skin. By the time the ambulances and police cruisers got there, the neighborhood was buzzing.

Chief Johnson is crouched in the woods, scrounging around for clues. Yellow caution tape being put up by his fellow officers surrounds the crime scene. He hears someone shout, "Oh my God! One of them is alive!"

Johnson slowly stands upright, exhaling heavily from the exertion. He pulls his pants up to cover his drooping potbelly and rushes toward the scene. The police converge toward the man. He's barely hanging on to his life. They bring over a stretcher and cautiously slide his dirt-covered body onto it. An oxygen mask is placed over his face as a paramedic straps him in and brushes off some dirt and leaves. The officers help paramedics take the stretcher into the ambulance.

Johnson decides to get in the back and catch a ride to the hospital.

"Take my cruiser back to the station." He tosses the keys to the assistant of the county coroner and tries to catch his breath.

The wounded man's pulse is irregular. Within ten minutes, they arrive at the hospital, where a team of nurses and doctors are waiting at the emergency entrance. As the ambulance pulls up to the hospital, the man is conscious. The chief gets his chance.

"What's your name?"

"Brown. Michael," the injured man manages to expel.

"Do you know who did this to you, sir?" Johnson asks him.

"Help!" he whispers. "Help!"

"We got help for you, sir. You're gonna be okay. Who did this to you?"

"A boy . . ." The man pauses while catching his breath. "A boy saw it. I don't know. 'Help!' I yelled."

"All right! That's enough! He needs to save his energy," the medic says.

"Just one more thing. Can you identify the boy?" the chief presses.

The man nods his head. "Yes."

"How old was he?"

"Nine"—his short, abnormal breathing interrupts—"or ten."

"Okay. Now these people will take care of you. Get some rest and get better. We'll get these people that did this to you. I'll send a sketch artist to the hospital as soon as I can."

The victim's eyes drift toward the ambulance ceiling and close.

The chief gets on his radio and contacts his deputy.

"Yeah, Chief," the deputy responds.

"I was able to get a quick statement from our victim. He identified himself as one Michael Brown. He said something about a boy. Estimated that the witness was around nine or ten years of age."

"That would put him in fourth, maybe fifth grade."

"Once he's awake and feeling better, we'll get a sketch of the witness. Get the principal at the elementary school up to speed on the situation and ask for his cooperation. We'll get moving on this as soon as we can."

"No problem, Chief. I was just there yesterday speaking with him while picking up my daughter," his deputy informs him.

The neighborhood is alive, as the adults are outside of their houses trying to figure out what's going on in the woods. They're congregated in front of their driveways speaking to one another, speculating about endless possibilities. Neighbors and fellow citizens who rarely say more than hello are thrust into conversations that have pulled them away from their routine weeknight. The news filters through the crowd like sand in a gold miner's pan; three bodies were found. Ben stays up watching the mess unfold outside his window. He can't make much out. Just the fact that the neighborhood is buzzing. His mom comes in the house, and he meets her at the front door.

"What's going on?" he asks.

"Nothing, honey. Get some sleep," she says, trying to reassure him.

But Ben can feel the butterflies starting to flutter.

He turns back to his room to try to get some sleep for the big day ahead. Tomorrow is Halloween.

4

HALLOWEEN

Ben didn't sleep much last night, with the events going on in the neighborhood, the butterflies in his stomach, and his excitement over this special holiday. He wore his costume to school yesterday. The school celebrates Halloween the day before to educate the children about safety. His costume was a hit with the other kids. It was not as big of a hit as Brian's, but it was good enough for him and a major improvement from last year. He gets dressed as fast as he can this morning, making sure his costume is on his bed, ready for this afternoon when he arrives back from school. The sooner he gets ready, the sooner he can get through the school day, so he can meet up with his friends and retrieve as much candy as possible. He's a human candy vacuum. He bolts out of his room and lands at the breakfast table. He overhears his mother on the phone with one of the neighbors. "Can you believe one of them is still alive?"

Ben cannot believe what he's just heard. He downs his cereal as fast as he can, inhaling it like an anteater. He races to the bathroom and runs the water in the sink—a trick he's learned to make his mother think he's brushed his teeth. He knows she's always listening. He rushes out of the house and waves to her, shouting, "Bye, Mom," as he closes the door behind him.

She waves; covering the phone with her other hand, she yells, "Love you!" Then she continues her conversation with the neighbor.

Ben bounces down the porch steps and looks to his right, toward the dead end.

Amid a small morning fog, a cop sits in a patrol car. It makes Ben nervous as he continues across the street to meet up with Brian. They walk to school together every morning. He catches Brian walking out of his house. Their neighborhood is covered in fall-colored leaves.

"Hey," Brian says to him.

Ben decides to tell him about what he overheard his mom say on the phone. "I have to tell you something"—he pauses—"about one of the guys that got shot." He pauses again.

"Well?" Brian asks.

"Well, he-he," Ben stutters, "he is . . . still alive."

"What do you mean? You saw him get shot!"

"I just know all right! I heard my mom talking on the phone with Mr. Richards," he says as he nods toward the Richardses' house.

"Wow." Brian has a puzzled look on his face.

"Yeah, but there's something else," Ben leads on.

"What?"

"I think one of them saw me."

"How? We were behind the bushes and leaves!"

"Before they got shot, the one that yelled 'Help!' looked at me," Ben informs him.

"Why didn't you tell me before?" Brian asks angrily.

"I didn't know for sure; it all happened so fast," Ben tells his friend.

"I wonder if he's the one who's still alive," Brian ponders.

"I wonder if who's the one?" A red-cheeked, chubby boy runs up on them from the sidewalk and questions.

"No one!" Ben and Brian respond simultaneously.

"You won't tell me. Come on! I won't tell anyone. Who are you guys talking about?" Rob begs them for an answer.

"*I'll* tell you." Their friend Mike steps out from behind the bushes. He peels a mask off his face, and the rubber band jostles his dark hair. His Guns N' Roses shirt shows his and his friends' affinity for their favorite band. "I was following them for two blocks. I was gonna jump out and scare you guys. That's when I heard you talkin'. So I listened in. Now I know your secrets," he says.

"What did you hear?" Ben asks.

"Everything. Every single thing," Mike divulges.

"Listen," Ben says, "we need to talk. We can't ever say anything to anyone. We need to keep our mouths shut. Understand?" Ben asks seriously.

The other boys nod in agreement.

"You swear?" he asks them again.

"Yeah I swear," Mike answers.

"Yeah," Rob replies.

"We can't tell anyone—not the cops, not your mom, not your dad, no one. We saw something we shouldn't have—something so bad that, if we tell anyone what we saw, we could wind up dead."

Ben watches Rob react to the news; his face becomes flush white. Some other children are making their way up the street, heading to school. Ben decides to walk to a secluded area where he and Brian can tell Mike and Rob the entire story.

"Let's go over here and talk," he says.

He tells them the story, detail by detail, from his majestic home run to one of the victims seeing him before he was shot to overhearing his mother's conversation this morning.

"What happens if the guy who got shot saw you and remembers what you look like?" Rob asks.

"That's something I've already thought about. I'll deny I was ever there. Deny, deny, deny. That's what everyone always says to do when you're guilty. I'll tell them that me and Brian were playing baseball on the other side of the neighborhood. You'll have to back me up," he says, looking at Brian.

"Sure. Whatever we gotta do," Brian answers.

"I want to see," Mike states.

"See what?" Rob asks.

"See where it happened, idiot! But we gotta get to school. Let's take the back way," Mike suggests. "It's quicker."

The boys make their way through the woods. They jump over a fence to the baseball field and scuttle across the open yard to the back of the school. Ben's the first to see one of the older students on the way in.

"Look who it is." The boy, dressed in a Mötley Crüe T-shirt pauses. "The Dead-End Boys. All together again."

The boy and his friends laugh at the Dead-End Boys.

Ben, who's crazy enough to do something, gives the bully a dirty look and says, "Fuck off!"

His friends coerce him to keep moving to get to class.

"Come on! We don't need another detention!" Brian tells him.

Mike follows behind, unafraid and unaffected by the older boys' comments. He walks in the building, still looking at the other boys. They rush into class as the bell rings and take their seats. The boys will not get a detention on this day.

Their teacher, Miss Lindley, steps into the room and closes the wood door. The noise from the hallway cuts out. Only one small, rectangular pane of glass stands between the class and the outside world.

Ben looks over at his grade-school crush. Janet is the prettiest girl in class, maybe the whole school. Little does he know that his three friends have checked her out just the same.

The regular morning announcements travel through the PA system as the class quiets down. Brian nervously doodles with his pencil.

When the announcements are complete, Miss Lindley steps to the front of the class, her high heels clicking on the solid floor with each step. "Class. Class. Listen up."

The chatter in the room starts to settle down.

"We have some visitors here today that'll need to speak to the boys in the classroom. Chief Johnson and his colleagues from the police department need to see all of the boys in the school. I'm sure everything is fine, so don't be worried. Would all of the boys please stand up and make your way down to the cafeteria? One single file line and please do not talk and disrupt the other classes on the way down. Thank you."

The Dead-End Boys look around at each other with eyes blaring wide open. They reluctantly get out of their seats and make it into the corridor. Ben tries to reassure them.

The boys make their way into the cafeteria. They see Chief Johnson with a couple of other officers.

"Please take your seats gentlemen," he says with a deep, stern voice.

Ben looks over at his friends. Brian's shaken by this quick turn of events. Ben sees him tapping his foot anxiously. He gulps his saliva down, and his Adam's apple moves up and down. His forehead sweat starts building like condensation inside a car windshield.

Ben whispers, "Just relax. Don't worry about a thing. Just tell them we were on the other side of the neighborhood. If we stick to the story, they can't do anything."

Brian takes a deep breath to try to calm himself.

"I'm sure y'all heard 'bout the recent incident in this town by now. There was a serious crime committed. We're just looking for information from anyone who may who committed this violent act. We have reason to believe that one of you gentlemen may have heard or seen something. If anyone knows anything about this incident, you would save us a lot of time and yourselves a lot of trouble by coming forward with the information. We're going to give you about thirty minutes to think about this and to allow you to come forward. No one will be in any trouble. We'll be outside." Johnson and his colleague head out of the room.

The boys look at each other.

About thirty minutes pass on the clock. The chief and his fellow officer return to the cafeteria.

"All right. We want you to know that one of the victims of this horrible crime has survived. We spoke with him at the hospital where he's recovering from his injuries." The chief pauses as the boys in the room all try to process what they've just heard.

"He was able to give information to a sketch artist. So what we'll do is call one row up at a time. See if any of you possibly match the description that was given to us. Please do not be alarmed. We just want to narrow it down to a few people and go from there." He pauses again. "Myself and my colleague will be seated here with the sketch. First row, please stand up; you'll walk by one at a time, and we'll tell you either to walk back to class or to take a seat back in your row."

The first row slowly rises out of their seats and proceeds out of their aisle. They walk up the small staircase to the top of the stage, where Chief Johnson is seated with his fellow officer. The first boy is told that he can go back to class. The same with the next. Another student with features somewhat similar to Ben's is examined more closely. After a few long seconds though, he's told to sit back down. The next row is called up.

The next group of boys stands up and slowly shuffles up the staircase. All except one are told to go back to class. The boy who remains has the same hair color, same eye color, and is roughly the same height and weight as Ben. Ben's starting to get a lump in his throat. He tries to stay calm.

"Third row, please stand." The boys from row three make their way up the small staircase. One by one, they are sent back to class.

Brian's so nervous he's visibly shaking. He makes it up to the stage, and there's a commotion. He's fallen face-first on the stage. Mike and Rob shake him until he opens his eyes. Chief Johnson takes a look at Brian while his friends sit him in the first row.

"He's been sick since yesterday," Mike blurts out, trying to cover for his friend.

"What's his name?" the chief asks.

"It's Brian, Brian Robertson," Mike responds.

The chief jots down a note in his notebook.

"Sit tight here, boy," he says. "Once you're good enough, make your way back to class," Johnson adds.

Ben slowly walks up to the chief. Johnson and his colleague examine him and look back at the photo. They spend extra time looking him over, and they tell him to go sit down back in his row. Rob and Mike grab Brian and drag him back to class. They both turn to look at Ben as they exit the cafeteria, worried about what will happen. Ben's seated, trying to hide his nerves. He rubs his sweaty palms on his pant leg.

"Last row please." The final group of boys proceeds to the stage, and each, with the exception of one, who's told to have a seat as well, is told to go back to class.

5

THE QUESTIONING

Ben is sitting in the stiff desk chair and trying to convince himself that everything will work out. He hears the footsteps approach his door and slide to a stop.

The doorknob slowly turns, and Ben looks over to see Johnson walk in. He can't believe it's Johnson already.

"Well, boy. One down, two to go. If you're any kind of mathematician, you know that leaves a fifty-fifty chance that you're my boy."

"Only if the boy you're looking for goes to this school," Ben whips back.

Johnson shoots an evil look in his direction. "Listen up, smart guy. I'm gonna ask you some questions. And I want straight answers in return. If I find out that you're holdin' out on me, you could be charged as an accessory to a major crime. Got that?"

"Yes, sir."

Chief Johnson pauses. "Where were you on the night of October 28? That was Tuesday."

"I was playing baseball after school on the other side of town. Near Indian Creek."

"And who were you with, son?"

"I was playing with my friend. We play against each other in Little League."

"What's your friend's name?"

"Brian."

"Brian what?"

"Robertson."

The chief pauses and then pulls out his notepad. "If I asked him where you were, he would tell me the same thing?"

"Uh-huh," Ben says as he nods his head.

"Did you go anywhere else at all that night? Maybe the woods?"

"No. Just baseball."

"Didn't see anything strange or out of the ordinary, son?"

"No. No, sir."

"All right. Sit tight. We're gonna go talk to your friend."

Chief Johnson steps out of the room and into the hallway. He sees the other officer, whose walking toward him.

"Sir?"

"Yeah, what is it?"

"I just confirmed the first boy's story with his mom."

"All right. I need you to grab Brian Robertson out of the fourth grade please. We need to verify this boy's story as well." The chief nods toward the room Ben is sequestered in.

6

THE DEAD MAN

Brian is seated in class, but he can't keep his attention in the room. His eyes are focused outside, out through the window. His heart races, and his thoughts are zipping around his head. Suddenly, a knock comes from the door. It's Johnson's deputy.

Brian sees him lean his body into the room. "Is Brian Robertson here?"

The whole class turns their heads toward Brian, like people following a ball at a tennis match.

"Yes, he's right here," Brian's teacher answers. "Do you need to see him?"

"Yes, please," the deputy answers.

"Brian?" His teacher motions him toward the door.

Brian gets up and walks toward the door, feeling the eyes of everyone on him. He exits the door as the deputy closes it behind him. "We're going downstairs," Brian is told.

Brian reluctantly walks a few steps in front of him with his head down. They take a turn into the hall from the stairwell. He knows he's in for one of the longest walks of his life.

"This is the boy that passed out this morning," Brian hears Johnson say to the deputy. "Just when I thought there was no hope left," he says, as he's done questioning the three boys. "Get these last two boys' phone numbers and verify their stories with their parents," he says to the other officer.

"Sure thing, boss."

"Take a seat in here, son." Johnson motions to a side room.

Brian steps toward the room. He takes a look across the hall to see Ben seated in the chair. Ben gives him a confident nod to tell him everything is all right. He takes his seat, thinking about their story, the one he and Ben agreed on.

"Where were you last Tuesday night, son?" The chief asks sternly.

"I was playing baseball with Ben." He nods his head toward the other room, where Ben is located.

"Where were y'all playing baseball at, son?"

"We were over near Indian Creek. I was kicking his butt, too," he says, trying to embellish the story to make it seem more believable. He looks up and sees Johnson's red face seething. "I mean, uh, I was winning."

"What time did you boys play there till?"

"Uh, I don't really remember. Maybe like six o'clock. It must have been because I would have to be home for dinner. My mom gets mad when she cooks and I'm late," he tells Johnson.

"Son," he leans forward in his chair, while pausing in midsentence, "I don't have to tell you how important this is, do I?"

"No, sir."

Brian's been holding it together very well since fainting, but after this question, he's now starting to feel like he did the moment before he fainted. Pressure bears down on his head like he's swimming underwater at the bottom of a pool. He's starting to realize that Johnson doesn't believe him.

"Do you know that some people got murdered?"

"Yes, sir. It was all around the neighborhood last night and this morning."

"Did you stop anywhere on the way home with your friend over there?"

"No, sir. We went straight home."

Johnson's colleague steps into the room. "Sir?"

"Can't you see I'm with the kid?! What is it?"

"Well, sir, Mr. Brown is awake at St. Mary's Hospital and seems to be feeling well. He's responsive. I thought you should know."

Johnson's priority is to speak with the victim to find out the details of the attempted murder firsthand. "Do me a favor, get all of these two boys' information," he tells the deputy. "I wanna go speak with him while he's conscious." He turns to Brian. "This ain't over yet, son." He wags his finger in Brian's direction.

Brian is horrified. He quivers. "Yes. Yes, sir," he nervously replies, knowing Johnson has it out for them.

Brian exits the room after Johnson and walks down the hall. He hears the radio coming from the school nurse's office.

"He's doing very well considering what he went through," the doctor being interviewed states. "He was packed tightly with the other two. This is what most likely kept him alive. It kept his body temperature up. The bullet barely scraped his skull. He'll be extremely lucky if he gets away with just a concussion. Most people don't survive a run-in like that with the Mafia." He pauses. "We have to do a few more tests, but he may be released soon."

Brian gets a tap on the shoulder from Ben. As they head back to class, he tells Ben what he just heard.

7

THE STATION

At Ben's house, a knock sounds from the front door. His mother puts down the dishes and walks out of the kitchen to answer.

"Who is it?" she asks.

"It's Officer Hayes. Spoke with you yesterday. I'm here to pick up your son."

"Just give us a minute," she nervously tells him as she rushes to get Ben away from the breakfast table and out of the door.

Ben's mother believes it's a case of mistaken identity and hopes this will all be over with today. "Now, Ben, make sure you don't let them talk you into saying anything. Stick to your guns and tell them the truth. I spoke with this officer yesterday. They said they just needed to ask you a few more questions. I'm sure that it will all be over once you do that." She takes a second while helping him put on his jacket. "Are you worried?"

"Nah." He's done well at consoling her over the past twenty-four hours. He plays it off. "I just hope they believe me; that's all. Seems like they don't—like they're just tryin' to stick words in my mouth."

"Well, like I said, honey, just tell them the truth. It always works." She pauses. "The policeman is waiting. Let's go. I'll be here if you need anything. They told me you can call, if you're scared or anything, all right?"

"Okay," he answers while sighing.

"Okay. Love you, honey. Be good." She pats his back to calm him as the butterflies fill up inside of her.

Ben walks down the hall to the front of the house with his mom following close behind. She gives him a hug and opens up the door. Ben sees the policeman standing on the porch, his revolver in the holster. "You ready, kid?"

Nodding, he answers, "Yeah."

They walk across the driveway to the cherry-topped four-door. "I'm gonna have you sit in front. Just give me a second," says Officer Hayes, clearing a clipboard off of the seat. The policeman's leather belt makes noise as it stretches and moves with his body. Ben sits down on the passenger side.

The car slowly cruises down the street and out of sight as Ben's mom watches from the door. He's being taken to police headquarters.

Ben thinks about the man who survived the incident and wonders whether the man will be able to identify him. He and Brian have kept their mouths shut so far, but he's still worried about Brian cracking under the pressure of Johnson's questioning. It will only be worse if the man can point them out.

Ben's ushered out of the car and into police headquarters. He sees the other two boys from school in the lobby. They're told not to speak to one another and are seated in separate chairs around the room. After a few minutes of silence, one of the officers comes in, leading them into a back room. Two other, older boys are in there. They all take their seats. Ben notices one of them. It's one of the older boys who makes fun of the "Dead-End Boys" at school. The police officer turns to them. "Hang tight in here. It'll just be a few minutes."

8

THE LINEUP

At the same time the boys are moved inside, Johnson pulls up to the station with Michael. A few of the officers come outside to greet them, providing Michael with some help getting out of the car. He looks like an Egyptian mummy just emerging from the tomb. Bandaging is wrapped completely around his head, exposing only his eyes and nose. He's surprisingly healthy despite his ordeal. The officers wheel him into the back of the building and escort him into a room with a glass partition.

Michael looks around and begins to realize that, in a few minutes, he may see the boy who saw him get killed. His palms begin to sweat as he thinks about those moments he thought would be his last. The thoughts at that moment replay in his mind—his life, flashing by like an old, eight-by-eight film reel. He thinks about the man who pulled the trigger and the boy who can help put him away, about what the people who did this could do to him or any of the witnesses if the police collect enough evidence to prosecute. Either way, he's overwhelmed. His body is shaking.

A voice comes through on the monitor where the boys are waiting. "Gentlemen, please exit to your right." It's Johnson.

The boys get up and walk through the door into a room with a bright light. Ben realizes he's in a lineup. He's seen it on TV before. His hands hide in his pockets as he sheepishly looks straight forward into the glass and the dark room in front of him, trying to look relaxed.

Chief Johnson enters the room, taking a seat next to Michael. "Now listen, Michael. I know you're probably nervous. Before you look up, just remember that they can't see you. Only we can see them. I know this is probably going to bring back some recent bad memories, but try and stay calm. If we got your boy, then we're gonna be able to bring those dirtbags to justice. If not, we'll continue to search for the murderers and eventually put them away."

"Okay." Michael nods his head and slowly turns toward the lineup. He looks over the first and then the second. Then he sees Ben, who is third. "That's him. Right there. That's him," he says, pointing to the glass.

"Now take your time. Are you sure he's the one?" Johnson asks.

He pauses. "Yes. I'm sure. I remember those eyes. I thought they'd be the last eyes I'd ever see. How *could* I forget?" The feelings overcome him. "*Oh man!*" He gasps as his eyes swell while he tries to hold back the leaking tears, his hands covering his face.

"Take him outside and get him some water. We got him!" Johnson says victoriously.

9

LOW TIDE WITH THE EAST WIND

Thoughts are barreling through Ben's mind like a runaway train. Johnson and his officers keep him in an interrogation room alone with these thoughts. The sound from the wall clock's second hand lightly taps in unison with his foot against the floor. He feels like everyone is starting to look at him like *he* was the one that committed the crime.

Johnson walks into the room with another officer. He sits down at the table across from Ben. "Listen, son, you're not in *any* trouble *right now*. But if you don't tell us the truth, you could be charged and sent to juvy. You'll go there alone! Away from your mama! She'll be alone then too." He pauses. "This is the deal. The man who got shot just identified you in the lineup as the boy who was there at the scene. So now, son, I'm going ask you again. Where were you on the night of the twenty-eighth?" he demands as the vein pulses out of his neck like something's inside of his skin trying to break out.

"I already told you," Ben pleads. "I don't know why he thinks it's me! This guy gets shot in the head and is supposed to remember things a few days after? I wasn't there." Ben's heart pumps harder as the sweat starts to slowly trickle from his skin.

"Son, I'm not gonna tell you again!" Johnson slams his fist on the table. "Tell me the truth, or we are gonna charge you as an accessory and put you in a cell!" His reddening face demands again.

Ben sees through Johnson's anger. He knows he has to stick with his story and nothing will happen. Johnson's frustration is transparent. This interaction will not go anywhere. "I'm sorry. I don't know what happened." He shakes his head back and forth.

"All right then. If this is how you want it, son. This is how you're gonna get it. We're gonna call all of your friends down here—see if they know anything. We'll keep you here in the meantime to think all this over. Whaddya think about that son?" Johnson puts it to him.

"I guess do what you have to. I mean, if I didn't see anything and I don't know anything, what are they gonna tell you?" Ben answers.

"We'll see, son. We'll see." The chief gets up and walks out of the room with the other officer.

As they exit the room, the officer turns to Johnson. "Still think he's lyin', Chief?"

"Something smells fishier than low tide with the east wind," Johnson says. "We'll get one of his friends to crack. Then he'll have to talk. Round up the other boys we talked to—specially the one we called down at the school. I'll work on him for a little."

"No problem. I'll get right on it," the officer says.

Ben has been inside the room for about an hour, and he's resting his head on his arms across the cold, metal table when the door opens and the officer who drove him to the station steps into the room. "I'm here to take you home."

"I thought they were gonna keep me here while they talked with my friends?"

"Change of plans. They're gonna bring your friends down here tomorrow. Give you and them some time to think about things," he says, pausing. "Plus your mother called and made a big stink. Let's go."

They get in the car. As they leave the station, Ben starts to worry about Brian.

"You're under strict orders to not speak with any of your friends tonight. You got that?"

"Sure," Ben says.

10

SLIM JIMMY

After the questioning at the police headquarters, Ben is back at home when his mother asks him to get the mail. Ben descends off his porch and crosses his lawn. He takes a look down the quiet street toward Brian's house and turns toward the mailbox, facing his house. As he reaches in to get the mail, he notices a car coming toward him. He grabs the envelopes, thinking it's a cop making sure he doesn't come in contact with any of his friends. But the car rolls up a few feet away and stops. A man steps out of the passenger side and makes his way toward Ben. The driver exits the car as well. The passenger takes off his hat, and Ben sees that it's the skinny man who pulled the trigger.

The fear causes his body to start moving backward. But the driver is behind him. He bumps into the driver and drops the mail. He knows he has nowhere to go.

"Listen, kid, we ain't gonna hurt ya. I already know you didn't say nothin'. We got friends in low places. You know what I'm sayin'?" Jimmy asks him.

"Uh-huh," Ben manages to expel.

"Well great then. Smart kid. You didn't rat. Nobody likes a rat. We know they're gonna be talking to your friends. Now just make sure that none of your friends talk either. Got it?"

"Uh-huh." Ben nods his head and continues to shake.

"Everything will work out fine if no one says nuttin'. But if someone does . . ." The slim man brings his hand to his throat and makes a gesture, as if he's slicing it with a knife, and pauses. "And I wouldn't want anything bad to happen to you; your friends; or your pretty, little mom in there. Would *you?*" he asks Ben.

"No, sir."

"Remember, we know where you live. And you don't know nuttin' about us." He pauses. "Be a good boy and take care of business. It'll all be over soon." He steps back into the car, and it rolls out of sight.

Ben walks back into the house in a catatonic state and collapses on the couch.

11

HEADQUARTERS

Brian, Mike, and Rob are picked up in separate cars and taken down to the police headquarters at 9:00 a.m. The police have asked about Ben's friends, and they learned pretty quickly that the foursome is known as the Dead-End Boys. Stories of them running around the neighborhood together, "causing trouble," as one kid's mother put it, abound. The boys are walking under a raincloud of suspicion and feeling like it's going to rain.

They're brought into headquarters and give each other one last look before they're ushered into separate rooms, each hoping this will be over soon and that Brian keeps his nerves in check, as they all see that his hands are already shaking.

Brian's questioned first by Johnson. "Son, we know that one or more of you boys saw something that night. But we still don't have any answers from y'all. I need to talk to you about something. Do you know that, if a person lies about a crime, he can be charged as an accomplice to that crime?"

Brian's a deer caught in the headlights.

"Well do ya, boy?!" Johnson slams his fist on the table and lets out his frustration.

Brian is jolted by his interrogator's reaction and starts to shake. "No, sir."

"Well that's right." The chief sits back in his chair and takes a breath. "So if someone lies about a murder, that kid can be charged with murder. And in this state, that means a life sentence. How old are you, son?"

"I'm ten."

"Hmmm." He scratches his head. "Ten years old, huh. That means a person your age charged with murder could spend, hmm, let's say"—he looks at the ceiling and tallies the numbers in the air with his finger—"fifty years in jail. Man! That's a long time to be away from your momma, son! Now tell me somethin'," he bellows. "What did you see last Tuesday night!?"

"I was playing baseball over at Indian Creek. It was getting late so we started heading home. I got back and ate dinner with my family."

"Son, what I don't understand is why you were playing baseball over at Indian Creek—all the way on the other side of town. Why wouldn't you just be a good little Dead-End Boy and play on your street?"

Brian can't believe that Johnson knows about their nickname. He wonders what else he knows.

"Well," Brian states, "we don't have a field."

"Yeah? Well we spoke with a couple of your neighbors who were home that night. They said that two boys were playing baseball at the end of *your* street near the woods. I wonder which two boys that could've been. Maybe you and Ben!" he yells.

Brian can feel his heart beat faster and his breaths get quicker and shallow. He blurts out, "No, sir. We were playing baseball at Indian Creek! I already told you!" The lie has become the truth. Brian's not going to budge.

After a moment, Johnson realizes that the boy isn't going to change his story, at least for the time being. His experience tells him he needs to play more tricks with the youngster—try to catch him in a lie.

He calls the deputy into the room.

"Yeah, Sarge?" the deputy answers.

"We need to interview some of those people we spoke with who saw those boys playing ball. Get them in here so they can identify the boys."

"Okay," the deputy says. "I'll get right on it."

Johnson knows full well that the neighbors he and his officers spoke with saw two boys playing ball but could not identify for certain who they were.

"Well, we're going to keep you here until they get a chance to come down," Johnson tells Brian. "In the meantime, if you happen to remember anything, we'll see if we can't take away any criminal charges that could possibly be filed against *you*." He points directly at Brian's face. "You got me, son!?"

"Yes, sir," Brian responds.

As Johnson and his colleague leave the room, Brian slumps his head over on the metal table in disbelief. He wonders who saw him and Ben playing ball on the street and whether the neighbors would be able to point them out. He starts to think about telling the truth. But Brian knows where his loyalties lie and can't let his friends down, even though he's worried about the consequences.

12

THE BAIT AND SWITCH

Chief Johnson enters the next room where Mike is, and he takes a seat. "Well, since this is the first time we're meeting, allow me to introduce myself. My name is Chief Johnson," he says, as if Mike doesn't already know this. The boys have seen him all of their young lives so far—sitting in his car, twirling donuts in his coffee, parked under a shaded tree while they're playing football. Mike knows older kids in the neighborhood who have played pranks on the chief, like sticking bananas in the tailpipe of his cruiser while he was sleeping. And he's heard stories of some kids around town who've had the experience of being arrested by him. Mike's not scared of Johnson at all. Actually, he is enjoying this. Mike likes to challenge authority. He feels like he's on a stage for himself and showing off. His natural competitive nature is poking through. It's something he's already been showing when he and Ben are on the schoolyard or playing sports in the neighborhood.

"I'm trying to find out some information on a case you may have heard about. A few men were shot behind the woods over in your area of town."

"Yeah I heard about that," Mike responds.

They're interrupted with a knock at the door. A police officer steps inside. "Sir? Could you step outside?" The officer asks.

"Right now goddammit?!" Johnson yells.

"Yes, sir. It's important," the officer answers.

"Excuse me, son," Johnson tells Mike as he steps out of the room. The door closes behind him.

"This better be good!" The chief pins the officer with a glare.

"Sir, Michael Brown has been found dead," the officer tells him.

"What!" Johnson yells. "What the fuck happened? We've had two guards in front of his room since we delivered him there!" he demands.

"Well, sir, as you know, we had to station two new guards since yesterday afternoon—after Dickerson and O'Toole were arrested 'n' all."

"So!"

"Well, we put two of the newbies on detail, and it looks like one of them went to lunch. Only one was left on duty. There was an emergency at the hospital. Someone was having a seizure. The remaining guard grabbed the man having the seizure so he wouldn't fall to the ground. He called for a nurse, and the newbie raced over to help. When he went back to guard the room, he saw Michael Brown in the bed and thought nothing of it. The nurse did her rounds an hour later and discovered he wasn't breathing. They think he was suffocated. He's dead."

"Son of a bitch! We're all over the news already! This is gonna look bad!" Johnson pauses as the vein in his forehead pulses, his face growing red like a ripening tomato on a vine. "It's gonna look really bad for us—me *and* you," he says. "Our whole case is gone unless these kids talk."

"What do you think the chances of that are?"

"Not good."

13

SOMETIMES YOU HAVE TO
KILL A MAN TWICE

The district attorney of Atlantic County steps into the room where Ben is waiting.

"Hello, son. My name is John J. Harrison, district attorney for Atlantic County. I'm here to take a statement from you. Please speak slowly and clearly into the microphone to answer my questions, and let me remind you that you are under oath."

"Yes, sir."

"Where were you on the night of the twenty-eighth?"

Mr. Harrison proceeds to ask Ben questions similar to the ones Johnson already questioned him with. He sticks with his previous responses, embellishing every now and again when he feels like he has to.

Once Mr. Harrison's done with the questioning, he turns off the microphone. "Well it's too bad you couldn't give us more information, son, especially now that Mr. Brown is dead. We would've possibly been able to arrest the men who committed this horrible act."

"Mr. Brown died?" he asks, a look of shock flying across his face faster than a speeding train. His jaw drops like a hundred-pound dumbbell.

"Yes. Oh that's right. I guess you didn't know. They've had you locked up in here for a few hours, haven't they? Actually it looks like murder. I guess sometimes you have to kill a man twice."

Mr. Harrison packs up and moves into the next room to question Brian and get his statement on record. He goes through his routine with Brian, and he's let go. Both of the boys are driven back home. Mr. Harrison tells Chief Johnson that, without Michael and with no evidence or information from the boys, "This case will go cold I know you think Slim Jimmy did this, but there's nothing to pin the crime to him," He adds.

The Dead-End Boys learned two things from their run-in with Slim Jimmy—that they would need to weigh the consequences of telling the truth for the rest of their lives and that they could truly trust only each other. Their loyalty would, now and forever, grows stronger, and these lessons would remain with them like a scar.

14

THE CITY: MIKE'S STORY

The Port Authority Path train makes its last turn around a bend as light appears from the outer world. The rail straightens to the final stop. A map of the subway showing an imaginary line separating New York and New Jersey lines the wall inside of the car. The tunnel rats begin to gather their belongings as the car sways the bodies back and forth like jellyfish in a soft current. Brakes screech as they grab the rails. A voice breaks out: "Thirty-third and Broadway."

The view out of the subway car window of still frames begins to slow. Random, scattered bodies appear on the platform as eyes peer into the car as if it were a fishbowl. Mike tightens his grip on his briefcase and folds the newspaper, tucking it under his arm. The date on the front page of *The Wall Street Journal* is February 11, 2001. He rises to his feet as the riders flow out of the doors like rushing water. The crowd slows again as they make their way through the turnstile—a metronomic tick as each person exits. Mike feels the metal slide against his hip. The crowd moves like it has its own mind, pushing everyone along without anyone's individual effort, all sharing a common brain.

Mike's leather shoe soles gently tap and scratch on each step. He balances his coffee in one hand while bouncing up and down, eyeing the sipping hole as if it's a geyser waiting to erupt. At the end of the underground tunnel, a hole filled with light makes him focus. He emerges from the tunnel as monolithic buildings rise into the sky like glass gods. The crowd is losing its common mind as people begin to break off in different directions like birds from the flock. Mike checks his watch and simultaneously picks up his speed.

"Fuck!" he expels under his breath.

He avoids a small line at a newspaper stand and bolts across the street as the sign turns to "Don't walk." Mike enters a revolving door, swipes his security card, and walks through another turnstile, squeezing into an elevator before the door closes. He checks his hair in his reflection from the inside of the elevator as it races up to the forty-second floor. A single strand of hair is out of place. Mike fixes it and gently moves his fingers over the rest of his head. He exits and walks past a secretary.

"Kathy wants to see you," she says to him. "She said, go straight to her office when you get in."

"Okay. Thanks." He nods to her while trying not to show a look of discontent on his face.

He makes his way down a hallway past executive offices. It's an extra-long walk. He's been warned about being late before and is hoping his get out of jail for free card works again. Mike knocks on the door before stepping in.

"Good morning."

"Good morning. Come in. Please close the door." Kathy motions for him to have a seat. She takes out her earpiece.

He closes the door and, after taking a few eggshell steps, sits down.

"Mike"—she pauses while sighing—"what are we going to with you?"

"I don't know. I'm sorry," he manages to expel as his eyes glance over the diplomas hanging on the wall behind her. The picture of her husband on her desk stares right through him.

"'I'm sorry' only goes so far, Mike. We've been over this before. You know I run a tight ship. What's it going to look like if you're the only one who I allow to show up late?"

"I know. You're right."

"Do you want people to find out what we're doing? Do you want me to not get promoted, or worse yet, lose my job? Do you realize they could fire me for this?"

"Just relax. You're not going to lose your job. If you have to give me a formal warning, then go ahead. I promise it won't happen again."

"I'm going to write it up. I'll have my secretary send it to you via e-mail within forty-eight hours."

"Fine. If you send it to me by tomorrow, I'll respond—give you a good reason. If it's after that, I'll be out of the office."

"That's right. You're going to Miami with your little friends. I forgot," she reminds herself in a condescending fashion.

"They're not my little friends." He angrily shakes his head. "You never give them any credit."

"I just think you're better than them."

"Well, you don't know them like I do. They're better than you think." As he says this, he gets up out of the chair and heads over toward the door.

"Well, I'll be waiting for you when you get back. Enjoy the weather."

"Yeah, thanks," he says while turning around.

She gives him a flirtatious smile, and he grins back at her.

Mike is an only child. He found out just after Ben's run-in with Slim Jimmy that he was adopted. It gave him a permanent chip on his shoulder for the rest of his life and helped feed his competitive nature. He never felt like he fit in with anyone, other than the Dead-End Boys of course. He made himself the consummate outsider, even if it looked like he fit in to others because he *did* look like he fit in. He knew how to dress, not necessarily in expensive clothes but any clothing looked good on him.

Mike's family had a little more money than those of the rest of the boys. They weren't necessarily comfortable, but they had did have a small, well-kept house. He eventually became the high school quarterback and excelled in sports. The world of athletics was a place where the chip on his shoulder did him some good. Notoriety followed as a result. It caused a little friction between him and Ben, but they also pushed each other to be better at their efforts.

He could be compulsive, looking for instant gratification and didn't worry about consequences like Ben. Some of his decisions could be morally borderline. It's always been more important for him to do what *he* wanted to do when he wanted to do it.

Mike has always known how to talk his way in *and* out of trouble. The boys have seen this many times before. Their quick-lipped friend earned his law degree and is working at the National Association of Securities Dealers in New York. The NASD is a regulatory agency that oversees financial institutions, and although working there has been great experience, Mike is starting to look elsewhere for a job. One reason is his astronomical law school loans—the size of some people's mortgages. His chances for advancement within the NASD are not looking so great. He showed up to his job on the first day of work with a black eye that was achieved on one of his wild, drunken nights. Although Mike has no recollection of how this happened, at least so far as he tells his friends, all of the guys came to a conclusion. It was Mike's mouth that got him into trouble. Then there's also the issue of his relationship with his boss.

Mike walks back down the hall to his small office and turns on his desktop. A coworker stops by on his way back from the watercooler.

"Hey, Mike." He knocks on the door. "I was able to hook you and your friends up. I got that dinner reservation for you at BED in South Beach."

"Oh thanks, man! You didn't have to."

"No problem. It was easy. My counterpart in the Miami office has some great connections down there. Have a great time. I'll see you when you get back. You can repay me by telling me your wild stories over a beer."

"Yeah, sounds great. We'll grab drinks, and I'll tell you some stories."

"I wouldn't expect any less."

Mike checks his desktop and studies the screen. His cell phone buzzes against the leather portfolio on his wood desk. His office shows some of the markings of his bachelor status. There are no pictures of a significant other or children.

"Hey, man!" he answers.

"What's up? You ready to get out of here?" Brian asks him.

"Yeah, I can't wait to get away," Mike tells him.

"Me too. I'm in the doghouse with Melissa."

"Doghouse? Again?" Mike asks.

"Yeah, we're still talking', tryin' to figure things out. It's not that easy."

"Well it should be. At least now you can do whatever you want down there and take advantage."

"Yeah, we'll see. I'll catch hell for it either way."

"Great!" Mike sarcastically adds. "Something I'll be able to look forward to when we come back from vacation—listening to my roommate argue with his on-again, off-again girlfriend. That'll be something new."

Brian changes the conversation. "Anyway, I wanted to see if you made it on time today. I know you left late."

"Yeah, I was late. Kathy's gonna have to give me a written warning."

"You're the only guy I know who screws his boss and gets written warnings for being late."

"It's part of the game, Bri; keeps it spicy. You should try it sometime."

"And risk fuckin' up my career like you? No way!" He pauses. "Oh, I almost forgot. I'm trying to get in touch with our old buddy, Aaron, from college. He works at one of the best clubs in South Beach. We'll see if we can get in for free or something. Haven't heard back as of yet."

"Sounds good. I got us reservations for dinner at some swanky place through my coworker."

"Great! I'll see you later on at the apartment; the market is about to open in a few minutes."

"Yeah, time for me to make my money too."

"That's all you really care about."

"What else is there? Plus, between undergrad and law school, I got a mortgage payment on my back."

"Don't remind me. I can barely pay mine. See ya," Brian says.

15

BRIAN'S STORY

Brian sits at his desk watching the clock on the wall as it drifts toward the opening bell. A framed photo, taken when Brian was eight years old, of he and his brother just before his older brother passed sits on his leather portfolio. The phone starts to ring; his computer lights up with different colors as the numbers start to appear. The chatter increases, a rush of adrenaline starts to flow like when he's standing next to a craps table in Atlantic City. It isn't too much different either. Bets on positions, numbers, directions. He glances up at the calendar that's thumbtacked to his cube. It's got the day circled in red. February 17—one long day ahead.

He loosens his tie and then sips his coffee while thinking about how he got into a job like this. He starts to reminisce about the days he spent with fewer responsibilities—the days with his Dead-End Boys. Maybe he should've stayed in South Jersey and lived a simpler life—one with no college loans, lower rents, and less congestion and stress. His phone lights up. It's Melissa. He sees the name on the caller ID. He thinks about answering but just lets it ring.

"Good morning Brian," the voice greets him at his cube.

"Good morning," Brian replies while realizing it's his boss.

"I wanted to hand you this month's numbers." His boss pauses while handing him the sheet. Brian sees that he's just hanging on to mediocrity and, with one small move, a job. "You know I'm expecting a lot from you this month. It could make or break your year."

You expect a lot from me every month!

"I know. I'm working on it. Thanks," he says, finishing the conversation as his boss moves on to the next target.

The realization that this will be the rest of his life washes over him like a tsunami. He can't run. He can only find something to hold on to for dear life.

16

ROB'S STORY

Rob hands the turnpike worker change for toll. He exits off the jug handle that cuts through the pine trees that make an imaginary dividing line between North and South Jersey. He's officially near his childhood home. The memories roll in like waves in his mind.

Rob parks in front of the doctor's office—a place he's been to before when he injured his arm in a wrestling match in high school. It's located about ten miles away from where he grew up. He walks into the waiting room with his briefcase; the office staff barely acknowledges him, even though he's visited several times over the past year.

"I'm here to see Dr. Letterman."

"Whom should I say is asking?" the woman in the office asks behind a small window.

"Rob O'Sullivan."

"He knows you're coming to see him?" she asks him.

"Yes he does. We spoke on Friday," he informs her.

"I'll let him know you're here. Take a seat. It will be a few minutes," the woman directs him.

He takes a seat and sees another man in a suit. They don't acknowledge each other at all, as they both know they're competing for business. A few minutes pass, and the woman at the desk speaks up. "Rob?" She motions for him to come closer.

"The doctor said he has an emergency to take care of, that he will call you to reschedule and that he's sorry."

Rob reaches through the window above the desk and hands her his business card. He knows it's futile, a waste of paper. Rob exits the office and walks back to the car, knowing he's just been brushed off. He doesn't take any offense, as it's not the first time it's happened and surely won't be the last.

He places a call to Ben.

"Hello?" Ben answers.

Rob hears Ben's truck shifting gears in the background. "Looks like my vacation is going to start early. My last appointment just cancelled."

"Cool. I'll see you in an hour," Ben replies as he honks his truck's horn.

Rob has recently broken up with his longtime girlfriend. All of the Dead-End Boys agree that Rob has a habit of getting too close to his girlfriends. Rob puts his phone down and thinks about stopping by his family's home. He has two older sisters who don't live there anymore. They're extremely overweight. As a matter of fact, his mother and father, who both work at the post office, are even bigger. If there was a person in the family who didn't look like he fit in with the rest of the family, it was Rob. He's always been embarrassed by his family members' weight and has always tried to make sure that he doesn't follow down the same path.

His mother always blames the family's weight issues on genetics, stating it's a glandular problem, but Rob knows better. He saw how they ate firsthand.

Since he had been teased a few times about his family's weight issue as a child, he had a vision of himself as being bigger than he actually was. He carried a disproportionate body image of himself.

Rob decides not to drop by his childhood home, knowing that his parents would be at work. His trip down memory lane spurred on by his proximity to his house is enough for him to handle now. He's looking forward toward the getaway with his friends. His friends are the only thing he has.

17

THE DAY

At 310 Washington, Ben's alarm violently rings out as he's awakened to start the day. His eyelids open and reveal the ceiling. He turns his head to read the clock. 7:01 a.m. His robotic morning arm reaches over, turning off the blaring noise. It's Wednesday. Any other day, he'd be slowly pulling himself out of bed, but today is no ordinary day. It's *the* day they've been waiting for. It's finally here—their Presidents' Day holiday weekend. Rob is rumbling around the apartment getting the last of his things together.

"Are you up in there?" Rob says, leaning his ears against Ben's door for the sounds of movement.

"Yeah. I'm up," Ben answers.

"I got a cab coming in fifteen. Let's get rollin'."

The buzzer for the building entrance goes off. Ben hears Rob answer. It's Mike and Brian; they're already here. Ben sits up on the side of his bed to shake out the morning cobwebs. He makes his way into the bathroom as the boys continue their chatter. "We're just gonna hang down here with our things. You gonna be out here soon?" Mike asks him.

"Sure thing. The cab will be here in about ten or fifteen."

A few minutes go by, and Ben throws the last of his things in his suitcase. He wheels it into the living area, and it clunks through the doorway. Rob is standing there waiting and checking out his messages on his cell. He looks up at Ben. "You ready?"

"Yeah. Whaddayou think?" Ben manages to mutter, rolling his eyes. He's not much of a morning talker.

Rob looks out of the window. "The taxi just got here. Let's do this."

They make their way down the stairs and out of the building. Mike, Brian, and the taxi driver are putting their suitcases in the trunk. The taxi's parked next to the trash on the sidewalk that's still covered with a dusting of snow from last week's cold front. The exhaust cloud floats into the cold air before disappearing. Small drips of condensation drop to the street from the tailpipe.

Ben and Rob squeeze the last of the luggage into the trunk and jump in the taxi. The cab heads down Washington and crawls through the morning traffic out of Hoboken onto Route 1. Within about ten minutes, they see the smokestack of the Budweiser Brewery.

"We've kept *that* place in business." Mike motions to the brewery.

The cab driver lurches forward in his seat as he laughs, breaking the tired morning silence. The boys crack a smile and chuckle.

Fifteen miles south of midtown Manhattan, the driver pulls up to Terminal C and announces that they have arrived at Newark International. "Newark to Ft. Lauderdale," the cabbie announces as he stops the vehicle. The driver hands them their bags from the trunk one by one. Brian is the first to grab his bag from the cabbie and hands him a dollar for a tip.

"Hey, Bri. I don't have any cash. Could you give him a dollar for me? I'll get you inside," Ben says.

"Oh? *You* don't have any money? What a shocker? You *never* have any money." Brian turns, searching for the others, "Hey, guys, Ben doesn't have any cash on him. You believe that?"

"Yeah, yeah. You're holdin' the guy up. Just give him a dollar," Ben tells him.

They step inside the airport, and it feels like they've just arrived at the circus. The line is snaking around in circles with many people clamoring around to check in. The automatic doors open and close as people spill inside the terminal, each time letting the cold wind sneak in. A black Town Car horn sounds off as the driver lowers his window and extends his finger.

"Asshole!" The driver yells.

It's chaos at the tenth busiest airport in the country.

"Well, looks like we're at the right airport," Rob sarcastically adds.

The four boys get in line and notice a young blond in front of them. As she moves forward, the line turns, and she is now heading back toward them. She's oblivious to their looks until she picks her head up and sees them all looking in her direction—all four checking her out in order, like monkey see, monkey do. She pretends not to notice and bends over to place her bag containing her mini poodle on the floor. As she does, their eyes all glance down to the same place. A pink thong pops out of the top of her low-rise jeans.

Rob, who is in front, turns and says, "I can't wait to get to Florida."

They smile, thinking about the opportunities they have ahead of them on the trip. An older woman catches eyes with Mike and Brian and gives them a dirty look. They turn to each other, cracking up and trying to cover their hysteria with their hands.

The boys head through security and step on the moving walkway. This place is cavernous. It seems like miles past the shops selling T-shirts that say "I love NY" and "Welcome to New York, Now Give Me Your Money," along with NY Yankees shirts and hats. Even *The Sopranos* T-shirts are selling off the rack. They have one hour to board.

Ben places a call to his mom to let her know that he's at the airport and the flight is on time.

"Okay. Have a safe flight. Be careful. I love you."

"I will. Love you too."

Mike suggests they grab a drink.

"What, are you crazy? It's nine thirty in the morning." Brian responds.

"Can't you ever just relax?" Mike says.

"It'll help me take the edge off," Ben responds.

"I'm in," says Rob. "I don't have work today. Let's start the vacation early!"

"This is a bad idea. You think we have enough time?" Brian asks.

"Pipe down. Of course we do. We're fine," Mike answers.

"Well, I gotta grab something to read for the flight," Brian says. He walks away toward a store avoiding the nonsense.

The boys take a seat at the bar. The bartender yawns before dragging himself over to them and takes their order with zero enthusiasm. The bar is empty at this time of the morning, a lonely traveling airport soul reading the newspaper in the corner its sole occupant. "Kegs and eggs," Mike says. "Just like in college. We used to do this every Sunday morning instead of going to church."

After two rounds and not having much in their bellies, the trio already feeling buzzed. Just a few more minutes to go, as the last round is on its way, along with the tab. They quickly throw they're final drinks down as they see the plane is starting to board. The boys clumsily gather their bags and saunter toward the gate. Rob drops a bag. Brian almost bumps into him as Rob bends down to grab it.

They show their tickets and board the plane. The stewardess gets on the intercom and rushes through the emergency procedures. Within minutes, the plane thrusts the engines. The fast forward ground rushes by. They enter the airspace and catch a glimpse of the New York skyline before it fades in the distance. Ben looks out of the window, checking the sights from a different point of view. It's one of a handful of times that he's been on a plane. His palms are sweaty as he holds on to the handrails of the seat, as if that would help if the plane went down. The nervousness he's getting from flying makes him realize how fragile life is. He thinks about not taking things for granted when he gets back.

Sandy Hook is clearly visible. The military Navy pier stretches out 2.2 miles. The flight heads all the way down the coast toward Atlantic City. Ben thinks about his family below.

"There's the AC Airport," Mike states out loud. "Nothing but trees."

"We're from the sticks of South Jersey," Brian reminds them.

"It looks like Kentucky down there," Rob jokes, getting a laugh from fellow passengers.

"There's nothing but trees down there. I've never been to Atlantic City, but I didn't expect the airport to be in the middle of the woods," a passenger remarks.

The fasten seat belt sign goes off. Mike heads to the bathroom and tries to make eye contact with two pretty girls he noticed while boarding the plane. It's no use. They don't pay any attention and continue reading their magazines as the flight attendants service passengers with the beverage cart. Rob decides to order a few more.

After some magazine articles, some two-liner jokes, television and radio distractions, and a terrible excuse for a sandwich, the pilot starts their descent. Ben looks at his watch. They're on time.

"I mean, why even bother with the sandwich?" Ben asks out loud.

Brian just shrugs his shoulders.

Rob is out cold after finishing his last beverage. Mike decides to touch his face gently while he's sleeping. Rob's hand reflexively moves toward his face to scratch his skin. Childish, but Mike still gets a laugh from the other two. As the flight descends, the passengers are able to see the turquoise waters of South Florida. The different colors of blues and greens are appetizing to the boys' eager eyes, which have seen nothing but charcoal skies and lifeless flora for the past few months.

The plane flies in low enough to see the coastline. High-rise condos stretch into the sky up and down the coast. Fishing piers every couple of miles line the Atlantic. Canals and water seem to be everywhere from up here.

Rob is awakened with the sound of screeching wheels as the jolting plane touches down on the hot tarmac. They've made it to Miami International. Passenger hands move in and out of bags while cell phones light up to send messages to loved ones through the great Internet sky. Rob slowly opens his eyes to see his friends all looking in his direction.

"You could sleep through anything," Brian tells him. "Unbelievable."

"We're here?" he asks.

"No, we're fuckin' dead, stupid. You slept right through," Mike says.

"Fuck you," Rob answers matter-of-factly.

18

MIAMI INTERNATIONAL

Patterson sits in his unmarked vehicle outside the Miami International Airport. His elbow is resting on the door, the window slightly cracked open and his dark fingers clutching the top of the vehicle. One of his phalanges is disfigured from a sports injury. He watches the people flooding out of the air-conditioned airport, the Miami heat hitting some of them, especially the vacationers, like a warm stove. Some of their expressions are priceless. One man lowers his bags and arms while holding his head up toward the sky and closes his eyes like he's showering or being baptized.

A taxi pulls up in front of Patterson. A man in a Fedora steps out of the cab and enters the luggage carousel area for arrivals. The man bumps into two people on the way inside and politely nods his head.

Patterson sees his partner, Stokes, exiting among them. His white skin make him easy to spot among the many shades of brown. Stokes makes eye contact and just shakes his head. Patterson knows that the man they're looking for is gone.

"Shit," Patterson expels under his breath.

The two men worked together since graduating from the academy together ten years ago. Verbal communication is overrated at this point.

"He left on the eleven a.m. flight to Columbia," Stokes informs him as he leans in through the passenger-side window. "If he's smart, he'll never come back."

"Another one slips right through our fingers. Thought we had him for a second," Patterson states, frustrated, as he waits for Stokes to say something sarcastic.

"Well, look at this way, one less crook in Miami. Of course, there's probably ten walking through those doors today alone," Stokes finally replies as he gets into the car.

Patterson doesn't even respond. He just stares out of the window, knowing that Stokes is right. Without any words, Stokes knows his partner agrees with him.

19

WASHINGTON TO WASHINGTON

The boys somehow find the patience to keep their mouths shut as an out-of-shape, older passenger grunts while trying to grab his luggage from the overhead compartments. The man narrowly misses decapitating a fellow passenger as his biceps shake and convulse from the weight of the bag. A baby coughs and smells like it needs to be changed. Ben shakes his head in disgust, sighing deeply as his patience is wearing thin like ice in a springtime river flow.

After a few more minutes, the Dead-End Boys meander out of the gate. Mike, never one to waste an opportunity to impress his friends, finally has the chance to make small talk with the two girls he saw on the plane as they walk to the luggage carousel.

"Been to Miami before?" he asks.

"No," says one. "This is our first time." They both look unimpressed.

"Oh cool. I'm Mike," he responds nonplussed.

The girls reluctantly exchange introductions.

"We know this place like the back of our hand." Mike nods toward the Dead-End Boys.

"I know what place he knows with the *palm* of his hand," Brian jokes, loud enough for Ben and Rob to hear, and the two have to hold in their laughter.

"You girls looking to have some fun this weekend? Hang out? We got a couple of really good hookups down here."

"We don't have any hookups down here," Rob says.

"*They* don't know that," Ben tells him.

"Yeah we're just looking to get away from the weather and have some fun. We had to beg our boyfriends to let us have a girls' weekend." The taller blond throws the dagger straight into the heart of the conversation.

"Ouch, the old boyfriend line. Kiss of death," Brian says.

"Yeah, we can watch his boat slowly sink now. This should be fun," Rob tells them.

"He'll never recover from that," Ben chimes in.

"Oh yeah? I had to beg my girlfriend too," the Dead-End Boys hear him say.

"Not a bad recovery; still a lot of water in the boat though, and that little bucket of his ain't gonna do," Ben quips.

The group of travelers stops at the carousel and sees their bags are already coming out.

"Well, listen. Let's exchange numbers, and if you girls wanna hang out or something, we can do that." Mike opens his cell and takes down their number. He says good-bye and walks back over to join the boys.

"How did it go?" Brian asks.

"I got their numbers," he states. "It's a start."

"Way to see the empty glass half full," Brian chides him, prompting a chuckle from Ben.

Once their luggage appears through the endless monotony of bags rolling to reggae music that pours through muffled speakers, the boys grab their belongings and head toward the exit to hail a taxi to their hotel.

A man in a fedora sees the boys exit the plane and places a call to a cab driver.

The cab driver, who's leaning against a yellow taxi outside the airport, answers.

"Four twenty-something males. Coming your way.

"I thought you wanted three?" the driver asks.

"I know. It's the best I could do. Looks like they got their vacation early."

"No problema," the cab driver says into his phone and then places another quick call. "Yeah, boss. Looks like I got a pickup." He listens for a second. "Okay, no problema." He closes the phone. He sees the boys coming his way.

"Right this way, gentlemen."

"Oh great." They throw their luggage into the trunk as the cab bounces with the weight of their bags. They squeeze into the car and slam the doors.

"We're going to the Catalina Hotel," Brian tells the driver as the taxi departs. "Do you know where it is?"

"Absolutely. Know this place very well." The driver puts his finger in the air.

Mike chimes in. "How is it there?"

"You will like it. Lots of fun, party time." The driver informs them.

"How far is it from the bars and clubs?" Brian asks.

"You can walk there," the driver abruptly answers.

"Maybe we should ask him if he knows where to get some shit," Mike mentions to Ben.

"Take it easy, man. We just got here!" Ben tries to settle him down.

"I mean we *are* in South Beach. Know what I mean? Land of the cocaine cowboys?" Mike explains.

"Yeah I know what you mean," Ben responds.

"By the way, what's your name?" Mike asks the driver.

"Why? Gonna call immigration?" he says dryly.

The response sends an awkward shockwave through the cab. The boys don't know how to react, so they don't.

The driver got the response he wanted. "It's Miguel."

Ben checks over the driver. The driver's dark five o'clock shadow glistens with droplets of drying sweat. Dark sunglasses hide his eyes.

They make their trek to South Beach and cross the intercoastal as the excitement fills the cab. The driver makes a turn onto Washington.

"So, let me get this straight. We live on Washington and we just flew to Washington?" Rob observes.

"Pretty deep thought there, Einstein," Brian says to him.

"Except it's like eighty degrees warmer dipshit," Mike responds.

"Yeah. And a thousand miles away from all the bullshit," Ben reminds them.

They're spotting pretty girls walking down the street without a care, wearing clothes that covered only parts of their bodies and clung like a mountain climber to their skin. One slip and you're in heaven.

"This is going to be a crazy weekend," Brian says devilishly.

They pull up to the Catalina Hotel, where they're greeted by the doorman. He takes their belongings and helps them check in.

A doorman dressed in all white, from head to toe, flies off the steps of the hotel. His jet-black, slicked-back hair doesn't move in the slightest. His mocha skin is genetically manufactured and farm-raised.

"Hola! My name is Julio," the doorman says, opening his teeth to the outside world.

Brian notices jagged teeth pointing in different directions, like rocks forming a jetty.

"Hola," Rob answers.

"Hi, Julio," the other three chime in.

The bellboy and Julio help them upstairs. Ben puts his bag down and opens the door with the room key. They all walk in, except Ben, who goes back out to grab his bag.

"Yeah, boss," Julio says into his cell phone, "there are four of them. I'll keep an eye on them."

He turns around to see Ben grabbing the bag. "Oh, hey *cabrón*! I just was letting my boss know, uh, that I'll take care of you guys this weekend. Anything you need, you let me know."

"Yeah," Ben answers hesitantly. "Uh, okay," he adds, heading back into the room.

There are two bedrooms and a common area all furnished with trendy South Beach stylings. White sheets are on the bed. White curtains line the windows that look down to the Washington strip below. It's not a big room, but it'll do. Ben opens the curtain and peers out of the window to see the pedestrians and traffic. He and Rob each take the single rooms that they paid for, leaving Mike and Brian to fend for the foldout bed and couch. For now, they just have one thing on their minds.

"Let's get to the beach!" Mike excitedly demands, slapping his hands together. He looks directly at Ben, who's exactly his height and eye level. Ben nods back in agreement.

They unpack a few things and start to get dressed in their bathing suits. Rob clicks on the TV. The local news station has live footage of a waterspout that was over Biscayne Bay today in Miami.

"I didn't know they got tornadoes down here," Rob says.

"They do, but that, that's a waterspout, dumbass!" Brian tells him.

"We ain't in Jersey anymore, Toto," Ben quips. "And it looks like they'll be keeping a close eye on us too. I heard Julio talking to his boss. They probably see that we're here to party. Let's try not to trash the place." He pauses while searching for his bag. "Shit! I forgot my cell phone charger." Ben tries to call his mom back home, but the phone doesn't work. "No service in here? Damn!"

They head across the street to the beach. Excitement and anticipation mix with the heat of the air as they float onto Washington off the steps of the Catalina. The traffic is flowing. They pass by girls in bikinis and guys in swim trunks—all of them covered in oil, glistening in the sun and cooking like a rotisserie. A Yellow Cab taxi whisks by, displaying its phone number. Ben puts the number in his phone, thinking they may need that later on.

They walk down Eighteenth Street pass the Delano to the entrance of the beach. It's a Chamber of Commerce, mid-eighties degree South Florida day. A man who looks like he's been sleeping on the beach for a few days and in need of a shower walks by, his purgatory tan tucked gently underneath a cowboy hat. He's strumming an acoustic guitar and singing.

Variously colored umbrellas are splayed out across the beach, each different color representing the different hotels on the strip. The boys spot the red umbrellas for the Catalina and get their free chairs and towels courtesy of the hotel. They drop their belongings and take a walk to the water. Large, anchored yachts wade in the water just off shore. Mike takes off running. Groups of young women, some with their tops on, some without, are scattered all over the beach. The boys spot a group of Latin girls who sit up in their chairs, shooting looks right back. Rob doesn't seem to notice, since he's still affected by the morning refreshments. Ben's heart skips a beat as he catches eye contact with one of the girls. He coolly cracks a smile.

"You see that?" Ben asks Brian.

"How could I miss it?" Brian responds.

Mike is the first in the clear water. "It's awesome. Come on in!"

The others follow him in. In an instant, Rob is waking up. The January water is a warm seventy-four degrees.

"The water's not even this warm in Jersey for most of the summer! This is awesome!" Brian says.

"What's that ugly thing with teeth?" Brian says, pointing at a fish.

The boys look. "Barracuda!" Mike yells. The boys each take off in a different direction.

After a few minutes of splashing and dunking each other, the boys see some topless girls make their way past them in the water.

"Now why can't every beach be like this?" Rob asks as their horseplay is interrupted.

After a few more minutes, they've had enough of the ocean and decide to get some sun. As they walk up the beach, they pass by the group of Latin girls, who are still checking them out.

"Hola," Mike says.

The girls giggle and reply, "Hola."

Rob whispers to Brian, "I guess those guys aren't their boyfriends?"

"Guess not," Brian replies.

Mike says, "What guys?" as he looks up. "Those girls *sure* weren't acting like they were with their boyfriends."

"When we went in the water, there were only two of them. It looks like another guy is there too," Brian says, referring to a man who is fully dressed and wearing a fedora.

The boys sit back and soak up the endless sun. A flock of seagulls fly overhead and squawk. Each scantily clad girl walks by looking better than the last.

After some time relaxing on the beach, Mike and Ben make their way down to the water. They don't quite make it there, stopping instead to talk with the girls who've been flirting with them from a distance.

Ben steps up to the girls who he's had his eye on. Cool, calm, and collected, he begins, "I came over here to, uh"—he pauses and finishes with an inflection in his tone—"hit on you." The pause was to build the anticipation, not because of nerves. He cracks a smile.

The girls laugh, and just like that, the ice is broken.

"My name is Dianna. You would like to sit?"

"Hi, Dianna. I'm Ben. You have such a beautiful accent."

"Muchas gracias, Ben. Where are you from?"

"New Jersey. You?"

"I live in Miami. We are staying at a friend's place for the weekend—the Continuum. You boys are here on vacation?"

"Yeah."

"Where are you staying?"

"The Catalina. You know where that is?"

"Oh, yes. It's beautiful."

Brian and Rob walk toward the girls and their friends and get introduced. They let Mike and Ben handle things and jump back in the ocean.

"Where is the place to party tonight?" Ben asks.

"We're going to Mansion. You should come," Dianna adds in a flirtatious tone.

"Definitely. We are going to dinner at a place called BED. One of my buddy's lawyer friends recommended it. Have been there before?" Ben asks her.

"Yes, it's very good."

"Let me get your number, and we'll get in touch."

They exchange numbers and promise to call. But the night is full of promise, and after all, no one wants to settle for the first thing that comes along this weekend. They grab their belongings to head back to the hotel and get ready for dinner.

"Not bad for a couple of minutes at the beach," Ben says to Brian.

"Yeah. We got some work in during our vacation," Rob says.

"We?" Mike says, and they all laugh.

"The night is young my friend," Ben says as he puts his arm around Rob's shoulder.

The boys walk off the beach as the sun is starting to go down. They float onto the street to Washington and back to the Catalina.

20

Neon Nightlife

"Dinner reservations are at nine. Let's get ready." Mike smacks Brian, who's napping on the couch, on the shoulder.

Mike heads into the bathroom where Rob is getting ready. "Who would've thought that it takes that long to get your hair to look that shitty?"

"I look good," Rob tells him.

"Compared to what?" Mike whips back.

"Shut up and get in the shower," Rob responds.

When they're ready, the boys head down to the hotel bar to have a drink. House music is filing out of the speakers.

"Where's the fun spot tonight?" Ben asks the bartender, who's bobbing his head up and down to the beat of the music.

"You guys should go to Mansion. You will like very much. I'll tell Julio to set it up for you," the bartender tells him.

The doorman makes his way over to the boys. "Hola," he says to Ben.

"Julio, right?" Ben says to him.

"Sí, you remember!"

"Sure, I remember. I overheard you talking to your boss and saying you'd keep an eye on us," Ben says to him.

"Uh, oh yeah."

"They want to go to Mansion tonight."

"I will set that up for you. Who's name should I put on the list?"

"Mike."

"Let me know if there is anything that I can do for you guys this weekend. I want your stay here at the Catalina to be perfecto. Okay?" Julio tells him as he slips away.

"Thanks; we will," Ben informs him.

The boys finish up their drinks, jump into a taxi, and head toward one of the best and most exclusive restaurants in all of South Beach. No signs mark the restaurant, and tables are hard to come by. Their taxi drops them off, and the boys head toward the velvet rope that awaits them at the door. Inside the restaurant, the dance music is blasting through the sound system.

"Party of four. We have reservations. The name is Jersey," Mike says to the hostess at the door. He nods and winks at the rest of the guys, drawing a half-embarrassed chuckle from Ben.

"Sure. Follow me," she says.

They follow the hostess inside the restaurant and are told to take off their shoes before being seated. The table is an oversized, circular bed. It's dark inside. Only flashing disco lights and candles light the way. They're seated across from a couple in their forties who are all over each other.

"That's what I'll be doin' in a little bit," Rob says.

"Yeah, with another guy," Mike strikes back.

Three girls are ushered into the restaurant and seated on their bed. The girls are all smiles, so Mike wastes no time. "You girls from Miami?"

Dinner is a mixture of appetizers, cocktails, entrées, flirtatious conversations with the girls, cocktails, desert, and more cocktails. When dinner is over, the boys order some more cocktails. The waitress comes around multiple times to take away the empty glasses, and the thirsty party becomes more boisterous with each passing second. They're a rocket ship waiting for takeoff; each moment of the imminent countdown builds on the last.

The dinner crowd is clearing out. The number of people around the bar and on the dance floor swells. The place is filling up with South Beach partiers out for the rest of the evening. Flashing lights search the walls of the room like a floodlight searching for an escapee at Alcatraz. The music being spun by the DJ is growing louder. Mike buys a round of shots, playing his never-ending role of the impresser.

"We're going to hop over to Mansion. We have a connection there and should be getting set up in the VIP area. You girls should come," Mike recommends.

Mike's phone reads twelve midnight; the lights continue to flash in and out with the beat of the music. The drinking has taken its toll on the boys' senses. They're anxious to leave the club. It's agreed that Club Mansion is the next stop. *It* is on. The boys and their newfound companions step outside and are whisked away by two taxis. They travel down Washington, packed shoulder to shoulder inside the vehicle, the girls borrowing the boys' laps. The cab approaches the club.

"There it is!" Brian says.

"It's so packed. How are y'all gonna get in? It'll take all night," one of the girls remarks.

"We know people," Mike flashes back.

The line to get in the bar flows all the way down the street and wraps around the corner. Brian walks to the front of the line, which is filled with local wannabes and vacationers who are clamoring to get in.

Hope this works, he thinks, considering the group he has behind him. Everyone in the front of the line has their eyes on their crew as well.

"Where do they think *they're* going?" they hear a girl from the line ask her friend.

"Life all comes down to a few special moments," Rob says.

The boys just look at each other and shake their heads, laughing at him.

Mike steps up to the bouncer. "Hey, man. We're on the guest list. Can we get these girls in too?"

"What name are you under?"

"Mike. There should be a total of four," he tells the man at the door.

"Mike." The bouncer's eyes scan the papers in the clipboard. "Oh, here it is. Come right in."

They follow the bouncer into the bar. Their plans are in motion.

"Act like you've been here before," Ben says to his friends.

They're given bracelets by a beautiful hostess and do not have to pay cover. She sends all of them a smile.

"Did you see that look she gave us? She knows she's hot!" Brian says.

Ben nods in agreement but looks unimpressed.

"It's the only reason she has a job. Stand there, look pretty, and make sure everyone sees you." Mike jumps in to the conversation.

"That's what *I'm* doin'," Rob says as the rest of boys shake their heads.

The manager's told that they're friends of Julio from the Catalina. They're ushered upstairs into the VIP section that's separated from the downstairs bar. The floor has its own personal DJ. The boys make their way to their table.

"Remember, Rob," he says pausing, "cucumber cool."

Rob nods back. "Cool as a cucumber."

The bottle of Kettle One is opened, and the drinks begin to flow at their table like a never-ending spigot.

Ben takes his look around the room, pretending not to notice anyone, leans into Mike and says, "The girls from today." He pauses. "They're here."

"Where?" Mike says, looking directly at the table of girls and guys Ben's referring to.

Two of the girls notice him looking before Ben has a chance to stop him.

"Whaddaya stupid?" Ben scolds him.

"What'd I do?" Mike responds.

Smiles are sent across the room by the girls, like an open invitation.

"Try to play it cool for a little bit. Remember, we got the *whole* weekend here!" Ben advises him.

Rob has disappeared into the crowd; it's something the boys have grown accustomed to with him. The club is energized as the DJ picks up the tempo, and Mike stands up to dance at their table. The boys look over at the girls from the beach. Rob is already dancing with one of them. The other girls are dancing by themselves.

Ben floats over to Dianna. He moves right in behind her. She looks over her shoulder and sees him coming. As she continues to dance with her back to him, he slides behind and puts his hands gently on her hips.

"Hola," he whispers in her ear.

She turns her head and gives a flirtatious smile.

Ben checks her voluptuous body like a Homeland Security guard checking passengers at the airport. He catches some glances from the guys Dianna is with.

"Who are those guys you're with?" Ben asks her. "You seem to know a lot of 'em in here."

"You noticed that? Guess I'm a popular girl. They're just, how do you say, acquaintances, of my brother." Dianna shrugs the question off.

"Your brother? Where's he tonight?"

"He had something to do. Couldn't make it," she answers.

The time disappears like the sun in the night sky as the boys try to control their intoxication.

Dianna walks up to Ben from the crowd. "I think we're going to go back to my friend Oscar's place. Wanna come?" she asks him playfully.

"*His* place? Why not yours?" Ben questions.

"This is South Beach. It's only three a.m."

"Your friend hasn't looked so happy that you girls are hangin' with us."

"Which one?" Dianna asks.

"The guy with the hat."

"Oh, don't worry about him. Just worry about me."

"Good answer. Where is this guy's place?"

"The Continuum. Remember I told you about it today at the beach?"

"Yeah. I remember."

"It's just down the road from here at the end of South Beach. We'll get a ride with these guys."

"Let me talk to my boys, but it sounds good." Ben turns to look for Rob and Mike, but they're all locked up with the girls. "Looks like they won't mind."

Ben walks over to Rob and Mike and says, "We're going back over to this guy Oscar's place with the girls. Dianna hooked it up. You guys wanna go, right?"

"Let's go," Mike says.

"Listen, let's be cool though. I'm catching this shady vibe from these dudes they're with," Ben informs him.

"I'm sure it's all good. They're the same guys from the beach, right? If they had a problem with us, wouldn't they have done something already?" Mike says.

"Good point. But let's not get too crazy over there," Ben warns.

They walk out, heading down the staircase to a side door. It leads them onto the street at the side of the club so they don't have to deal with the crowd. Two Chevy Yukon SUVs pull up, and Dianna turns to Ben. "Come with me, Ben!"

She whisks him in the back as the boys are split up in the two different cars.

"You guys got a car service to drive you around?" Ben asks her.

"Oh, no; this is Jorge. He's been hanging at our pad at the Continuum." Jorge gives him a quick look in the rearview mirror.

"Oh, there are people hanging out there?" he asks.

"Just a couple. Don't worry." She tries to calm his nerves.

Jorge has a black baseball cap on that's slanted to the side. He's a Hispanic male with tattoos on his arms showing through the tank top he's wearing. He leans back and to the side while he's driving. He doesn't have much to say for someone who just picked up a group of people in his car just after three in the morning.

They make it down Washington Avenue with the music pumping in the Yukon. The car has twenty-two-inch tires with expensive rims that spin. Monitors are on the back of the seats with music videos playing. Some new song by a Hispanic rapper in Spanish is on. The girls gyrate to the beats. An Xbox is hooked up to the monitors. Jorge pulls up to the last condo on the south side of South Beach. They've made it to the Continuum. Getting out of the Yukons, the Dead-End Boys slowly migrate back to the equator that's their friendship—a magnetic force always pulling them together. It's obvious that they're all highly intoxicated as they move into the condo.

The lobby is luxurious. Oversized chairs fit for kings stand in each corner. Windows race from the floor to high ceilings against each other, competing for sunlight in the day and the stars at night, and affording a view of the walk-in pool outside and the expensive beach cabanas that are more like houses with everything that you could possibly want. Marble floors and a giant chandelier add to the ambiance.

Ben sees that Rob, Mike, and Brian are in really bad shape. Jorge and the three guys who were in the club walk inside. Ben feels as if he has sobered up a little bit after walking into the lobby and catching a strange vibe from these guys.

Jorge and the driver of the other Yukon walk to the elevator. Jorge says, "Let's go." He puts a key in the elevator. It moves down as the lights on the elevator signal the floor number. The doors open. They squeeze in. Mike is in the back and making out with Evora. The elevator is quiet as Ben looks around. Two of the girls let out a giggle. After what feels like a lifetime, the doors open.

I've never been in an elevator that opens right into an apartment, Ben realizes.

They enter the foyer and into the party that's taking place. A handful of people are scattered about the apartment. Ben sees the man with the fedora. The brim hides his eyes. Jorge and the other driver make their way over to where he is seated at the table. They step over, giving him a handshake and hug. Ben assumes that this is his place. He pays no attention to Ben or his boys. A couple of girls make their way over to greet the two drivers.

"Is that the guy that owns this place?" Ben asks Dianna.

"It is," she tells him.

One of men sitting next to him gives Ben a look and Ben looks away immediately. He feels the need to watch out for himself and the boys. Ben tries to sober himself up and grabs a water bottle.

Rob and Mike are far more intoxicated than anyone else. They enter the kitchen of the condo and grab drinks with the girls. Brian follows them in. Rob goes right for the vodka.

"You need to chill a little bit. We're at someone else's place, and we don't know these guys," Ben tells him.

Rob laughs and, after finishing pouring a round of drinks, clicks Evora's glass with his before slamming it back. Ben doesn't know whether Rob ignored him or is so far off in never never land that he can't hear. Ben has done all he can to calm his friend's rowdiness. He steps out of the room with Dianna.

"What's his deal?" Mike asks, looking at Brian.

"He's right. You guys need to chill out," Brian answers.

"I think he's in love," Rob responds.

Ben takes Dianna out to the balcony to get some privacy with her and to get away from his friends.

"Sorry about them," Ben apologizes.

"It's okay. My girls like them, so it's cool," she replies.

"This view is amazing. I could stare out here the whole night."

"Yes, it's very nice," she softly agrees.

"I was talking about you," he slyly follows up.

She smiles and shoots him a look. "Over there"—she points toward the south—"that's Fisher Island. People like Oprah and J-Lo live there. You can only get there by boat. Over there," she says, pointing west, "that's the Port of Miami and the arena downtown. And that's where we came from tonight." She points north to the South Beach strip.

"Almost a three hundred sixty-degree view; not bad."

She chuckles. "I like you, Ben. You're different."

"Thanks." He pauses. "I think."

She laughs again. "It's a good thing."

"Yeah, well then, I like you too."

She looks at him, and he leans in to kiss her.

Ben looks inside through the sliding glass doors and sees Mike and Rob leading two of the girls into the bedroom. Rob steps into a table and knocks a glass bowl onto the tiled floor. There's a loud crash. It breaks into a thousand pieces. Ben sees that Jorge and the other driver are moving toward Rob.

"I'm sorry, man. I didn't mean it!" Rob tells them.

Ben flies through the hurricane-proof glass doors from the balcony and is able to step in between Rob and the other guys. Brian rushes out of the kitchen to see what's going on.

"Listen we are getting out of here right now!" he says to Mike and turns. "Sorry, guys. It's time for us to go."

Ben quickly says good-bye to Dianna and tells her he will call her tomorrow. He pushes Mike toward the door as Brian follows.

21

REVOLVER

The boys rush down the elevator in a daze.

"That was a close one," Rob tells them.

"Yeah too close," Brian responds. "If it wasn't for Ben, we would've been toast."

"I think we could've taken them." Rob is barely audible as his body gets pulled to the wall like it's a magnet. He can barely stay on his feet.

The boys shake their heads, knowing he's intoxicated.

"Too many of them," Mike says matter-of-factly.

Rob checks his watch and sees it's 3:30 a.m. He's only has one thing on his mind as they have the doorman grab them a cab.

They enter the taxi and head down Washington. Blurry lights appear in Rob's slowly blinking eyes. Lights that seem to connect and reach out to each other. Lights that have no beginning and no end. They pull up to the Catalina in a blur and fall out of the cab. Rob exits and bumps into Ben while he pays the taxi driver. The driver accepts the money and nods his head. No words. Not because he's tired from a long night of driving, but because he's seen it all before. Four obnoxious, drunk twentysomethings on vacation is far from original.

Rob stumbles like a drunken sailor across the shag carpets, up the stairs to the elevator, and they climb to their room on the third floor. They race to the door as Rob fumbles in his pockets for the room key.

"Outta the way, idiot!" Rob hears from behind and feels Ben's shoulder nudge him out of the doorway. Ben opens the door for them.

The flame is flickering on the night. Rob pours a drink of vodka for himself, Mike, and Brian. He's trying to hold onto a night that will last forever but is already gone. He sees Ben walk into his room and fall face first onto the mattress in his clothes.

Complete exhaustion overtakes Ben. He hopes the sun will never come up.

Rob and the boys laugh their drunken laughs and slur their drunken talk until the night fades to the mind's eye and into that closing hole where the will to sleep reigns.

When all of the others have gone to bed, Rob punches numbers on his cell.

There's no answer, but within a minute, he receives a call back from a different number.

"Evora?"

"Sí."

"Jump in a taxi and come over to the Catalina," he tells her. "You know how to get here?" he asks her.

"Yes, I've been there a few times to hang out."

"Cool. I'm on the third floor. Call me when you get here. I'll let you in."

She calls from the lobby, and Rob meets her downstairs. After greeting her with a hug, he grabs her by the hand to lead her upstairs. No small talk needed. The lights go out. When it's all over, they lock each other up in their arms and pass out from the long and wild night.

The door to his room opens while Rob is fast asleep. He is awakened by the movement. His arm searches the bed, but Evora is not there. He closes his eyes and waits for her to get back into bed, thinking that it must be her coming back into the room. Rob is violently hit over the head with the butt of a revolver.

The first light of day sneaks through the curtains as the room is growing bright. Ben doesn't want to get out of bed to close the heavy drapes that block out the sunlight. He chooses instead to try to fall back asleep and, hearing some movement outside of his room, thinks it must be one of the boys. The door to his room opens slowly, and at the last second he hears a footstep right behind him. As he turns around, he is thumped on the back of the head and blacks out.

22

THE ABDUCTION

The boys are dragged out of the room down the stairwell. One of Castro's crew checks his watch. It reads 6:00 a.m., Thursday, February 15. The back emergency exit door is opened. Two of the men carrying Mike use his head to keep the steel door opened as he's taken outside. The boys are shaken back and forth as they're hurriedly carried down the stairwell. Ben is completely blacked out. Rob and Brian barely hang on to consciousness.

The Escalade waits with its doors open. The boys are thrown in like laundry into a pile. They're driven down the street as the leftovers make their way home from the parties. The driver sees a police car sitting at the intersection.

"No worries," one of the men in the car says. "He's with us."

No one pays much attention as the car heads to Castro's Hialeah hideout. After a fifteen-minute drive, weaving in and out of traffic, past slow cars that try to avoid detection themselves, the Escalade pulls into the Hialeah neighborhood.

The boys awake in the early morning with their hands and mouths duct-taped. The room they're in is dark. A small amount of sunlight shines through the steel hurricane shutters that are fixed on the window. Every once in a while, one of the thugs enters to check on them—just to make sure they're breathing. Then after a few times, they only check Ben, who is moving in and out of consciousness and is in the worst shape of the four.

Mike tries to get some help for Ben when one of the thugs checks on them but is backhanded across the face. Brian decides he needs to relieve himself. His jeans pay the price. Rob follows suit. The day wears on, and as the night falls, the three boys are taken into the Escalade again. Ben is left behind.

Brian, Mike, and Rob are in the backseat. Dark, tinted windows hide them inside the vehicle. Their hands tied with plastic handcuffs, and their eyes are blindfolded. Brian thinks about the one time in his life that he saw men with blindfolds on. All of the men wound up dead. His mental scar from that time starts to bubble to the surface.

Two Hispanic men drive them down US 1, speaking to each other in their native tongue.

Then one of the men speaks to the boys. "Listen up, gringos. Your friend is dead. You will be okay as long as you do everything we say. We'll let you go after the weekend. No funny business, or it will end up the same way for you."

Tears well up in Brian's eyes as Mike kicks the seat in front of him.

"I don't believe you! You're lying!" Brian tried to yell, but only a muffled blur is audible.

The thug leans back into the car and slaps Rob on the shoulder, but there's no movement. "Looks like he's still sleepy," he tells his associate, laughing.

Mike feels something in his back pocket. It's his cell phone. His hands are tied so tightly that he cannot reach it. He remembers that he put it in vibrate mode last night and yearns for a moment when he can use it. But the boys are at the mercy of Castro's crew. All they can do is sit back and wait.

They travel down the turnpike. Mike tries to squirm around. The ride has been uncomfortable, hellish. Two long hours have gone by. He decides to speak up. "Mmm."

The passenger turns around.

"Mmmm!"

"What you want? Damn!" He rips the tape off Mike's mouth.

"Ahhh. That shit hurts," Mike yells.

"What you want, gringo?" One of the thugs asks him.

"Where are we going?" Mike asks.

"Don't worry about that. We'll be there soon," the thug informs him.

"I gotta go to the bathroom. And unless we stop, I'm gonna go all over the floor—like we all did in the house."

"Can't you hold it?" the thug asks.

"No. I gotta go now!" Mike insists. "How long before we get to wherever you're taking us?"

"Another hour," the man answers.

"I gotta go now!" Mike pleads.

"Shut up! Next place we see, we'll pull over and you can go. We'll go one by one. Now shut the fuck up!" He rips the duct tape around his mouth again to make sure he stays quiet. He tells the driver to pull over at the next scenic stop—that he'll take a look around to make sure no one is there. If all is clear, he'll take them one by one to go to the bathroom.

At least fifteen different scenic stops invite drivers along Route 1 to Key West from the main part of Florida to take a break. Visitors— some fishing, sitting on top of white coolers, some homeless and sleeping, others just taking a rest from the drive—are scattered about on all of these stops at all times, day and night. Countless people have traveled down this corridor for infinite reasons—most of those reasons to disappear. All are here to take in the view.

Minutes and miles roll by as the boys make eye contact with each other. Mike uses his foot to get Rob's attention. He uses his head and feet to try to relay that this is their chance—their opportunity to get away. Rob and Brian don't have to be told. They get it. They just hope that it's going to work.

A sign reads scenic overview up ahead.

"Yo, cabrón, let's pull over. I'll check it out, make sure we're okay," the thug tells the driver.

"They told us not to stop! For *anything!*"

"You want them to piss all over the car? We still got an hour. I don't want it smelling like piss. You know how hard it is to get that smell out? This is our work ride, fool!"

"Damn! I'm pullin' over," the driver says.

They pull off of US 1 and roll onto the gravel on the side of the road. Two cars are in the lot when they pull in. The driver rolls as far past them as he can. Small trees line up an area up ahead past the parking area. The driver turns around at the end of the lot. He positions the driver side toward the trees so they can step out of the Escalade without being seen. The passenger steps out to take a look around. He walks toward an area that's extremely dark. He turns on his cell phone for some light and hears things moving in the sand.

"What the fuck?" He hears something. It's not loud enough to be humans, but maybe an animal. He shines his light again. It looks like the sand is moving. "What the fuck, cabrón? Oh shit!" He pauses. "Thought I been smoking too much chronic." He sees hundreds of ugly crabs make their way under the sand back into their little hiding spots as he takes each step. They're scattering from the light.

He walks back to the Escalade and opens the rear passenger door. "Everything looks good," he says to the driver. "You first." He grabs Mike, pulling him out of the car.

The driver turns off the lights on the Escalade. Rob and Brian are in the back trying to get ready for anything. The passenger walks Mike over toward the trees.

Mike groans.

"If you yell, I will kill you on the spot!" The man hisses as he points his gun in his ear. He rips the duct tape off Mike.

"I need my hands free. Unless you *wanna* hold it for me," Mike tells him.

"Motherfucker!" He pauses to think. "Okay. I'll untie your hands so they can be tied in front." He puts the gun away and takes a knife out of a holster on the inside of his pant leg. He slices the knife through the duct tape around Mike's wrists. Mike feels the blood circulate to his hands. Pins and needles. The thug slowly kneels down with his head up, keeping an eye on Mike. He puts the knife away and starts to duct-tape Mike's hands, this time in front.

Mike knows this is his only chance. He backhands the man across the face. The man falls to the ground as the gun flies out of his pocket. The Hispanic man reaches over to grab the gun out of the sand.

Mike pounces on his stomach as his captor's hand comes up just inches short of the weapon. The thug pulls his hand back reflexively to protect his body and swings his other arm, punching Mike in the face. Mike falls off of him for a second. His captor leans back over to grab the firearm. Mike lurches at him, landing a punch on the side of his face. Mike is able to grab the pistol, but the man lands an overhand on his forearm. His hand automatically opens up, releasing the weapon. Mike feels like his arm is broken. He slaps the gun away with his left hand. The thug reaches down his leg, going for the knife.

In the car, Rob throws himself over the backseat to try to exit the vehicle. He knows he doesn't have many other options. The driver turns around to grab him as he tries to right himself up in the seat, but Rob reacts and kicks him. The driver is stunned. Rob tries to use his head to unlock the power doors. Brian gets over the backseat as the driver jumps at Rob and shoves his head against the door. Rob is dazed as the driver then kicks him from behind. Brian kicks the driver in the ribs. He tries the kick again, but the driver thrusts his arm down, blocking it. The driver slams his knuckles across Brian's face.

Back in the brush, the passenger pulls the knife back and tries to stab down at Mike. Mike is able to grab the man's wrist as the tip of the knife grazes his forearm. Mike throws him to the side like an arm wrestler. The knife flies out of the man's hand. Castro's boy is thrown a few feet, and he's able to grab the gun.

"Hold it right there, motherfucker!" He points the gun at Mike. "Get on your knees! I said get on your knees!"

Mike, exhausted, knows it's over. "Okay! Okay!"

"That's right, motherfucker!" He hits him in the back of the head with the gun, and Mike falls to the ground, dazed. The man ties him up again with the duct tape and heads back to the car. "I need your help to bring him back. He tried some shit," he says to the driver.

"Yeah, so did these two bitches. But I handled them. No problema."

Castro's boys drag Mike back into the Escalade and throw him in the back. The boys now have the luxury of having their legs hog-tied the rest of the way. "You boys get comfortable now. We got about an hour left," he sneers. "You can pee yourselves now," he adds sarcastically.

The Escalade pulls off the road down a dirt driveway to a house set back behind the trees and comes to a stop. The driver switches the engine off, and the two men exit the car and open the back doors.

"Time to get out, gringos. Or should we leave them in there for a little while?" he says to the other, laughing. "What's that? I can't hear you. Sounds like you have duct tape"—he pauses—"on your face?" They both laugh.

The man leans into the car and cuts the duct tape off their legs with his knife. He and the driver pull the boys out of the Escalade one by one. A light comes on the porch. The front door slowly creeks open. An almost inhumanely large figure steps out of the house and into the porch light. He doesn't say a word. The tattoos on his muscular, dark skin come into focus under the light. His big lips and thick, protruding nose accent a frightening stare.

"Raul?" the driver asks, but there's no response.

"Take them to the shed next to the pool. Tie them to the chairs. Make sure you do it right!" Raul says sternly.

"No problema." The man pushes Brian forward. "Let's go. I said move it!"

The boys and their captors start to walk to the side of the house toward a shed. The door to the shed is opened, and one of them turns on the light. Three chairs are already set up.

"Raul? *The* Raul? Damn. Things must be serious! Raul's only brought in for the shit that *has* to go down right," the thug tells the other.

"That's one of the meanest faces I've ever seen! You've seen him before?" the driver asks.

"Only once," the thug tells him.

"You did a job with him?"

"No. Never. Raul doesn't work with anyone. Just himself," he informs the driver.

"I thought he was a myth. Like the Chupacabra. Where did you see him?"

"Let's put it this way. Last time, I saw him with a few other people. Those other people won't see him no more."

"Oh shit."

"Yeah, oh shit," the thug says, looking at the driver with worried eyes. "Castro rarely uses him. Raul does the dirty work, the stuff that's too risky for us—things that are out of our league and need to get done. He's a hired gun. And he's the best." The thug pauses as he realizes his partner is trying to process the information. "During the eighties, he served in an elite, highly trained paramilitary team known as the Kaibiles in Guatemala—kind of like the Navy SEALs. But these dudes were badass. They even slaughtered their own people."

The boys can't believe their ears. They are led to the chairs, tied down, and left alone. Mike's still clinging to the hope that his cell phone will help them. He reaches into his back pocket and is able to grab it. He feels around on the keys with his hands still behind his back.

He then enters the numbers 911 on his phone and hits call.

"Hello? This is 911. What is your emergency?"

"I repeat, hello. This is 911. What is your emergency?"

"Hello. Hello?"

But Mike cannot answer. "Hmmm! Hmmm!"

Brian and Rob can't believe he's got his phone. It gives them their first sign of hope.

"I'm so tired of this!" the 911 operator states.

"What's that?" her coworker responds.

"These emergency cell phone calls. I mean we get them all the time now. The ones calling on accident, but also the ones that don't respond. We can't track them. They could be calling from a faraway city or county, and there's no way for us to track them. We can't help even if they're for real," the 911 operator tells her coworker.

"It's frustrating. Can't wait for the day when they can track signals in the air," the coworker responds.

The line goes dead.

The door slowly opens, and a large figure enters the boathouse. He drops a bag on the floor and closes the door behind him. Mike gently tucks the phone back into his back pocket.

"As you know, you're in trouble. But if you do what we want, no one will get hurt, and you will get to go home from here. Got that? Good." He pauses. "Now listen to me. I don't repeat myself. I don't put up with any gringo shit. We have a shipment that we need to pick up. It's just a few miles offshore. Some of us are being watched, and we cannot take the chances of being caught, as you say, red-handed. I will show two of you how you will use a GPS, find the packages, and then dive into the shallow water. I will keep one of you here for insurance. One of my men will come with you on the boat. Got it?" He pauses. "Good."

The door opens again and two thugs walk in. "We're gonna untie two of you. No funny shit or we'll take care of you gringos. We're gonna have these two put on the gear and get in the pool. Leave that one alone," he says, talking about Rob.

The two thugs walk over and start to untie Mike and Brian.

23

OVERTOWN

Four Haitian boys in their ragtag clothes are playing soccer on a dead-end street. The street ends at a highway overpass. Sounds of passing cars zipping along the highway fill the air. They're playing on a street where, when the sun goes down, drugs and prostitution take over. Gunshots echo throughout the night sky. It's not unusual for the police helicopters to fly over during the day. The locals call them "Ghetto Birds." Overtown, Miami, is one of the poorest and highest crime ridden neighborhoods in all South Florida.

The Haitian boys kick the ball and run down the street, past abandoned homes and other ones that are barely standing. They kick the ball past an open yard that is filled with debris and follow it into an open area. Amid the garbage, discarded tires, and overgrown grass that's waist high, they make their way to the ball and see something lying in the field. It's a body. They don't gasp or seem surprised, except by the fact that the boy is white and in their neighborhood. They gather around the body without saying a word. One of the boys puts his foot on the ball and looks down at the body.

Ben's eyes open. He's on his back and staring up toward the sky. The world comes into focus. He looks to his left and sees the four Haitian boys that have stumbled upon him. The pain is unbearable. Everything in his frame is hurting. His body feels like it was hit by a freight train. He struggles to sit up, moans, and asks the boys, "Where am I?"

They look at each other, say something in Haitian Creole, and run back to the street. They continue to kick the ball and play soccer, ignoring him. Ben is perplexed, trying to remember what has happened. He can't remember *anything*. While sitting up, he rolls over to his left side to make it easier to stand but falls back to the ground. The dust kicks up in the air, and his face falls into the dirt.

"Motherfucker!"

He tries again in the same fashion. This time, he succeeds and looks down at his feet. His sneakers are gone. The blazing South Florida sun is beating down on his back. He wonders how he got there.

Ben turns around in a circle to get a three hundred sixty-degree view. He's trying to figure out where he is. His head is spinning as he peers around the desolate lot in a godforsaken part of town. It looks like he's in the ghetto. Ben is so dehydrated his hands are shaking. The lightheadedness overwhelms him. But he needs to get out of here and get something to drink.

Slowly limping through the yard like a damaged dog, he stumbles over some debris on his way to the street. He stops and looks to his left where the street ends. He looks to his right and sees down a street that cuts right through the neighborhood.

Ben heads to his right and tries to quicken his limping walk down the street toward the neighborhood houses, away from the underbelly of the highway overpass. His clothes are dirty like the rest of him. Dry blood has crusted under his nose to his lips, and droplets have stained his shirt. He touches his pounding head and feels a swollen eye.

Heading down the street past the open field, among the cracks on the misshapen sidewalks, he looks at the first home on his right and sees bars on the windows. A weight bench sits inside a broken fenced yard. He looks over to the other side of the street. He sees an older black woman sitting on a chair on the porch. She's extremely overweight. The woman is dressed in a dirty wifebeater, shorts, and sandals and obviously isn't wearing a bra. Her hair is unkempt. A fan is pointing in her direction, and it doesn't look like she will be leaving the porch at all that day, or maybe any other. She's a permanent fixture of sorts. She's staring at him, and they catch each other's eyes as Ben glances over. He notices that the all of the houses on the street have their windows open, even though the temperature is in the eighties.

As foggy-headed Ben lumbers down the street, his cell phone rings.

He searches his pockets. It reads Saturday. "Hello?" he groggily answers.

"Yo, dude! You were so fucked up the other night. You still alive?" the caller asks.

"Who is this?" Ben asks.

"Yo, it's me, Sean!"

Ben is still trying to gather his thoughts.

"'Member calling me? Holy shit, man! You *musta* been fucked up. Sounds like South Beach is crazy. You sons a bitches!"

"I talked to you the other night?" Ben is perplexed.

"Yeah, man. You gave me a call, and you were goin' on about all sorts of shit. I couldn't really make sense of it all," Sean tells him.

"*I* called *you?*"

"Yes, *you* called *me*. Is there an echo? Musta been a booty call. It was like five a.m.! What the hell were you guys doing?"

"I called you at five a.m.? What night was that?" Ben questions.

"Dude. You were outta your mind, huh? It was last night. Well, Friday morning—this morning."

"There's no way today is Friday!" Ben whispers under his breath. Sean doesn't hear him.

"You were telling me that, if I spoke to you again, to make sure that I gave you an address and this guy's name. What was his name again? Oh yeah. It was Oscar. I got that address for you too. Wrote it down on a piece of paper." He pauses. "Where did I put it?

Hmmmm. Let's see, is that it? No." He fumbles through some papers. "Oh yeah, here we go. His address is 12364 Southwest 178 Terrace, Overtown, Florida. Is that your connection or something?"

"Hold on," Ben says as he puts the address in his phone. He notices that the battery on his cell phone is running low. "Did I tell you anything else?"

"No, man. I just thought you guys were partying hard or something. I really didn't want to find out at five a.m. You scared me a little bit; you were pretty intense. And oh, by the way, you woke up my wife, and she was pissed. Thank you so very much for that; probably won't get laid for at least two weeks now. Everything okay?" He asks without really wanting to hear the answer. "Well, I gotta go" Ben can hear the kids in the background screaming, "I gotta take care of this. Call me when you get back, and we'll grab some lunch. Later." He hangs up.

Ben is left clueless on the street, more confused than ever.

He walks to the nearest intersection to read the street names and, hopefully, call a taxi if his cell phone doesn't die first. In one of the houses diagonally across the street, a man steps out of his house and onto the porch, where he sees Ben. Ben decides not to look in his direction and lock eyes with him.

But Ben can feel the man's stare. Through the corner of his eye, he sees the man get on his cell phone. He makes it to the intersection. The wires hang down from the street lamps, not fixed since the last hurricane. The telephone poles look like they're drunk and can't stand up straight. One strong breeze and look out below. He starts to look at the street signs. One reads Martin Luther King Blvd. The other has bullet holes in it, so it's hard to read. It doesn't make him feel any safer than before. He makes out the sign and calls the number for the taxi service that he put in his phone upon first arriving in South Beach.

"Hello. You've reached the party taxi, mon," a man answers with a heavy Jamaican accent.

"Yeah, I need a ride," Ben tells him.

"Where you at, mon?" the man asks.

"I'm at the corner of MLK and SW 148th Street."

"Where you goin'?"

"To the Catalina Hotel in South Beach," Ben directs.

"All right, mon. I will be there in ten minutes."

"Could you make it any faster? I'm in a bad part of town, and I want to get out of here as soon as possible."

"I will be there when I get there, mon—as fast I can, I assure you. Hang tight. Be there in a jiffy," the man responds.

"Thanks."

Ben hangs up and continues to wait on the corner. A car pulls up to the house across the street. It's a Chevy Lumina that's blasting some rap music that Ben has never heard of before. The license plate reads "D-Reaper." The car has gold rims that must be twenty-two inches. The man from the house walks up to the car and leans in to talk. He looks across the street at him. Ben knows the man is talking about him. The passenger door slowly opens, and out steps another adult male. He's a little overweight. His belly rounds out the bottom of the white tank top. He closes the door of the car. He sizes Ben up with a quick glance.

Ben knows he's in trouble. The man makes it around the car to the driver's side, his gold chains swaying with each step, where the men seem to be deciding what to do. Ben makes sure he doesn't make any eye contact, but he is trying to survey the scene out of the corner of his eye. He needs to get out of here quick and wonders if these guys know anything about what happened to him.

The men stand around and converse. All of a sudden, the car turns off. The music cuts out. The silence is paralyzing. The two men outside the car step back as the door slowly opens. Ben is frozen with fear on the hottest February day he's ever experienced. Another guy steps out of the vehicle from the backseat. The man, who has a gold-plated grill, gold-rimmed sunglasses, and a diamond-studded watch, buttons his sport coat and says something to the other men. They look over at Ben. Ben's heart is racing faster and faster.

The men take a step in Ben's direction. One of them reaches into his pants to pull out his gun.

Out of nowhere, a car rips around the corner, and Ben realizes it's his taxi.

"Get in, mon!" the Jamaican shouts to him.

Ben jumps in the backseat as the car is moving, and before he closes the door, the taxi screeches down the street. "Think you are goin' to owe me a big tip, mon." He laughs. "Looks like you were in some trouble there."

"Yeah? I thought I had the whole thing under control," Ben sarcastically quips and looks back at the men out of the window as the car races. He pauses. "What's your name?"

"My name is Bahama. I'm from the beautiful country of Jamaica, mon."

"Well thanks for saving me . . . I probably do owe you a big tip."

"Where we goin', mon?"

"Take me to the Catalina Hotel in South Beach."

"Catalina Hotel." The driver slowly ponders as he rubs his chin. "Sure. No problem. What you doin' way out here?"

"Your guess is as good as mine," Ben answers.

"Oh, I gotchya, mon." He laughs. "You were lookin' for some of that dark meat huh?" The Jamaican laughs again.

"Yeah whatever." Ben shakes his head and chuckles.

They make their way to the Catalina Hotel. Ben peers around the taxi and sees the colorful flag of Jamaica. Some incense is on the dashboard, along with a picture that shows Bahama's a certified Florida taxi driver. The taxi smells like marijuana, although Ben is sure that the driver has tried to cover up the smell.

"Smells good in here," Ben says sarcastically.

"What? Oh yeah, mon. Those are some good incense. Straight from Jamaica," the driver answers as he bobs his head back and forth to the beat of the reggae music coming from the radio.

Yeah right, Ben thinks.

They're headed across the Venetian Causeway, and Ben starts to think about all the things that could have happened to him. He knows he drank a ton of red bull and vodka, but he remembers most of the night. He thought at first that maybe he got lost, or mugged, but remembers that he made it back to the Catalina with the boys.

The myriad of thoughts consumes Ben's mind. He wonders if he was too drunk and went back out on his own. He still has his cell phone and wallet. He can recharge the battery when he gets back.

Ben tries to calm himself, knowing that, as soon as he sees the boys, they'll probably know what happened, or he'll be able to put the pieces together from the information that they tell him. But he also knows he will never hear the end of it from them. He feels sick, dirty, and tired. His shirt is stained with sweat, blood, and dirt. Ben can't believe he will be walking into the hotel looking like this. It will be embarrassing. He can't wait to get clean.

The taxi makes it down Washington to the hotel. "Here we are, mon. That'll be thirty-six dollars."

Ben hands him his debit card. The driver slides it through the credit card machine, and Ben leaves him a tip.

"Oh no! Not again!" the driver yells and leaps out of the car.

Ben looks up to see smoke coming from under the hood. The car's overheating. The driver stands in front of the car and opens the hood. Ben steps out of the taxi to head into the hotel and, hopefully, put an end to this nightmare.

"Good luck, bro." He waves to the taxi driver, who coughs from the smoke.

Ben makes his way up the steps. The doorman Julio moves toward him and says, "Where you been?" He looks Ben over and adds, "God damn! You look like shit! What happened to you?"

"Where are the guys at?" Ben asks him.

"What you mean, man? I haven't seen you guys in two days. Did you go on an excursion or something? The Keys?"

"Hey, stop messin' around!" Ben's voice grows louder. His anger pulls the skin above his nose and between his eyes together, creasing his future wrinkles. His demeanor changes in a moment's time. It's obvious he's becoming frustrated with the situation. People are stepping in and out of the lobby giving him strange looks. He's embarrassed and wants to get to his room.

"Man, I already told you! I haven't seen you or your friends in two days. You all right, man? You guys get involved in some shit you shouldn't have?" Julio asks.

"Man, I don't know what's goin' on. I'm gonna go to my room and start to figure this shit out."

He steps into the hotel lobby, puts his head down, and jumps on the elevator to the third floor. He wonders where his friends are. Three other hotel guests step away from him. He can feel their eyes on him as the elevator slowly climbs. Two, the number for the second floor lights up. Three, the number lights up. Ding, the bell rings and the doors open up to his floor. His heart is pounding. He tries to swallow but is parched.

He searches his pockets for the room key and puts it in the door. "Come on!" The red light flickers. He tries it again. Eternities flash by as he waits for the light to turn green. It flashes. He turns the door handle. Ben walks into the hotel room, hoping to see the boys or any sign of them. He glances up into the kitchen where beer cans, liquor bottles, glasses, and snack bags are strewn around the room.

"Hey! Are you guys here?" he shouts. His voice rings out unanswered.

He swings the door to his bedroom open, checking where he was sleeping. The covers are on the floor. He looks around the room, searching for something, anything. There's nothing. He wonders if the others went somewhere without him.

"What the fuck?" he yells in frustration.

He flies into the other room. He finds only bags by the couch and clothes scattered about. He sees blood on the floor—droplets of blood that start near the bed and lead out of the hotel room to the front door. Ben opens up the door and sees another drop, but it ends there. *Something* must have happened here. He goes back into the room and sees something on the floor as he moves the sheets around. It's a scrunchie. He picks it up. A long strand of dark hair hangs from it—a girl's hair, like Evora's.

Ben twirls the scrunchie in his hands, pondering his next move. He needs to charge his phone and speak with Julio. Ben plugs in the phone and tries to call Rob, but there's still no service in the room. Ben steps into the bathroom to wash his face and then grabs a shirt to change. He grabs the room key on the way out and hits the button for the elevator.

He taps his foot impatiently, instead making his way down the hall to the stairwell. He rushes down and opens the door into the lobby. Looking across the lounge area, he sees Julio standing at a podium near the entrance to the hotel. Julio has his back turned to him. Ben starts to make his way over.

Not even one step is finished when he spots Dianna stepping out of the bathroom. She catches Ben's eyes, and her face turns pale white. She turns in the opposite direction, trying to ignore him. Her hair whips behind her. She's trying to leave through the back.

"Dianna!"

But she continues to walk. Ben follows her and is a few steps behind before she makes it out of the lobby.

"Dianna!" he pleads.

She stops and slowly turns around. She has a confused and scared look on her face.

"Wha-what are you doing here?" she stutters.

"What do you mean what am I doing here? I'm staying at the hotel, remember?"

"I mean, you, you're okay?"

"Yeah I'm okay. I guess. I don't know. Do you know something I don't? I can't find the guys. Have you seen them?"

"How are you here? I thought you were, uh . . ."

"You thought I was what? Dead? Do you know what happened? Listen, I need to find the guys; please help me!"

"Things aren't safe here. I can't talk to you."

"Listen, I know one of your girls was in the room with Rob."

"You do?"

"Yeah I do. Where is he? *Why* are you acting like this?"

"I can't talk. We aren't safe."

"Why do you keep saying that?! Why aren't we safe? What are you not telling me?!" he demands.

"Oh my God!" she says and grabs Ben and pulls him out of a door at the back of the hotel lobby. A little garden area with a small fountain provides the sound of tranquility that only lasts for a fleeting second. Ben looks through a glass window and sees the man with the hat from the other night. He stops and talks to Julio. Ben sees them leave quickly after talking and head toward the elevator.

"What? Does he have something to do with all of this?"

"Listen, you are in big trouble. I didn't know what they were gonna do to you guys." Dianna looks around to check whether anyone is watching them.

"What?"

"Listen, my brother owed Castro some money, and he was going to hurt him if I didn't do him a favor."

"Who's Castro?"

"He's a bad man—the kind you don't mess with down here. He's got the city under his thumb. I didn't know he was going to hurt you guys. Please believe me! They just told us to flirt with you guys, party, and get you back to the Continuum." Her head continues to be on a swivel, surveying the scene like a referee in a game of life-and-death.

"You mean you guys set us up from the start? At the beach?" Ben is trying to process the information.

"They were at the beach with us too, remember?" Dianna asks him.

The thoughts of the day on the beach fly through Ben's faded memory. It was only days back but seems like another lifetime, considering the events that have unfolded. He remembers the men at the beach. "Yeah, I do now."

She pauses. "Listen, I'm sorry. They were going to hurt my brother, or worse. Since my father's been gone, *I* take care of my mother. She's been in bad shape. She couldn't take it if something happened to Kelvin!"

She's pleading, but for what? Ben wonders. *Forgiveness?* Then Ben is hit with the proverbial ton of bricks—the guys are in serious trouble.

"What did they do with my friends?" he demands with blazing eyes.

"I don't know." Her worried eyes dart around like a mouse in a snakepit, searching to see if hungry predators are lurking to feast on their prey.

"Dianna, you *have* to tell me! Please!" he begs her.

"Listen. When I was at the Continuum, after you guys left, I heard one of Castro's guys talking about taking you guys to the Keys—something about taking a boat out and picking up a package using a GPS. But that is all I know." She turns to look back into the hotel through the window of the outside garden area and sees another one of Castro's men enter the hotel. "See." She points to the man, knowing that she and Ben are in the middle of the lions' den. "You can't do anything to Castro. He even has the police on his side."

Ben looks back through the window and keeps himself hidden behind the curtain. He sees the man Dianna is speaking about. "The police? He's a cop?"

"He's Miami PD. There's a whole bunch of them under investigation right now for running drugs. They were giving protection to Castro and his crew." Dianna finishes, "Look, I already told you too much. You're in danger. One of the girls told me that you were dead, and from the looks of it, they tried. Good luck, Ben." She kisses him and slips out of the back of the hotel.

"Please, Dianna, if there's anything you can do to help me . . ." he pleads as she disappears back into the hotel.

Ben looks through the window into the lobby once again, still keeping his body hidden behind the curtains. He can't trust anyone here. They're all in on it. He can't believe this whole thing was a setup. Just at that moment, he realizes he needs to speak with this guy, Oscar.

24

DIANNA

Julio is talking to the policeman. Ben sees them head out of the lobby up the stair and wonders if they're going to his room.

Ben walks as discreetly as possible through the lobby. A man glances up from his newspaper. Paranoia takes over. *Everyone* looks suspicious. He doesn't know who's there for business or pleasure and who has more twisted motives. He grabs a lunch knife off one of the tables and is about to slip out the door when he feels an arm grab him from behind. He whips around and sees a hotel manager.

"I want to talk to you about the other night. We've had some complaints about noise in the room early in the morning. I would like you to come with me into the room over here so we can discuss this." The manager motions to the room on the side of the lobby. Ben is extremely frightened and knows that this may be a setup. Even if it's not, Castro's buddy and the cop are lurking in the hotel.

"Listen, man, I have an emergency I have to deal with. Can we take care of this later?"

"I think we need to take care of this now, sir." He again motions to the room.

A family of tourists is entering the door, and Ben sees this as the chance to get out. He slips in between them and says on the way out, "Listen, I will be back in a few hours, and we can talk then."

He steps outside and sees the Jamaican taxi driver who is closing the hood on the taxi and stepping around the vehicle to leave.

"Hey! Can you take me to 12364 SW 178 terrace in Overton, Florida?"

"Sure, mon. You must be a glutton for punishment." The driver shakes his head.

"Yeah," Ben barely answers while looking out of the window, not interested in small talk.

"But seriously, everything okay with you, mon? You in trouble?"

"That's what I'm trying to figure out right now. I don't really remember what happened to me." He pauses.

"Yeah that used to happen to me in Jamaica, mon, but it was from the rum." He chuckles.

"Seriously, man, I'm not fucking around!"

"Gotchya, mon. Sorry."

"Yeah. I think my boys are in some kind of trouble. This address where you're taking me—I think this guy knows something. I hope he tells me something, anything, so I can figure out what's going on. Some guy named Castro is involved; that's all I know, and no one wants to talk to me about it."

"Castro? *The* Castro?"

"Yeah." Ben sits up in his seat. "You know him?"

"Yeah, mon. Everyone in South Beach knows him. Castro's the boss. I heard he's got a place in South Beach, but he's rarely seen around town. He's got this city wrapped around his finger. A lot of people are on his payroll. He brings in drugs and stolen items through the port. Even has the police in his pocket. Heard he's got some childhood friends on the force. Information flows back and forth, all so he can benefit. I heard the feds been watchin' him, so he's been staying low-key." Bahama pauses. "I got a connection through one of his boys; know what I mean?"

"Yeah," Ben says.

They travel Interstate 395 across the MacArthur Causeway. They take an exit to Overtown. The neighborhood does not look like the images Ben has seen on the television for Miami. Ben doesn't know what he's going to say to this guy, Oscar, or what he will do if Oscar tells him nothing. This whole thing is a long shot. Dianna was frightened to tell him anything. She even thought he was dead.

Ben wonders how he got this address and number. He wonders if this guy, Oscar, had something to do with his boys disappearing, if he was the one who left him for dead.

Ben doesn't know where else to turn. He can't go to the cops and knows that his boys would do anything for him. He will stop at nothing to help them, even if the chances are slim to none.

"Let me see, mon. This is SW 178 Ct. Hmmm. This must be it here. Yeah this is the street. Let's see. 12364? Here it is, mon."

Ben slowly gets out of the taxi, closes the door, and steps up to the passenger side. He leans in to the car. "Can you hang out here for a few minutes?"

"No problem. As long as this ride doesn't overheat again, everything will be fine."

"Thanks."

Ben looks at the house and walks up the driveway. In front of the house sits a Dodge Charger. It looks brand new. Too bad the neighborhood doesn't look the same.

The house is the best kept house on this street. The lawn is manicured, and the roof has barrel Spanish tile. All of the other houses look a little more dated and tired, like they're ready to fall apart. The bars on the windows don't send a welcoming message, but Ben nonetheless opens the gate and makes his way to the front door. The welcome mat reads, "GET OUT!"

Ben lifts his hand and presses the button to ring the doorbell. He's sweating and extremely nervous. The sun, still burning in the sky like a ball of fire, follows his every move. He knows he may well be about to confront one of the men who left him for dead. He clutches the knife in his pocket.

"I hope this works," he whispers under his breath.

The door is slightly open. Nothing stirs inside, so Ben rings the doorbell again. Again no movement. He ponders his next move.

"Oh no, mon!"

Ben turns around to see that the taxi is overheating once again. He decides to take a look around back to see if anyone is there. He opens the gate and walks along the side of the house, peering into the backyard. Nothing. No one is there. He leans on the fence for a minute to figure his next move.

Ben finally walks back around to the front of the house and sees that the car is no longer overheating.

"You fixed it quick this time."

"No, mon. Not me. This gentleman came from across the street and helped me fix it. Nice guy. He went into the house you were just trying to ring. I'll introduce you to him."

Ben can't believe his luck. He runs up the driveway and to the steps to the front of the house, knocking on the door. There's no answer. He hears the sound of water running in the kitchen. Ben knocks harder this time, and in his best Jamaican accent says, "Hay lo?"

The man answers, "Yeah come on in. Just filling up some water for you."

Ben opens the door and steps into the house. He makes his way across the living room toward the kitchen where the water is running. The view of the kitchen is blocked by a wall. He's slowly stepping into the dining room, where he'll soon be able to see the man inside the kitchen.

His body turns to the right as he sets foot in the dining room. They catch each other's eyes immediately. The man's standing in the kitchen with two one-gallons milk jugs filled with water in each hand. The jugs immediately fall to the kitchen floor. The look on the man's face is familiar—it's the same one he saw before on Dianna's face.

"Are you Oscar?"

"What are you doing here?" The man snarls, "Get out of my house!"

"Listen, man, I need to ask you some questions," Ben replies.

"Get out of my house, man!" the man shouts even more loudly.

"Where are my friends?" Ben takes a shot in the dark.

"I don't know anything about you or your friends! Get out of my house before you get hurt, gringo!" The man steps up toward Ben to threaten him.

"How do I know your name then?"

"The taxi guy probably told you!" Oscar motions outside the house.

"I'm not leaving until you tell me about what happened to me and my friends!"

Oscar makes a run at Ben and shoves him back a few feet. Ben stumbles backward over the coffee table.

"I said get out, motherfucker!" Oscar growls. He makes another run at Ben, but this time Ben is ready. He squares up his shoulders and lands a left jab. Then with a right-hand blow to Oscar's head, he slows Oscar down and knocks him back a few feet into the dining room. The couch is knocked a foot back and over during the scuffle, and Ben sees something.

"What's that?" he says, as Oscar is trying to knock the cobwebs out. He sees a pair of Diesel sneakers—the same ones he bought before the trip to Miami. "Those are mine, motherfucker!" Ben rushes over to grab them.

Oscar darts at Ben with a roundhouse, but Ben puts his hands up and brushes the blow away. He steps back a few feet in defense and looks at the one sneaker he was able to grab. "These are mine," Ben screams. "The same size and stains. I *know* you know *something*. Tell me what happened!" he demands.

"Fuck you. I ain't telling you shit. I'd be in more trouble if I told you," he yells.

"You're gonna catch the beating of your life then, bitch," Ben warns him.

"Yeah? You see this neighborhood I live in? Think I'm scared of some fuckin' gringo? Not a chance, man!"

"We'll see about that."

Ben steps toward Oscar and squares up his shoulders while putting his hands up. He takes a left jab at the thinner Oscar, but Oscar blocks it and lands a hard right hand on the side of Ben's face that knocks him back. Ben has been in his share of fights in his life. The one thing he knows is that he can take a punch, but he sees a look in his opponent's eye, despite Oscar's attempt to hide it, that this isn't his first rodeo. Ben shakes it off as Oscar comes in to finish him off. Oscar tries to connect with another punch, but Ben steps out of the way. Oscar is way off balance and has left himself in a vulnerable position. Ben pounces on the opportunity, and his opponent's body. Ben hits him with a right on the side of his face. Oscar is down from being off balance and the hard blow. Ben jumps on top of Oscar and is pummeling him with a right, left, right, left.

"You scared of the gringo now aren't you, bitch!"

It's a bloody and violent scene, but Ben needs to beat the truth out of this man. He needs to prove that he could kill him, and he needs Oscar to believe it as well. Soon, Oscar is motionless and barely hanging on to consciousness.

Ben pulls the knife out from his pocket and presses it against Oscar's throat. "You gonna tell me what happened to me and my friends? Or are you gonna die?"

Oscar, with barely enough energy to speak, grunts out, "You won't kill me. If you do, you won't find out shit." He spits blood out of his mouth.

"Yeah?" Ben asks. He lifts the knife up in the air and slams it into the skin of Oscar's shoulder, purposely not quite catching any muscle.

"Oh!" Oscar screams in agony.

Ben rips the knife out of Oscar's shoulder, and blood starts to ooze out of the gaping wound. Oscar grabs his shoulder while screaming in agony. Ben gets up, off of Oscar, and heads into the kitchen. Filling up a glass of water, he gulps it down and then fills it up again. He searches the house and finds some rope in the laundry closet and grabs a chair from the dining room. He brings the chair and the rope into the room and props Oscar up on it. He ties Oscar up and makes him take a drink. Oscar is barely moving. Ben throws some of the water in Oscar's face.

"I got all day, motherfucker. And I'm gonna do whatever it takes to get you to talk." He reaches back and punches Oscar in his bloody shoulder.

"Ohh!" Oscar yells out in excruciating pain. "I'll tell you!" He gives in.

Ben can't believe that he is going to crack already.

"Listen, man, all I know is that I get a call from Castro. They tell me to make sure that I am home—that they're coming over. You don't say no to Castro. I owe him some money. So they show up at my house the other morning. The sun is coming up and shit, and they bring you in. I tried to tell them that I didn't want you here. They got you wrapped up in a carpet. You were in and out of consciousness. Before I saw you, I thought you was already dead. They open up the carpet and you look bad, man—not much worse than you do now. They tell me they got your friends and they are making an example out of you. They figure your friends will do whatever they want them to do."

"What do they want them to do?"

"They took them to Big Pine Key. Castro runs drugs from down there. He's got these Colombians that drive a boat that can't be tracked by radar. They stop a few miles offshore and drop the goods in the water. Sometimes, they make the drop by plane; hell, there's even word that he's got a sub. Castro picks the shit up by GPS in the middle of the night. This way there's no meeting. No shit that can go wrong during the switch. Castro does the same thing with the cash—tells the sellers the location and it's all done. The thing is the Coast Guard and the Feds are on to him, even some of the straight local cops, and he knows it. He's being watched too."

"So he took my friends to do this for them? Why them?"

"I don't know. They probably needed three people to do the job. They get rid of you and your friends know they mean business; that's my best guess. You're one lucky motherfucka, gringo. Tough too."

Ben can't believe this. He walks around in a circle to think about his next move.

"What you gonna do now?" Oscar asks.

Ben doesn't say anything.

"If you're smart, you don't do shit. Unless you got a death wish, man."

"Nah. I just watch out for my boys. And if you say anything, I'll tell your thugs what you told me," Ben responds.

"My lips are sealed, gringo."

Ben starts to leave.

"Yo, man, can you untie me?" Oscar pleads.

Ben turns to look at him. "No," he says and walks out the door.

He gets near the taxi and sees Bahama is fast asleep. The reggae music is still on, and the car is still overheating.

"Bahama," Ben says through the driver's-side window.

Bahama is startled and jumps up. "Hey, mon, can't you tell a brotha been sleepin'?"

"Yeah I could. But I got bigger problems. You know where Big Pine Key is?"

"Yeah. What you wanna go there for, mon?"

"Don't worry about it. Can you take me there?"

"It doesn't look like I'm gonna be able to take you anywhere in this."

"Fine." He looks in Oscar's driveway. "We'll take that."

"Oh no, mon. I never steal nothin', mon. 'Cept for a couple of girl's virginity in Jamaica, mon. Know what I'm saying?" He laughs.

"I gave Oscar some money, man. Told him I had some problems. And I'll pay you. Two hundred fifty bucks."

"Oh. Since you put it that way, sure I'll take ya, mon."

Ben goes back into the house and sees Oscar trying to untie himself. He punches Oscar in the arm again and grabs the keys to the car from the dining room table.

"Where you going with those?"

"Don't you worry 'bout a thing," Ben replies and walks out of the house.

Ben walks over to the Charger, and as Bahama starts to walk toward the driver's door, Ben tells him, "I got this." Ben steps into the driver side and turns on the car.

Bahama turns to him, "Sure you do, mon. This way, I can participate in some extracurricular activities." He shows Ben a joint he pulls out of his pocket.

"Sure. Do whatever you want. Just get me to the highway so we can get out of here."

Ben and Bahama drive through the neighborhood and are on the highway in less than ten minutes, screaming in and out of traffic down I-95. The highway turns into Route 1. Just one road down to the Keys—the Overseas Highway. Ben is racing against time, racing against the time left in his friends' precious lives.

The windows are open. Ben looks pretty beat up. Bahama is stoned. Ben lights a cigarette and looks at the scenery. They're at the first key, Key Largo, which starts the first section of the Upper Keys. Ben turns to Bahama and says, "Listen, man. You got me headed in the right direction. I don't want you to get involved in any shit you don't need to be involved with. Thanks for everything, man. I won't be needing you anymore."

Ben pulls the car over at a rent-a-car store.

"Tryin' to find a house in the Keys where they be keepin' yo boys, Mr. Ben? That's like trying to find real boobs in South Beach."

"What if I know the name of the key?"

"Depends on which one."

"Big Pine Key."

"Well, that one is the biggest of them all. But none of them are that big. Locals don't like to talk though. They keep to themselves mostly." Bahama looks at him. "Thank you, mon. Good luck."

Ben hands Bahama the money, and Bahama steps out of the vehicle.

25

THE RIDE

Ben peels off in the Hemi-powered Charger as the sun starts to set and begins to put an end to another glorious day in South Florida. The colors in the indecisive sky illuminate the landscape. The water is ever changing as the sky tries to figure out which color it will be before it fades to darkness. Ben makes it down the lonesome, two-lane gypsy highway over a series of small, fixed bridges that connect these low-lying islands.

He rolls through the last toll plaza and hands the worker a dollar. The turnpike is over. Now to US 1 and the Florida Keys—one long, lonely road. A sign for the Last Chance Saloon sticks out from the gas stations that occupy each corner like gangs marking their neighborhood territory.

The Last Chance sign sends lonely shockwaves through his bones. Construction signs sit next to plastic, orange barrels on the side of the road. Headlights bounce off reflectors pasted on the barrels. Mounds of dirt and gravel dug up by the claws of dinosaur machines create a temporary buffer between the roadway and mangroves in the water that surround it on both sides. Different types of wildlife take off throughout the air. Some, like the slender-snouted crocodile, lurk beneath the surface of the brackish backcountry water.

It's the most beautiful sunset he has ever seen on one of the worst days of his life. Keys end and Keys begin in matters of minutes. Key Largo to Tavernier to Plantation Key, Windley Key, Islamorada, and so on. Bridges—some man-made, some dug by the hands of nature—cross over channel after channel. He sees tiny islands off the beaten path that dot the waters surrounding him—Shell Key and Indian Key and the 1,700 islands, islets, and sandbars in the surrounding waters. Sailboats are anchored all over in the distance. People are fishing on the boats and off the roadway.

Ben feels like he's in slow motion as the wind flows through the open windows and in from the sunroof. He's at one with the road. Speeding by cars on this two-lane highway can be dangerous, but he's on a mission, completely focused. Just one thing occupies his mind—making sure he finds his friends and somehow brings them to safety.

Ben looks in the mirror at his swollen face. He puts his hand on his head and feels a lump like he's never felt before. He thinks about his friends and wonders about their safety—about how they got into this mess. He recalls the times they've had in their lives, the good *and* the bad. He shakes his head and smiles.

A sign for a gas station is approaching. He checks the dashboard. The gas gauge reads empty. He checks the time on the phone. He's been driving for an hour and a half since he left Oscar's house. Stopping in Plantation Key, he steps out of the car and heads in to see the gas station attendant. He pulls the glass door open as the bells cling. She's standing behind a bulletproof glass case—a desperate soul from a methamphetamine land.

He leans his head into the communication hole and asks, "How far am I from Big Pine Key?"

"About ten miles," she answers him.

"Do you know anyplace that I can stop at to get something to eat?"

"There's a bar, No Name Pub." She gives him directions, but after the first couple of rights and lefts, Ben just nods, remembering that if he comes up to a bridge, he's gone too far. He's distracted by the scratches on her face. He realizes the bulletproof glass is protection for her and for him too.

"Thanks," he says, exiting the store.

Walking over to the car, he opens the gas tank and proceeds to fill up. On the other side of the pump, an older tourist with his family is fueling his car.

"Howdy there, stranger," the man says.

Ben nods his head.

"Staying in this here Plantation Key tonight?"

"No, sir," Ben answers.

"Nah, didn't think so. You look like your goin' all the way."

"Goin' all the way, sir?" Ben asks.

"That's right. A young buck like yourself I figured be heading all the way to Key West—ya know, where the real party's at."

"Nah. Stopping before I get there. Somethin' I gotta take care of."

"Oh sure. Some business instead of pleasure I see. We're doin' the opposite. Headed down here all the way from Illinois. I hoped to have the kids swimming with the manatees." He motions into the car to his kids and wife. "But the tour guy said there's less and less of them. More people equals more speeding boats . . ." The tourist tails off.

"That's too bad," Ben says, anxiously waiting for the tank to fill.

The pump clicks to a stop. "Well, gotta go." Ben steps back into the car and takes off into the night.

He barrels down Route 1, putting a cigarette in his mouth. He pulls out a lighter and takes a drag. On the west side of the highway is the Florida Bay. He sees a sign on the road that reads, "Crocodile Crossing." Ben looks to the west for the last moment of sunlight and watches it fade in the distance.

He turns the radio on and finds a local talk radio station for a momentary distraction. The program's host is speaking with an eighty-two-year-old local about surviving one of the worst hurricanes that ever hit this area.

"On the morning of September 2, 1935, I was ten years old. It was a day that I have never forgotten." The old man speaks slowly and pauses for a few seconds, his voice crackling with age and fear. "My father was working on the railroad line that was being built down here. The hurricane was getting real bad, and the foreman of my father's construction company called their headquarters in Miami to send a rescue train. Well, the train made it down here, and by then, the winds were blowin'. They say that the winds were around one hundred fifty miles per hour, though I don't know how fast; I just know it was bad. I was a scared little boy. We all got on that train knowing it was our only chance. Well, the train got stuck on something, and it took about an hour to free it. By then, the winds got even worse; they say something like two hundred miles per hour. Again, I don't know how fast just that it was really bad. All of a sudden, a tidal engulfed our train and nearly everyone died. Hundreds of people—I know that much—including my father."

"God, doesn't anything good happen down here," Ben says as he switches the station. He finds a rock station playing Guns N' Roses. "That's better."

He looks off in the distance and sees a screw-pile lighthouse. His mind goes back to his boys. Ben's tired eyes tell him that he could fall asleep any minute. He presses down on the pedal and takes the road on.

Ben's cell phone lights up. It's the Catalina Hotel. He decides to take the call. "Hello?" Ben answers.

"Hola, señor Ben. This is Julio."

Ben clenches his teeth but plays it cool. "Yeah, what's up, Julio?"

"Nothing much, man. Just wanted to check in on you. You were looking a little rough the last time I saw you. Is everything okay? Did you find your friends?"

Ben plays along. "I don't really know. The guys weren't in the room, and I haven't been able to get in touch with any of them. I have a feeling that something may have happened. Wouldn't be the first time with these guys."

"Oh no! That's not good, señor Ben. You must've ran out of the Catalina so quick I didn't get a chance to talk to you. I have a friend who's a local police officer who may be able to help. Where are you now?"

"Well, right now, I'm trying to see if I can come up with any clues as to where they would've went. I'm gonna start with police stations in the area—see if they got arrested or something like that."

"Ohh. I see," he says. "What kind of trouble you think they could be in?"

"Who knows? Hopefully I'll find out soon and let you know."

"Okay, señor Ben. How will you get around to check the police stations?" he asks.

"I rented a car."

"Oh. Will you be back here tonight?"

"Yes. I think so. I'll see you when I get back, Julio."

"Okay, señor Ben. See you then. Let me know if there is anything I can do."

Ben hangs up the phone.

He steps on the gas. Not much room to move. He reaches the bumper of the car in front of him. The speed limits or, rather, speed traps change often from key to key. Cops wait patiently with radar guns to bring in revenue. Ben approaches Bahia Honda Channel and sees a sign for the Seven Mile Bridge. To his east, he catches a glimpse of the Bahia Honda Beach.

The old Seven Mile Bridge sits next to it, corroding. It's dilapidated and rusting. Hanging, interrupted railings made out of iron pulled down by the weight of time line the side of the bridge on both sides, holding with them the ghosts of the past looking for the future. Off the bridge to the right, he sees a walkway made by the steel of the Flagler railroad tracks. Oncoming headlights shine toward him in this land of bridges. Concrete poles and wires line the road, reminding visitors of the fragility of communication.

Seven more miles, one long bridge, and he enters Big Pine Key.

26

BIG PINE KEY

Ben sees a sign up ahead that reads, "Welcome to Big Pine Key, Mile Marker 33." He's made it to his destination. Somewhere here, his friends need his help. He worries about their safety and tries to keep his hopes up.

A sign juts out from the side of the road. It reads, "No Name Pub." His stomach growls as he turns off US 1. He feels transported back in time. Houses hide down dirt driveways, not visible from the street. The only evidence of their existence is mailboxes poking out to the road like hitchhikers' thumbs. The small amount of man-made light allows falling stars to be easily visible as they race across the sky throughout the night.

Ben takes a fork in the road over a small bridge and heads over another slightly larger bridge over another neighborhood canal. The canals are everywhere. He pulls the Charger into the pub's dirt parking lot, kicking the dust up so it swirls through the air in the glow of the parking lot lights. He puts the car in park and, after turning it off, sighs deeply. A few cars are scattered around the lot, and a couple of locals are hanging out on the hoods and bumpers, drinking beers on the soft February night. Radio music emanates from one of the cars. Seventy degrees and no humidity—it's a rough living in the Keys' wintertime.

Ben steps out of the car and makes his way to the entrance. He feels the eyes of the locals in the parking lot on him as he steps through the saloon shutter doors. Pushing them open with his arms and body, he hears the hinges creak as they whip back to their resting position like a slinky. The place is dimly lit. Dollar bills signed by the patrons who left them cover the restaurant walls like wallpaper. The jukebox sits in the corner playing a tired tune.

Ben takes a seat at the smoke-filled bar. The waitress makes her way over.

"What can I get for ya?" she asks.

"You still serving food?"

"Yeah. We'll make you somethin'." She hands him the menu.

"I'll take a Miller Lite draft."

"Sure. Be right with ya."

After pouring the beer, the waitress makes her way back over to Ben.

"I'll take a steak sandwich please."

"Sure, honey. You want fries with that? That's our Saturday Night Special."

"Sure."

"No problem, sugar."

She makes her way to the kitchen, where she peels the slip off the order from her pad and sticks it in the wheel. "Order in," she yells back.

Ben looks over to see the unkempt cook peer from the kitchen with a dirty look on his face. The waitress heads back over to the bar area to clean some glasses.

Ben tries to talk in a low voice to her. "Excuse me. I'm from out of town and need a place to stay tonight. Is there any place around here that you know of?"

"Kind of figured you weren't local. Never seen you in here before. Yeah. I know a place right up the road. Friend of mine, Maggie, runs the place. You gotta ring the doorbell. Here's the address." She scribbles it down on her pad and rips it off, handing it to Ben. "Tell her Lisa sent you."

"Thank you. I appreciate that," Bens says.

He peers around the bar to see if anyone has noticed him. The smell of stale beer rises from the wood floors. It's what made Ben's sneakers stick as when he walked in.

The clock on the wall reads 10:30 p.m. He sees a man on his right who's passed out at the table, cigarette still smoking in the ashtray. The man on his left sitting at the bar is more interested in his beer than *anything* else in the world. The small L-shaped bar ends at the kitchen past the beer drinker. Dark wood tables are scattered around. Two pool tables sit lonely in the back. A couple of booths with dim lights hang down on a wire from the ceiling.

"I might be around for a few days. I had a long drive. Are there other places to eat or drink in Big Pine Key?"

"What? This place ain't good enough for you?" she whips back with an evil eye.

"No. Not that. Just wanted to see around town. That's all."

"Sure. Whatever. This is pretty much it. Just your share of fisherman and heavy drinkers who want to live by their own rules. Got it?"

As Ben takes it all in, an understanding of what this place means to people sinks in. These Keys are like life in the slow lane—just fishin' and eatin' and drinkin' and livin' your own way. Everyone has another lifetime on his or her mind. Maybe past mistakes. The reasons why they live here all add up to one thing—anonymity. Here, a new life washes like water over an adult at a baptism. And it doesn't need to be said. You can feel the aura of these islands—hanging, floating out there in the air. The Keys are filled with these types of people. You don't tell them what time it is. They just live and sit back and watch the sun rise and set, enjoying their precious time, like old people watching the grass grow.

"Sure. I can understand that."

"Plus, this is the most famous bar in this section of the keys, if you can find it."

The kitchen bell rings. "Food up. Kitchen closed," the cook yells.

Lisa grabs the food and brings it over to Ben. "Anything else?"

"That's it. Thanks."

He looks up at the television. The local news from Miami is on the small television as Ben starts to take care of his sandwich. Ben finishes eating and leaves a tip. "Thank you."

As he gets up to leave, his phone rings. He checks the number before answering. A 305 area code—Miami-Dade. Ben's curiosity gets the best of him.

"Hello?" he answers.

"Ben?" a girl's voice asks.

He realizes it's Dianna. He sighs aloud and shakes his head in disgust. "Yeah, what do you want? You tryin' to set me up again?" he growls.

"Ben. I'm so sorry!" Dianna says, her words almost bursting with urgency. "But you have to listen to me! I feel really bad about what happened to you and your friends. I've been thinking that I might be able to help you."

Ben doesn't know whether or not to believe her. "Why are you telling me this?"

"Listen. I'm really sorry. I had no choice, and I would feel even worse if something did happen to your friends. I'm also starting to worry about my brother now. I think they got him involved somehow. I'm trying to make this up to you!"

"So what can you do for me?"

"Are you in the Keys?"

"Maybe."

"I'm sorry, Ben."

"Sorry's not enough!"

"I know. I'm trying to find out the address of the house for you Ben."

Ben worries about whether he can trust her.

"My friend is reliable. I did a favor for him and he owed me one."

"Yeah, I can see that's how you operate."

"Please, Ben. I'll call you soon as I hear something. Good luck."
She hangs up the phone.

Ben realizes that she might be his only help. He takes off down the road to hopefully square away his sleeping arrangements for the evening—maybe the next few.

27

LITTLE HAVANA,
MAXIMO GÓMEZ PARK

At eleven in the morning, the temperature reads eighty-one degrees. The heat and humidity will be near all-time record highs today. Kelvin, Dianna's brother, is seated at a table playing dominoes with some of his boys in the heart of Little Havana—a park off of Calle Ocho. He wipes the sweat off his forehead. His phone rings. When he sees it's his sister's number calling, he decides not to answer. The aroma of café con leche permeates the air. Heineken bottles are scattered across the table. Tank tops expose tattoos and gold necklaces. Dark wraparound sunglasses help hide poker faces. A red bandana is wrapped around one of his boy's neck, cowboy bank robber style. The sun rages like an inferno.

Kelvin's phone rings again. He reaches into his pocket to see who it is. It's Malo, Castro's enforcer.

"Shit!" he says.

Kelvin decides he has to answer. "Hola."

"Hola, Kelvin."

"What can I do for you, Malo?" Kelvin asks.

"What? Not so happy to hear from me, Kelvin? That's too bad. Well, amigo, since you are asking, you know that you are overdue on that payment?"

"Yeah, I know, Malo. I'm workin' on that."

"Oh, I see. Workin' on that huh?"

The sarcasm isn't lost on Kelvin, whose face feels wet, as more sweat starts to rush down his forehead, cascading like Niagara Falls. Everyone at the table looks in his direction.

"Workin', workin', workin'. That's all I ever hear from you, man," says Malo. "You must be one busy guy. I see now. Let me tell you something, while you are at the park in Calle Ocho playing dominoes! I don't think you are that fuckin' busy!" he yells into the phone. "You got till the end of the weekend to come up with that money, or your sister"—he slows down and lowers his voice—"will be put in, let's say an uncomfortable situation."

"Listen, Malo, I'll get it, hombre. My sister has nothing to do with this, man. Please, I beg you; leave her out of this."

Malo lets out his sinister laugh and hangs up the phone.

Kelvin looks around the table that has turned completely silent. Only the sound of Latin music from a speaker in a house window floats across the air. Everyone in this neighborhood is frightened by the stories they've heard about what Malo does to Castro's enemies.

The latest tale going around the Calle Ocho neighborhood is that a Miami charter fishing crew from a boat named *Joe Camel* was helping Castro bring in some cocaine and marijuana to South Florida. The goods were dropped into the ocean by plane. Over the last few months, a couple of shipments had come up short. The boat crew's explanation was that, when they'd gone to pick up the shipment, some kilos must have broken off from the main cargo. Square groupers, the Florida locals call them, had been reported washing up on the beach, so the fishing crew had used that news as their excuse for the shortage. Once Castro got word that the captain of the boat had been partying around town, Malo and another enforcer, went out on a shark fishing excursion with the captain, his new girlfriend, and two of the crew. The boat was found floating near the Bahamas a few days later, with no sign of the crew. Word is, Malo and his associate fed the crew piece by piece to the sharks and then were picked up by another boat. The police are still investigating the crew's whereabouts and have no leads.

"Yo, Kelvin, what does Malo want witchya? You owe him some money, man?" Kelvin's friend Tre asks.

"Yeah. Malo is givin' me one more day. Threatening me about my sister. Damn!" he says in frustration. "But I got something I'm workin' on."

"I thought you just did somethin' for him?" he asks.

"Yeah. Set up some white boys for Castro. Stupid gringos from New Jersey. But this"—he pauses—"this is for somethin' else."

"Damn! Don't you know when to call it quits with your luck, man?" Kelvin's boy asks.

"Don't worry, man. I got it under control."

"Yeah." He looks at Kelvin. "A'ight."

Someone at the table slams his hand against the table and yells, "Dominoes!"

Kelvin stands up from the table and looks at a car that has stopped along the street next to the park. He leans over the table while looking at the car and whispers to his friend, "Give me a minute, amigo. I gotta take care of this."

His boy turns his head to the street to take a look at the car. It's a long Mercury Grand Marquis, with twenty-inch rims that sparkle in the sun. A collage on the back of the car says, "RIP Hermano, 6-21-06."

Kelvin walks across the park and steps into the street where the car is stopped. He leans into the driver's-side window while the boys set up the dominoes for the next game.

It's Sedano, an old acquaintance from the neighborhood. He's the closest thing that Kelvin has to a friend within the group of thugs that he sometimes pulls jobs with.

"We takin' care of that shit tonight?" Sedano asks Kelvin.

"Yeah."

"When?"

"We are rollin' up in there at the shift change. Around one. We got guys on the inside. Piece of cake, man," Kelvin informs him.

"I'll see you at one," Sedano says.

28

THE SAGAMORE

In South Beach, Dianna is laying out at the classic pool of the Sagamore Hotel, where she's the bar manager. Her voluptuous body is the desire of many men at the pool, single or married. Dianna sees her looks and body as her money ball lottery ticket. It's her way up and out of the neighborhood she grew up in. Her main priority in finding a partner is his ability to take care of her and her barely English-speaking mother. A little plastic surgery never hurt those lottery chances either and was a good long-term investment. A tiny scar from an incision hides just beneath her bikini top.

The sweat beads gather underneath the hot Miami sun on her smooth, olive skin. She decides to take a dip in the pool. She leaves her drink at the edge and jumps in. After a few submersions under the water, she comes up for air by her drink. Looking up, she makes out a male figure through her chlorine-blurred eyes.

"Hola, Dianna," a voice says.

She wipes the water out of her eyes and recognizes Tre, one of Kelvin's friends who's always gone out of his way to be nice to her.

She, on the other hand, has always had trouble with giving him anything more than the friend card.

"Hey, Papi!" she answers with her flirtatious voice.

"So you just lay out here, tease all the gringos here on vacation?" He chuckles.

"Oh shut up! I was out late last night, Papi. And they had some rooms available. I gotta work later anyway."

"Yeah, all right. Anyway, I talked to Kelvin at the park. We were playin' dominoes."

"Yeah. You know my brother. He and the thugs he's been running with lately like to chill there on the weekends. When they're done."

"Yeah, but I think he'll be workin' today, Mami."

"He doesn't work. Psss." She pauses. "What you mean, Papi?"

"I mean, I heard Malo be callin' him, yo."

"Malo? About what?"

"I don't know; nuthin', Mami. Just that he owes him some money or somethin'. You know he likes the hustle."

She smacks her hand on the edge of the pool and lifts herself out of the water. She lets out a worried sigh. Hurrying to her chair, she grabs her towel to dry off and heads into the hotel.

"Don't tell anyone I told ya," he says as she speeds away.

Dianna narrowly avoids a waiter who's on his way out of the hotel. He's able to save the tray full of sandwiches but a drink slides off onto the concrete. The plastic cup dances back and forth until it rolls to a stop. She pays no attention and heads to the elevator, hitting the call button over and over. It finally opens, and she jumps in and takes it to her floor. She hurries down the hallway while her wet flip-flops squeak against her feet. Making it to her doorway, she swipes her room key. It doesn't work. She has to swipe it again. "Come on!" The green light flashes.

She rushes through the door and paces in the room. She finally picks up her cell phone, placing a call to her brother. He answers this time.

"Kelvin, what you doin'?" she asks him.

"What you mean, Mijita?"

"You know what I mean. I thought after we set up those boys you were gonna be done with all of this."

"I am!" Kelvin tells her.

"You're lyin'. I heard something."

"What did you hear and who told you?"

"I'm not gonna tell you. But *Malo*? How could you get messed up with Malo, Kelvin?"

"I got something goin'. It's supposed to pay off tonight. Listen, it's a sure thing."

"Yeah. I've heard that all before."

"Don't worry, sis. I got it covered."

"I hope you do, Kelvin. Promise me that this is it—that once this is over, you won't get mixed up with Castro or Malo or any of his boys anymore."

"I promise, D."

"Okay, now listen. One of those Jersey boys came back to the hotel and found me."

"Which one?"

"The guy they had me flirting with, Ben."

"What! I thought they were goin' to take care of him."

"Yeah, me too. I heard they already did. I felt real bad when I heard that. Anyway, I was at the Catalina layin' out at the pool with my girl. I go inside and see him in the lounge. He sees me at the same time and runs me down."

"What did you tell him?"

"Nothin'. But he was goin' around tryin' to figure out what was goin' on."

"If he's around tryin' to figure out what happened, I'm sure someone's gonna see him and let Castro know. If you see him again, just stay away."

"No problema."

"I'll call you later," he says, hanging up the phone.

29

MALO

Dianna is in her bathrobe after finishing her shower when there's a knock at the door. She steps out of the bathroom and asks, "Who is it?"

There's no answer; instead a louder, more hurried knock. She makes her way to the door and slowly turns the knob. Opening it a few inches, she looks through the space between it and the metal safety lock. She's frightened when she sees Malo's face peering up against the small opening.

"Hey, chonga," he says.

"What you doing here, Malo?" she asks as her hands start to shake. "I'm getting ready for work."

"Work. Work. Work. That's all anyone does here in South Beach these days." He turns around and lets out his sinister laugh as his two thugs join in.

"What you want, Malo?" she demands. "I'm getting ready."

"What, you don't like me anymore? Now you listen to me!" his voice grows louder. "You know that I can open up this door here!"

A hotel guest is walking down the hall, and Malo turns to see the guest passing by. He decides to play it cooler. "Listen, open up the door. We won't hurt you. Just got something to say, Mami."

Dianna thinks about screaming, but she knows someone would call the hotel, her employer, or worse, the cops. It would only make the situation worse in the long run, and Malo would always know where to find her. "Okay, Malo." She closes the door and unlocks the safety lock. She steps back as the door opens, clutching her robe tighter to her body as the band of thugs steps into the room.

"See. That wasn't so hard, was it?" he says. "Me and your brother, well let's see, how should I put this? We have a little situation. He owes me some things." As he speaks, he looks her up and down in her robe with his dirty eyes.

She clutches the robe even tighter.

"What kind of things does he owe you, Malo? We just helped you guys take care of that thing with Castro!"

"This, you see, is something else. Let's just say that Kelvin had some business he wanted to do." He takes his finger and runs it on the lapel from her waist up to her neck. "He needed some, let's say tools and some backup. That's where I come in. I help him out with the"—he pauses, as if searching for the right words—"ammunition, some associates. He gives me a cut and my"—he pauses again—"inventory back. I make some money with no risk, and we all walk away happy."

"So what you want with me, Malo?"

"Well, I gave him a deadline. The clock is ticking. Time is money, Mami. You understand?"

She doesn't answer.

"Comprende?" he yells and steps closer.

"Sí," she answers as she steps back and turns her head away.

"He has till dawn tomorrow. And he can't come up short on the amount he promised me. If he does, he'll be in trouble. And I'll have some things I will need from you and from the hotel." He turns to look at his thugs. They start walking out of the door when Malo pauses to turn back to her. "By the way, Mami, lookin' real good." He belts out another loud laugh as he steps out of the room.

As soon as the door closes, Dianna runs to lock it. She turns around; leaning against it, she slides down to the floor, clutching her robe, and starts to cry. The bar she runs is a profitable business. It's a job she doesn't consider work. She gets to socialize with some of the biggest and brightest stars in South Beach. She doesn't want Malo or anyone to start moving in on the bar profits. Walking back over to the couch where her cell is charging, she sees that there's a message. "Who's this?" she thinks as she sees the 973 area code. "Ben!"

30

THE HEIST

It's eleven o' clock, and Kelvin's cell phone rings. "Hola," he answers.

"Hola, Kelvin. It's time," the voice on the other end tells him.

Kelvin checks his phone. It reads 11:56 p.m., Saturday.

"Muy bien. I will see you at the warehouse."

Kelvin jumps in his car and makes his way to the interstate. Thoughts flow through his head about this job. His jaw clenches. He tries to calm himself with a deep breath. It's no use. He's pulled other small-time jobs in the past, but this is his biggest by far, certainly the most dangerous. There's Homeland Security, airport security, and a huge police presence all around this facility. Kelvin has everything hanging on this job—his health, his safety, his sister, and their future (if there is one).

Kelvin has friends who work at the hangars at the Fort Lauderdale-Hollywood International Airport. They've told him that there's an international flight coming in. Onboard this flight will be many different currencies, but mostly unmarked US dollar bills. They think it will be somewhere around one hundred thousand dollars, maybe some more in other currencies.

On Old Griffin Road, he sees a sign for Tropical Acres Trailer Home Park. The mile marker indicates that the park is two miles from here.

Reasons why he's doing this glide through Kelvin's mind. He wants to get out of this game. After the heist, he'll buy a house up north where it's cheaper, take his mom and sister to a quieter place—away from all of this. North Carolina. A small town where his father took him fishing when he was a kid—back when his father was still a living being on this crazy earth. That all changed in an instant a few years ago. His father was the victim of a gunshot one night, and the crime still remains an unsolved mystery.

He makes the first right like he was told. The tires thump across the railroad tracks, and the car creeps slowly through the dilapidated neighborhood. On the right side of the street is a canal waterway that's linked to the open ocean. It's part of the Intracoastal Waterway that gives this area its unique title as the "Venice of America." Large, high-tension wires follow along the interstate for miles. This is the landmark he was told to look out for. He makes a left into a parking lot in front of an old, abandoned warehouse and pulls around back.

He steps out of the car, and out of the darkness someone approaches him from the side. "Are you Kelvin?" an unknown voice asks.

"Yes," he answers.

"Come with me."

He follows around the side of the warehouse to a door and sees the man is carrying an automatic weapon. The man opens the door and says, "Go ahead," as he motions Kelvin to go into the warehouse. Kelvin steps in and sees some of Malo's men. Six of them are there, seated and standing around a table underneath a light.

Sedano steps out from the group at the table and speaks. "Hola, Kelvin," he says, embraces him.

"Hola, Sedano."

"Kelvin will get us all up to speed on the plans in just a second. First, I want to introduce you to the men we will be working with."

Sedano introduces them. "They'll be with us when we enter the airport as your contacts have told us to. The man you met outside will be our eyes outside the warehouse. Are you ready to tell us how this will go down?" Sedano asks Kelvin.

"We have twenty-five minutes to load up the pallets. Myself, Sedano, and you two"—Kelvin points to two men—"will drive back to the warehouse, here, to meet up with our entire crew." Kelvin waves his hand around in a circular motion. He indicates another pair of men. "You two will be in the boat and be our backup if anything goes wrong. If we need an alternative escape route, we can get take the pallets to the boat if we have to. Keep an eye out for any movement on the canal," he tells the men. "Communicate with us on the walkie-talkies if you see anything." Kelvin waves his walkie-talkie. "If all goes as planned, me and Sedano will take our cut and head south on Federal Highway to the safe house in Hollywood." He nods toward Sedano. "These two," he motions toward the pair that will be on the boat, "will walk the other pallets out to the boat from the warehouse. Then they will take off to the safe house from the canal. You last two will head west on Old Griffin Road to I-95 and head south to meet all of us, where we have an alibi waiting. You guys got it?"

They all nod.

"Good."

At precisely 12:45 a.m., they head to their positions. Sedano takes off in his van with one associate and Kelvin takes off in his with another. The two other guys get in the boats, where they'll wait until 12:55 a.m. to crawl up the canal to the warehouse. Only large rocks on the bank of the canal, a barbed wire fence, and about a hundred feet of grass will stand between them and the hangar.

Kelvin gets on the walkie. "Everything is in motion."

His truck reaches the airport, and he and his passenger pull up to the checkpoint. The security guard is waiting at a gate to check their identification.

"Play it cool," Kelvin says to his hired gun.

"No sweat," the man replies.

"Can I see your ID?" the rotund security woman asks, looking half-asleep. Kelvin flashes his badge, as does his associate. She checks them for a second, rubs her eyes, and then reaches into the quarters and hits a button. The gate lifts up.

Kelvin says, "Have a good night."

"Uh-huh." She barely acknowledges the greeting as she yawns.

Kelvin gets on the radio. "We're in."

"Ten-four. Everything is looking good here too," the man waiting on the boats outside the hangar states.

Sedano's van sputters in behind. Same questions. Same result. He speeds up through the gate and sees Kelvin in front of him. He follows behind to the hangar, and the two vans slowly roll in. Kelvin can't believe how dark and deserted the area is. He looks into the night and sees the glowing lights of the airport. A plane's engines roar in the distance. After it takes off into the night sky, an eerie silence falls over the place. *This can't be this perfect*, Kelvin thinks.

They step out of the vans and head to the backroom.

Kelvin steps up to the secured area door and pulls. It opens immediately. Then after a few inches, it sticks. Kelvin sees that a simple theft safety lock is barring their entrance. One of his associates steps up with a crowbar and peels off the lock in a matter of seconds. The men quickly make their way through the door and are in the secured area without a hitch. Flashlights bounce across the darkness, illuminating a cage at the end of the room. As they hurry to the cache, the men make out what looks like pallets covered in a black tarp inside the wire cage. Upon examination, they determine that the lock on the cage requires a key and an electronic card.

"I got this." One of the men takes charge with his deep voice. He pulls out a torch and starts to blaze an opening in the gate in the shape of a large rectangle that extends from the floor to about six and a half feet at the top. The men enter the caged area and pull off the black tarp, revealing four waist-high pallets covered by another layer of material, their contents still unknown. They slice off the heavy material. The pallets are wrapped tight in plastic wrap. They're still unable to see anything.

Kelvin looks at Sedano and says, "Here we go." He stabs his knife into the plastic wrap and begins to tear through the covering. He makes a slit about a foot long and says, "Help me."

Sedano and one of the hired guns stick their hands in the plastic and pull the tear further open. They're amazed when they peer into the pallet. It looks like the whole thing is filled with US bills.

"This is it!" Kelvin says. "Go get the cart," he orders.

The other two men run back to the van and bring the cart in. They have only fifteen minutes left until the night crew makes it back to the hangar. They transfer the first pallet as the associates take the first load to the van. They see a security vehicle making its rounds in the lot and duck behind the van for cover.

"Oh shit! Did he see us?" one of the men asks.

They're startled for a second, but the van turns around and continues driving.

"Just a routine spot check," one of the associates declares. "They didn't see us."

They rush back inside with the cart.

"Ten more minutes," Kelvin alerts the others on the radio.

The second pallet is loaded and taken to the van. And then the third. The last one is very heavy.

"It must be filled with coins, this one," one of the men says.

"Five minutes," Kelvin states on the radio.

As the last pallet is loaded, the four men exit cautiously to their vans and leave the hangar, once again in a slow crawl. Kelvin's van is in the front and headed to the security gate.

They pull up and see the hangar employees entering. The female guard is busy checking their identifications as Kelvin's van rolls up. The gate is automatic, and Kelvin can't believe his luck. He keeps his head down so the employees don't see him and propels the van through. Sedano's van follows.

"We're out."

"Ten-four," the men on the boats respond.

The two vans lumber through the off roads of the airport and meander to US 1. The men follow south, make their first right, and traverse over the railroad tracks once again. The tires bump across the tracks as the van bounces up and down like a boat over a wave. They hear the rear of the van scrape the tires as it's forced downward from all of the weight. Home free.

The high tension wires are overhead as the vans turn into the parking lot. The associate opens the warehouse doors, and they back in up to a table in the middle of the room. The doors are shut to the warehouse.

The crew meets at the table. High fives are exchanged as the men, except for the two men who are unloading two of the pallets and transferring them to the boat beside the warehouse, take off their gear and weapons except for the two men who are starting to get two pallets out of the van to carry to the boat beside the warehouse.

Time to relax. Everything has gone as planned, Kelvin thinks for the first time tonight.

Behind Kelvin, a door opens, and four men enter as he's celebrating. He's tapped on the shoulder and turns around to see Malo. His face turns white. He can't believe his eyes. The celebration is over.

"Malo?"

31

THE NEW DEAL

"Hola, Kelvin. Yes. It *is* me, cabrón. I told you that I wanted my cut by this time. And it looks as if you are late," Malo tells him with a greasy smile and slicked-back, wet hair.

"Late? What do you mean? Everything is here."

"Sí, a little late. This may cost you. We shall see. We shall see." He smiles and rubs his hands together. He's dressed in a dark suit. His gold chain shows that he's trying hard to play the part of someone higher up in the organization. The second-day-old dark hair peaks through the skin on his face, providing a five o'clock shadow.

Malo looks at Sedano and barks out his orders. "Grab the money counter and count it up. Let's see what we got."

Sedano grabs the first stack and puts it in the money counter. In a matter of seconds, the machine reads ten thousand.

"How many rows?" Malo asks Sedano.

"Thirty. That's three hundred thousand on this pallet."

"Thank you, Einstein. I'm not too good at math." He lets out his laugh; his dark sunglasses hide his eyes. "I thought you told me that

the whole deal would probably be around one hundred? You holdin'
out on me, Kelvin?"

"No, Malo. I told you they thought it would be around that
amount. It's always different."

"Okey dokey," he says. "I have trouble believing that. It may
cost you." He shrugs his shoulders, cocking his head to the side as he
squints his eyes and the palms of his hands supinate. Malo is playing
with him.

"Check the next pallet," he orders.

Sedano puts the money in the machine, and the results are the
same.

"Not too bad, Kelvin," Malo states. "Not too bad."

Kelvin is growing nervous about his share. He's already supposed
to be giving a cut to two of the employees at the hangar.

"What about this one?" Malo asks.

"This one has twenty rows," Sedano says. "Ten thousand on this
one too. So"—he pauses—"two hundred thousand."

"Not bad," Malo says as he continues to rub his hands together.

"What about the last one?" he asks.

"Well," Sedano says, "this one has twenty rows. But they're all
different currencies. This one is Euro, this is, let me see, German
Franc? I think. They're all different, Malo. I'm not too sure."

"Load them up on the boat and make it to the rendezvous."

The associates grab the first pallet and scatter out of the
warehouse.

"But, Malo, we, we had a deal."

"Yes, my friend. We did. You told me I would have my cut by a
certain time. You told me a certain amount. And that time has come
and gone. You are late. Time for a new deal." He lets out another
laugh. "Take him back to the house, and we will talk from there."

32

PATTERSON AND STOKES

At the Miami Police Department, Chief Gonzales is briefing the officers. "Listen, as some of you may know, our informant has made us aware of a shipment coming in to South Florida. We don't know exact dates or where it will happen. I know the details are a little sketchy, but I've issued a BOLO. We think the major player involved will be our buddy Castro, but again, we are not 100 percent sure. But where there's smoke, there's usually fire. Okay. You guys are dismissed. I wanna see Sergeant Patterson and Sergeant Stokes please."

The officers file out of the room as Patterson and Stokes, who graduated together from the police academy fifteen years ago, make their way up to the front. They've been partners on the force ever since completing their rookie year, and both share a distinguished resume.

"I need to speak with you guys about something," Gonzales says. "And it's gotta stay with the three of us. You got that?"

"Sure thing, boss," Stokes replies as they both nod in agreement.

"What is it?" Patterson asks.

"Well, you know that we got this shipment comin' in. You guys are two of the most trusted men we have in this department. The last bust you guys pulled got us national headlines and was great police work. I'll never figure out how you two put that one together," he says shaking his head and smiling. "So as a reward, I'm gonna put you on something else now. I've gotten word, not only from an informant but also from internal affairs, that we may have some dirty officers here in the department. I know that I can trust the both of you to keep this quiet." He pauses. "Castro has been laying low. We think someone tipped him off that we're keeping tabs on him and that we're goin' to be on the lookout for this shipment. We've had a couple of our undercovers trying to keep tabs on him and his associates, but we've come up empty-handed. He may have gotten some mid—or low-level guys together to take care of this to throw us off track. Here's a picture of one of his right-hand men, a guy known as Malo."

"I know this scumbag," Stokes says.

"Well, he got on our radar after we shook down a couple of local dealers in Overtown. We were told he may have been involved in last month's missing person's case with that boat we found. Now word is he and some of his crew may try to take care of this shipment. We also heard he's been getting real cocky and may even want to try to take out Castro for the top spot in their band of scumbags."

"Why do we need to know this, Chief?" Patterson says.

"Well, we're gonna have you guys on the streets and in charge of this investigation. No one else in this department is to know about this. It's undercover. You two are to go about your regular routine. *Nothing* out of the ordinary. You are to report to me only. You got that?"

"Yes, sir," they answer in unison.

"Here are pictures of most of the crew." He shows them the pictures on a tackboard with their roles filled out underneath. "Great then! Get out there and we'll be in touch."

"Thanks, Chief."

Patterson and Stokes make their way into the locker room, where some of the officers are getting ready to go out on the night shift.

"What did the chief want with you guys?" an officer asks as a few other cops gather their things from their waffle door locker and look toward Patterson and Stokes.

"Ah, he just wanted to talk to us about our last arrest downtown," Patterson responds to the officer.

"Yeah? Looked like it was more important than that."

"Well, the guy said that we roughed him up. He had bruises on him from a beating he musta took from somebody on the streets. He wanted to let us know internal affairs is on it," Patterson tells him.

"God damn internal affairs. Always lookin' to get somebody in trouble," one of the officers says.

Patterson and Stokes get their things together and head out on their shift. They make their way out of police headquarters, and Patterson notices some of the guys' looks on the way out.

"Are you catchin' some weird vibes from some of the guys tonight?" Patterson asks him.

"Huh? No, not really. You?" Stokes responds.

"Think so."

"You're probly just lookin' into things too much. Let's get to Overtown and talk with our guy," Stokes directs.

They hop into their unmarked car and head up Interstate 95, exiting at a neighborhood where they can get some information from one of the local guys who owes them a favor. Patterson, who's black, grew up in this neighborhood in South Florida. He pulls up to the corner and rolls down the window. "Any of you guys see Darius hangin' round here tonight?"

One of the three guys on the corner answers, "Nah. Not tonight. I saw him today though."

"Well if you see him, let him know that Patterson and Stokes are lookin' for him."

"Yeah. We will," the corner boys answer.

They drive through the streets, waiting for Darius to contact them. Stokes always feels uneasy when he makes his way around here. He has two strikes against him—his badge and the color of his skin. A man on a bicycle drifts by their cruiser. Stokes sees the man weaving back and forth as the man checks them out. Unlit lampposts extend above the pavement. Other than a couple of headlights that pass them by and the man on the bike, the streets are deserted.

Patterson used to play basketball at the University of Florida and was a professional prospect until his knee blew out. Now he plays pickup games in the park with Stokes, where he still manages to keep his six-foot-three-inch frame slim. Despite the large knee brace he wears, he beats the smaller, stocky Stokes on the court on a consistent basis—enough for him to talk trash to Stokes as they ride around in the cruiser.

"You tired of waitin', boy?" Patterson asks.

"Waitin' for what? Darius?"

"Nah. Nah." He pauses as he looks over to Stokes in the passenger seat. "Waitin' to see me drain jumpers from the sky on yo' ass, white boy! Ha ha yeah!"

"You know I'm in better shape than you," Stokes tells him.

"You might be in better shape, son. But it don't help you out there on the court!"

In Hialeah, Castro is awaiting word from his crew in Big Pine Key. Castro's right-hand man, Cheo, is on the phone.

One of the cops on the take lets him in on the news. "The chief spoke to us tonight. They don't have any evidence, but they think it's you bringing in the shipment. 'Where there's smoke, there's usually fire,' he told us."

"All right. We got it." Cheo's call waiting beeps in on the line. "I gotta take this," Cheo tells the officer as he clicks over to the second call.

"Tell Castro we need to talk," the voice states.

"Castro doesn't speak on the phone, only directly through me. No taped conversations. You need to tell anything to him, you tell me, cabrón. I'm Castro as far as you're concerned. I'm his eyes and ears."

"Okay. We have a problem down here."

"What seems to be the problem?" Cheo asks as he takes off his fedora.

"Well, both of the guys are doing well with the scuba shit. Problem is, we're keeping one of these guys here on land as a security deposit—just to make sure they don't take off. Know what I mean?"

"Sure. So what's the problem?"

"Well, we could use another body to drive them out, another set of eyes while they're in the water. Everyone one down here has had felony charges. If they get stopped on the boat, it won't look good. I just want to make sure this thing goes off without a hitch—since I'm down here running this shit."

"I'll work on it," Cheo tells him.

Castro is at his hideout in a heavily populated, mostly Cuban part of town just a few miles outside of Miami. Only his most trusted men know where it is. They have this part of the city wired. If anyone who doesn't belong there comes into the area, they know about it in a matter of minutes. Castro's crew keeps the lookouts on the corner well-greased.

Cheo is Castro's sidekick. The two men came over from Cuba together with some members of their family and Marielitos packed into a 1955 Chevy. The vehicle was kept afloat with tire tubes that were rigged underneath its belly. On their journey over through the Florida Straits, a wave ripped through the gulf current and swept Castro away from the Chevy. Cheo was a great swimmer as a boy and risked his own life to save Castro's. He was finally able to pull his friend back to safety with the help of some of the other men. Castro is forever indebted to Cheo, and he's the only man Castro truly trusts.

He walks in to see Castro, barely looking like he fits in the door frame with his six-foot-three body, which is covered with gringo white skin and dark hair. "Castro?"

"Yeah, what is it?" Castro asks as a beautiful girl in a skintight dress brings him something to drink. Castro's a man of short stature, five foot seven, with somewhat light mocha skin. A dark mustache finishes off his small face. He's quick witted and sees many steps ahead like a great chess player. He sees himself as a successful business man who's married and has a daughter and son who attend the best schools.

"We got a problem down there in the Keys," Cheo tells him.

"Well?" Castro motions to Cheo.

"They're keeping one of the guys hostage for insurance so the other two don't take off on the water. They'll send the two out to receive the shipment, scaring the shit of 'em so that they come back to be with their friend. They want someone to drive them out to the pickup and to keep an eye on them so they don't just take off—someone without any felony convictions."

"Good idea. Some insurance. I like their thinking." He pauses. "Call Malo. I know he's had use of the boats for a while. And you know he likes the open water," he says with a smirk.

"I'll get right on it," Cheo tells him.

Cheo dials a number. "Hola, Cheo."

"Hola, Malo."

"What can I do for you?" Malo asks him.

"Well, I was told to call you. You know the New Jersey boys? We need someone to drive the boat out there to the pickup site. Someone without any prior convictions. Someone clean. We're keeping one of them on land."

"You need someone. Sure. I got someone in mind," Malo says.

Cheo realizes Malo considers himself to be simply playing his role for now. He knows Malo has ulterior motives and is waiting for the right opportunity to move up or take over the syndicate. He's eager, driven, and motivated; and he's impatient, like a shark chomping at the bit. Malo might not be the brains, but he's smarter than he's given credit for. His brutal thug tactics sometimes overshadow others' perception of him.

"I'm pretty busy right now, just wrapping something up. But I'll have a few of my crew take him down there," Malo tells him.

"Muy bien."

Malo and his crew make it back to the safe house and load the money into two vans. Malo looks at his crew. "Act like nothing has gone on. You will all get your cut, sooner or later." He turns on his greasy smile while looking at Kelvin. "And for you my friend, there's something else you will have to do before you get your cut."

"But—" Kelvin is cut off.

"But nothing. Sedano will take you to Big Pine Key. You will have to drive out there immediately. Kelvin, you will have to drive a boat out for a pickup. They will get you up to speed once you get there."

Kelvin can't believe that, after pulling this job, Malo is asking him to do more. His hands are tied; he knows what Malo can do to him.

Sedano says, "No problema, Malo. We will leave pronto." He looks at Kelvin to make sure he is calm. "Let's go," he says to Kelvin.

And with that, they whisk out of the front door into the night.

At the Sagamore Hotel, Dianna is at one of the busiest points of her Saturday night. She is busy socializing with the important people and making sure they're taken care of. It's two in the morning, and this party will last until at least four. Most of the people here partying are part of the "pretender crowd"—the people who want to tell their friends who they hung out with and where in South Beach. These aren't the people who are famous or rich, but those who keep the bar packed night after night. Her job is to keep the rich people coming back. Cater to the famous ones. As Dianna makes her way to the front of the bar, she looks into the mirror and sees Malo and some of his boys making their way in behind her. A glass falls off her tray as she tries to turn the other way and avoid contact with him. But it's too late.

Damn it! She has been busy tonight and almost forgot about Malo and the problem with her brother.

"Hola, Dianna. We're here to celebrate tonight. Do you have a table for us?"

"It's really busy in here, Malo. You'll have to give me a minute. Is everything all right?" she asks, referring to her brother.

"Sí, señorita. Things are working themselves out. Just one more thing—once we sit down at the table, it's where we've been since midnight, in case anyone asks. Got it, Mami?"

Malo's always at the clubs, hanging out with groups of women around town. He wants to make himself visible. He loves the attention, seeing people whisper to each other about him as he walks by their tables and pretending he doesn't see.

"Sure, Malo. Anything you say."

"Good. I will make sure that you and the table girl are taken care of at the end."

"I'll set it up," she says.

Malo and his crew are eventually seated at a table and order a bottle of Dom for the attention and females. They party for the next couple of hours and have some chongas meet them up at the club. They call for one of the crew to come pick them up and fade down Washington Avenue.

33

DARIUS

Darius is standing on the corner in the hood where Patterson and Stokes were searching for him earlier. He scrolls through his contacts until he finds the name PIG and he places a call.

"Darius, my man! How you doin' tonight?" Patterson answers.

Darius pictures the pig and his partner, Stokes, making their rounds in their cruiser.

"Chillin'. Chillin'. Heard you been asking for me," he says to Patterson through the gold-plated grill on his teeth. Darius got pinched a few months back, and the prosecution gave him a sweetheart deal. As long as he dropped the dime on an ongoing Miami PD investigation and agreed to provide some information on some future investigations, he wouldn't have to do jail time. Since Darius had already been to the clinker, he was going to do anything not to go back. "You know, ha ha,"—Darius giggles as he brushes his hand underneath his nose—"the corner boys done told me."

"We just wanted to talk," Patterson tells him.

"Time is money, homeboy. What you want?"

"Well, you hear anything about Castro lately?" Patterson asks.

"Damn, man! Why you gotta ask me about him?" Darius pauses. "Damn! Couldn't you ask me 'bout anyone else? Gotta be Castro!"

"Well? You hear anything?" Patterson persists.

"Sure. Hear stuff all the time. Some real. Some real *bullshit*. Know what I'm sayin'?"

"Listen," Patterson says, "you know we helped you out on that charge. You owe us. Let's go. Time is money, remember?"

"Yeah I know. I told *you* that. I heard he's been layin' real low lately. Heard he's got a tail and your guys have been keepin' a close watch on the man. Also heard he's got a couple of your boys in his pocket."

"Wouldn't be the first time I heard that." Patterson pauses. "What else? Anything about a shipment comin' in?" he inquires.

"Damn!" Darius pauses. "Yeah. Heard something about that. But he's got some of his boys takin' care of it."

"Where?" Patterson pushes.

"Somewhere in the Keys. Not sure exactly. Heard he's been layin' low somewhere over in Hialeah. He's got a place over there. Got the neighborhood on lockdown I hear. No one gets in there without him knowin' about it."

"Can you find out where in the Keys this thing might be goin' down? Or his Hialeah place?" Patterson probes further.

Darius snickers. "Listen to you tryin' to talk like you're down and shit. Yeah, I can find out. I'll call you when I do."

"I'll be waiting," Patterson hangs up.

Darius gets off the phone and pulls away in a purple car. The license plate reads D-Reaper.

"Time for us to find Castro's hideout," Patterson tells Stokes.

"Hopefully our man Darius will be good for something. We find the hideout *and* the place in the Keys, and we got something," Stokes says.

"Wish it were all that easy," Patterson tells him.

"Tell me about it."

34

OSCAR'S HOUSE

The new moon shines down in between gathering clouds on a South Florida evening. The night wind blows in lightly from the west. Patterson's cell phone lights up again.

"What's up, Darius?" Patterson says as he peers over at Stokes.

"Not a thing, yo. Listen up. I found out somethin' for you and your boy. By the way, tell Stokes I said what's up," he says to Patterson.

"I'll let him know you said hi," Patterson tells him.

"Shit, man, I give you guys a lot of 411," Darius grudgingly realizes.

"Yeah, well, let's remember what we did for you," Patterson reminds him.

"Yeah, *whateva*! I found out where Castro's stayin'. The place in Hialeah."

"You got that already?" Patterson wonders aloud.

"Yeah. I got the street anyway. You'll have to figure which house."

"How'd you find that out so quick?" he asks Darius.

"There's nothin' a crackhead won't do for a Benjamin. Know what I'm sayin'?" He chuckles.

"Yeah I got you," Patterson confirms.

"Yeah. *You* got *me*." Darius chuckles again. "There you go, talkin' like you're down again. Now check this shit out too. Some white boy woke up in my neighborhood yesterday. Motherfucker was lying in the field and shit over here."

"So what? Another homeless drug addict passin' out in the field. Wouldn't be the first time?"

"Nah man. Nah. This white boy was no homeless addict! He creeps through the neighborhood, whips out his cell phone, and calls a cab to get him outta here! What kind of homeless white boy gets on his cell and pays for a cab in the hood, yo?" Darius asks him.

"So what are gettin' at?"

"Word is Castro's boys took care of him and dumped him in the field. Only this cracker won't die. Heard this shit might be tied into that shipment. Thought you'd like to know."

"All right. We'll look into it. Let us know if you hear anything else."

"Shhh." Darius sighs. "You let *me* know if *you* hear anything?" he sarcastically adds. "Whatever."

Stokes turns to Patterson. "So. What's up?"

"We got a street address in Hialeah," Patterson relays to him.

"We gotta keep a low profile. We can't let shit hit the fan over there. If someone spots us, they'll know we're on to them," Stokes says to him.

"Yeah, I was thinkin' about that. Darius already told us that neighborhood 'Be on lockdown, yo!'" He points his finger toward the ground for extra emphasis. He turns and smiles at Stokes as he cracks a smile. "Oh yeah. He mentioned somethin' about some white boy wakin' up in a field in Overtown the other day. Says word is Castro's boys were supposed to take care of him, 'cept he survived somehow. Says it may be tied in to this shipment."

"Interesting," Stokes responds and pauses. "Those damn white boys; they just won't die, will they? Just like cockroaches!" Stokes cracks. He looks over at Patterson, and they both laugh. "Why don't we go and grab a bite to eat—talk over what we're gonna do about the Hialeah place?"

"Sounds good to me."

Patterson and Stokes head to the Gables Diner in West Miami and pull into the lot. They spot another squad car there. They see two Miami Police Department detectives heading out of the diner as they're walking in.

"Hey, fellas," Stokes says as they stop to chat.

"How you guys doin' this evening?" one of the detectives asks.

"Not bad," Stokes answers as Patterson nods.

"Just makin' our rounds," Patterson says.

"Yeah I hear that. Anything interesting?" the detective asks them.

"Not really. Same old shit. You guys?" Stokes returns the question.

"Just a stolen car follow-up. Seems pretty random."

"Yeah?" Patterson pushes.

"Just can't figure out how a white boy makes his way into a victim's house in Overtown and beats him, takes his keys, and drives away," the detective divulges.

"Huh?" Patterson questions.

"Yeah. And there was a taxi driver waiting outside too. Looks like the guy may have taken a cab there. Not sure about that one yet though."

Patterson looks over at Stokes. "We got a couple of friends in that neighborhood. We'll let you know if we hear anything," Patterson tells them.

"Yeah. Thanks. Looks like this one will just sit in the unsolved file though. Enjoy," the detective says, nodding toward inside the diner.

Patterson and Stokes slip inside as the other officer leaves.

"White boy, huh? Think it's the same guy?" Stokes asks him.

"Could be. Let's call the chief and get the address on the stolen car. Work it out from there."

35

SPECIAL TASK FORCE

Patterson and Stokes sit at the counter and order their usual eggs benedict. Stokes calls the chief and gets the name of the victim and address in Overtown. He writes it down on a napkin and hands it to Patterson.

"I think it would be better if we showed up at this guy's house here. What's his name? Oscar Hernandez. Then, if all goes well, we can head over to Hialeah really late and catch the neighborhood off guard. We'll drive by and get out—hopefully without anyone seeing us. What do you think?" Patterson asks.

"I'm in," Stokes agrees.

The meal disintegrates before their jaded eyes. They leave a tip and exit the diner before making their way back to I-95 in their patrol car; in a matter of minutes, they're back in Overtown. "Let's see. Here is SW 178 Terrace. Which one is it?" Patterson says.

"Is that it over there?" Stokes asks him.

"Where?"

"Over here on the right. This one," Stokes says, pointing to the house.

"Let's do it. We'll tell him we were sent to do a follow-up—that we're a special unit investigating a string of car thefts in the area we think are connected to the same crew."

"Got it. I think he'll be able to see that you *are* special," Stokes says, laughing. "Let's see what we get."

Patterson and Stokes get out of the car. They head up the driveway toward the front of the house. Stokes rings the doorbell. There's no answer. He rings it again. This time, there's movement inside. A light goes on in the room, and someone steps toward the door.

"Who is it?" the voice answers.

"It's Officers Patterson and Stokes from the Miami Police Department," Patterson says.

"Man. I already talked to you guys."

"Well, sir, you spoke with two of our colleagues today, but we're in charge of a special task force unit investigating a string of car thefts in the area and just wanted a few minutes of your time," Stokes tells him.

"Can you put your badges up to the door?"

They lift their badges up and hear multiple locks being opened. Oscar opens the door and immediately turns, walking back into the house. Patterson and Stokes follow.

"What can I answer for you guys that I didn't tell the other two? I wanna go back to sleep," Oscar asks as he turns around to face them.

"Yeah, we'll just take a few minutes of your time." Seeing the cuts and swelling on Oscar's face, Stokes glances at Patterson. "Please," Stokes nudges, "tell us what happened."

Oscar tells them that he was making his way back from a friend's house when he spotted a cab overheating. He decided to help the driver and went into the house to fill up some water for the engine. He heads back out to the street. While he and the cab driver are under the hood, he hears his car start up and sees it peeling out of the driveway. He caught up with the car, but it was too late, and he saw a gringo inside speeding off.

"What did this guy look like?" Patterson asks.

"Short hair. White T-shirt and jeans. Average build I guess. Like a white boy," Oscar explains, noticing as he does that Stokes is trying to look around his place. "Can I help you?"

"No. Not at all." Stokes pauses. "Just a curious, average white boy," he says, shooting Oscar a look.

Stokes also notices a deep cut on Oscar's arm. "You get into a fight recently or something?"

"I think I hit my arm on the side mirror when this gringo was peeling out of my driveway. Everything happened so fast. He had the window down as I was tryin' to reach in. Hit me real good in the face too, 'cept I didn't feel it. All the adrenaline and shit you know?"

"Yeah, I guess so. Well listen, thanks for the info," Stokes says as he and Patterson start to walk toward the door. Stokes gets the feeling he's not going to get any more information from this guy about his appearance. "Oh yeah, by the way, what was the taxi driver doing in front of the house?"

"I don't know. I guess he had a drop-off in the area. I didn't ask. Some Jamaican guy. Or Bahaman. Jamaican guy named Bahama or Jamaica from Bahama. Something like that," Oscar recalls.

"You talked to him?" Patterson asks.

"Yeah. I heard him cursing at his car when it was overheating and went over to check."

"Thank you. Here's our card. If we hear anything, we'll let you know." Stokes extends his hand.

"Yeah," Oscar says as he closes the door.

Patterson looks at Stokes. "Something was fishy in there, huh?" he notes as they walk back to the car.

"Yeah. The story about his face and arm doesn't add up," Stokes responds. "You think he knows something about the shipment? I mean it seems to be too random that a white boy who Castro might've tried to take out wakes up in Overtown not dead, jumps in a taxi directly to this guy's house, beats him up, and steals his car," Stokes explains.

"Hopefully we find out soon," Patterson answers.

"I was peeking around the house. Saw he had a hole in his wall. The cabinets in his kitchen looked like they were messed up too. Like there was a brawl in there. Unless this Oscar guy has some temper and likes to punch his own walls I would say there was a fight *inside* of the house. He was getting really jumpy when he saw me looking around."

"Yeah. I noticed that," Patterson agrees.

"And a cabbie in Overtown? You didn't buy that he caught his accent from him cursin', did you?" Stokes presses.

"Not at all."

"You wanna head over to Hialeah now?" Stokes suggests.

"Yeah. Let's do this."

36

GANGSTAS LIKE TO PARTY TOO

In Hialeah, Patterson and Stokes see an unmarked police cruiser parked on the street as they make their way into the neighborhood. A sound like someone tapping on a wood table floats into Patterson and Stokes's ears. It has started raining on their car. Patterson flicks on the windshield wipers as the heavy rain splashes on the glass. The blades from the wiper slop back and forth as Patterson and Stokes ride through the area. Stokes gets an eerie feeling about the unmarked vehicle. "Funny how that cruiser is hangin' outside the neighborhood we're here to take a look at," Stokes tells him.

"I think so too. Darius heard the whole neighborhood was on lockdown. Hope they're not part of the problem too," Patterson says thinking out loud.

"You get a look at who it was?" Stokes asks him.

"Nah. Too dark with the fog on this window," Patterson says, turning the switch for the defroster.

"Yeah. Same here."

"Now he said it was"—he looks down at the napkin—"NW 201st Terrace. Can you see that street sign?" Patterson asks him while driving, struggling to see through the rain.

"It's"—Stokes pauses to read—"198 Terrace. Just a couple more blocks."

As they approach the next intersection, the rain continues to descend. A car that's facing them flashes its headlights on. Suddenly without warning, the car's wheels peel, screaming in the street like an innocent girl fending off an attacker. It's heading straight at them. The screech tears through the night air, startling both of them.

"Move over!" Stokes yells.

Patterson swerves to his right with his hands clenched on the wheel, his muscles rippling out of his forearms, and narrowly avoids the car.

"What the hell was that?" Stokes yells as the vein in his neck pulses.

"I don't know!" Patterson expels.

"Here it is. 201st Terrace. Now which way?" Stokes asks him.

"I guess we should just try one way and then the other. See if we notice anything out of the ordinary?"

"Too late for that. Head right first," Stokes directs.

Patterson turns the wheel and heads down the street. Both of them have been through this neighborhood in the daytime. The arrests they've made over the years and days fade into one. Drugs, domestic disputes, even homicide have called them to these streets. Then again, most of these neighborhoods look the same.

"There are hundreds of houses here. It would take us days, maybe even weeks of surveillance to find out which one it is. It's probably under someone else's name," a dejected Patterson says.

"You remember that grow house the department raided a few weeks back?" Stokes doesn't wait for a response. "They tracked down the owner yesterday. Some guy who lives in Argentina. Don't even know if he exists."

"I wonder how many foreign criminals have gotten mortgages down here," Patterson asks aloud.

"We can't see shit in this rain anyway. Guess we'll start heading out so we don't waste any more time."

Patterson's cell phone lights up. He flips it open. It's the department headquarters. "Hello?"

"Patterson, this is the chief. How are you guys doin'?"

"Followin' some leads, sir. Got a couple of sparks. We'll see if a fire breaks out."

"Keep me posted," the chief tells him before hanging up.

The two officers see a car parked next to the cruiser as they make their way out of the neighborhood.

"You see that?"

"Ten-four," Stokes answers.

"I'm gonna pull around the corner. You can get out and take some shelter by that store under the overpass," Patterson directs.

"This is exactly why I signed on to do this," Stokes sarcastically adds as his door opens and he heads out into the wet evening.

"Make sure you keep your radio on," Patterson mentions before the passenger door closes and Stokes runs off.

Stokes takes cover and peeks across the street to view the two vehicles.

"Got a visual," Stokes says into his radio.

"Ten-four."

"No movement. Sit tight." Stokes relays.

A few minutes go by, and the driver turns the car's engine on. The lights flick on. Stokes sees it slowly turn around and head away from the neighborhood.

"We got movement. The car is leaving. Time to follow."

Patterson pulls the car around, and Stokes jumps in yelling and pointing, "That way! Let's go!"

Patterson puts the pedal to the floor, and after some tense seconds, they catch up to the car.

"There it is," Stokes tells him. "The dark-colored Escalade."

"What is it? Blue or black?"

"I think it's black. But don't get too close."

They follow the car onto I-95. The Escalade weaves in and out of traffic and makes a sharp exit off the interstate.

Patterson turns to Stokes. "Where are they going? South Beach?"

"Might be. Gangstas like to party too, right?"

A few minutes zip past, along with the white traffic lines. The Escalade takes a turn down Washington with Patterson and Stokes following. As the traffic snakes north between traffic lights, pedestrians, wannabes, and seemingly endless amount of taxis, the Escalade takes a right into the driveway of the Sagamore Hotel.

"The Sagamore?" Patterson asks as he turns and looks at Stokes with a puzzled look.

"Looks like we're going to party tonight. Let's see who they make friends with inside."

The keys to the Escalade are handed to the valet by the driver. The valet steps around the car and opens up the door. A Hispanic man exits the vehicle in all white linen pants and shirt. Another man meets him at the stairs, and they enter the hotel.

Patterson and Stokes pull up in "the unit." This is their term of endearment for their "other" partner—the police-issued, undercover cruiser, a Mercury Grand Marquis with all of the police necessities inside. The unit holds a portable flashing light, a radio, a computer, and a couple of metal nightsticks. Patterson gets out to hand the keys over to the valet. The valet can't hide his surprise. "Take very good care of this vehicle," he says with enough of a straight face to make the valet think he's serious.

"Yes, sir."

Patterson and Stokes head toward the steps of the Sagamore. "It's good that I always dress well," Patterson tells him matter-of-factly as they enter the hotel. "I'll fit in real well. You, on the other hand . . ." He rolls his eyes.

The doorman opens up the glass doors, and they enter the Sagamore.

"Have you stayed here before?" Stokes asks his partner.

"Nah. I always stay across the street at the Catalina when I come down here with Michelle. I figure four hundred dollars here, two hundred there. You know?" Patterson responds.

"On a cop's salary? Yeah. *I* know," Stokes confirms. "That's them. Up there." He nods toward the men they're looking for, and Patterson, who hasn't spotted them yet, follows his gaze. "Looks like they're getting a table. Must have the gangsta roll. Let's grab a beer over here at the bar."

"Drinking on duty? That's pretty rare for you." Patterson inquires.

"Well, duty calls," Stokes informs him.

They finagle their way over to the bar and set up there as the partygoers and vacationers come and go. Stokes nods toward the two men. "Looks like they got it hooked up in here."

They see a pretty Hispanic cocktail waitress make her way over to the table the men are seated at.

"Looks like somebody hooked her up too. Damn!" Patterson says.

"Yeah. *Not bad!* You wanna try to talk to her while I keep an eye on this crew." Stokes nods, motioning toward the two men.

"I thought you'd never ask." Patterson revels.

One of the girls seated next to Stokes is looking him over while he finishes up with Patterson. "Having fun tonight?"

"Yeah," she says with a smile. "How about yourself?"

Patterson makes his way to the back bar, dodging in and out of dancing people, some at their tables, some on the floor. Some are dancing by themselves, trying to find a partner, while others gyrate in groups. He makes his way up to the bar and keeps an eye on the waitress. She takes her table's order and heads back to the bar to put in the order.

"Bottle of Moet and Chandon. One bottle of Dom and one of Kettle One."

"Sounds like a party. Can we talk for a second?" he asks her.

She's filling ice into glasses at the waitress station. "I'm busy. If you need anything you can get it from the bar."

"If you're the cocktail waitress for that table I saw you serve, I *need* to talk to *you.*" Patterson shows her his badge.

"Not over here! Be careful! Meet me back there in two minutes. She nods toward the curtains behind the bar. By the way I'm *not* a cocktail waitress. I'm the weekend manager," she shoots back.

The pretty manager continues to fill up the ice bucket with a nervous hand. The ice spills out of the top as her arm twitches. The bartender delivers the bottles, and she's off to the table. Patterson makes his way to the curtains. He can still see the table from back there. The gangstas chat it up with her, and she flashes a smile as they look her up and down—the kind of forced smile that girls give when a group of guys makes them uncomfortable. She pours them their drinks, heads back to the bar, and drops off her tray at the waitress station before meeting Patterson at the curtains.

"What can I do for you?" she demands.

"Well, I need some information on the guys at your table. Do you know who they are?"

"Everyone in South Beach knows who they are. Why should I tell you?"

"Because I'm a police officer and I'm asking you for your help."

She pauses. "They come in here all the time. Hang out with a couple of guys in Castro's crew. You *do* know who Castro is, right?"

"Yeah, of course we do. What are their names and who do they normally come in with?"

"They normally come in here with a guy named Malo. But he doesn't seem to be around tonight."

He looks around the club and sees the crowd getting sexier as he thinks out loud. "Yeah. Doesn't seem like too many of them are around tonight."

"What? I can't hear you."

"Oh, nothing. Here's my card. Next time they come in here with Malo and his boys, please give me a call. What's your name?"

"My name is Dianna."

"Thank you for your time, Dianna. It was a pleasure."

"Before you go . . ." She pauses.

"What is it?"

"If I help you out, would you be able to help me out with something?" She thinks about telling him about Ben.

"Maybe. What is it?"

"Well, I know some of you guys are friends with Castro's crew."

"I've heard some things too, but I'm not one of them. Neither is my partner."

"Are you sure?"

"Yes."

"What is your partner's name?"

"Michael Stokes. And I am Patterson. David Patterson."

"Okay, David Patterson. I might give you a call—maybe let you in on something if you can help me, okay?"

"Sure. My phone is on all the time. Thank you."

Patterson heads back over to the bar, where Stokes is occupied with the same girl he was talking with before. They are cozied up to one another. "See anything?"

"Nah. I'm just trying to blend into the crowd," Stokes yells over the music. "They're just hanging out at the table. Couple of chongas showed up. They're drinkin' and hangin' out. Like everyone else."

"Yeah I can see. Just like everyone else huh?"

"Yeah!"

"Well not like us anymore. Let's go," Patterson demands.

"Aww come on! Look at what I got here," Stokes pleads.

"Let's go, Stokes. Got some information to work on."

"Shit!" Stokes says his good-byes. He tries to yell above the music while Patterson drags him out. "I'll call you soon!" he yells back to the girl he was cozied up with.

"So what did the waitress have to say?" he asks Patterson as he catches up with him.

"She's the night manager. Not too much. Just that those guys normally come in with Malo. It got me thinking that none of these guys are around—just these little shits."

"You think tonight may be *the* night?" Stokes inquires about the shipment.

"I don't know. But sure feels like they've been occupied. Probably going down soon." He pauses to think. "Anyway, we should get back to headquarters and let the captain know that we got an address in Hialeah. We got a place here where Malo and the rest of Castro's crew likes to party. We got a stolen car, a white boy, and maybe a little help from someone we met tonight."

"Oh yeah? I *bet* you want some help from someone we met tonight," Stokes cracks.

"Remember what I said about the car," Patterson says to the valet as he hands him the ticket.

"No problema, sir."

37

THE MEETING

The night slowly winds down at the Sagamore. The crowd thins out. Dianna grabs her phone and places a call to Tre.

Tre's phone vibrates. He reaches into his pocket as he drives. The girl in the passenger seat looks over at him. The phone reads Dianna.

"'Bout time, baby!" he says aloud.

"Hey, I need to see you. Can you meet me at the Sag at four?" Dianna asks.

"Yeah, I can get over there," Tre tells her.

"Who's that, baby? Bet she won't do to you what I will." She leans over and rubs her hand on his face.

"Man, shut up!"

"Psst." She sits back in her seat, upset and disappointed.

"I'll see you in a minute." He closes his phone.

"I got some work to do. Gotta drop you off. Where are your girls at?" he asks his passenger.

"Damn, Tre! You got some work to do? I thought we was chillin'."

"We was, but now we ain't!"

"Drop me off by Cameo."

"A'ight."

Tre parks the car and heads up to the Sagamore to grab a drink to loosen up his flow. He steps up to the bar. "Can I get a Kettle One and Cranberry?"

He leans against the bar checking his watch. It reads 3:45 a.m.

"Do you know where Dianna is?" he asks the bartender.

"The manager Dianna? Yeah, she should be in the back behind the other bar." She points him in the direction.

He walks across the room and sees her. "Dianna," He yells.

"Oh, hey, Papi." She gives him a hug and kiss. "I need to talk to you 'bout something."

"Anything for you, baby. What's up?"

"I need you to check on some cops for me. And I know that I can trust you to keep it quiet. I need to find out if they are legit."

"That's it, Mami? I came all this way, and I'm not gonna to get some?" he says, raising his voice.

"Damn, Tre! Yeah, that's it. It's really important to me though." She sends him flirtatious eyes.

"All right," he says, giving in. "What's his name?"

"Well, there are two of them. David Patterson and the other one is his partner, Stokes."

"I'll check them out."

"Can you find out tonight?" she pushes.

"Damn! Tonight?"

"Please!" she begs as she grabs his hand.

"All right. I'll see what I can do, Mami."

"Oh. Gracias, Tre!" She gives him a big hug and kiss. "And one more thing."

"What now, Mami!"

"I need the address for Castro's house in the Keys."

"I hope you know what you're doing. Don't get in over your head, Mami." He pauses. "I'll hit you up when I get the 411."

Tre picks up his cell and sends a text to his chonga.

An hour and a half later, Dianna receives a call from Tre. "None of my boys know them. Should be clean. By the way, your brother's still caught up in somethin' wit Malo. I heard he's messin' with him. The house is 1011 Cocoanut Path."

"Thanks, Papi. I owe you." She knows she's used all her favors.

Back in her apartment, Dianna finishes washing her face. She walks over to her bed and picks up her cell phone. It reads 4:30 a.m. She dials a number. "Patterson?"

"Yeah," he answers.

"I wanna meet tomorrow."

"Okay. Where?"

"Café Versailles. Be there at eight a.m."

"I'll be there."

"Good. I might have a way we can both help each other," Dianna informs him.

She hangs up the call and then thinks for a minute, tapping the phone against her face. She puts in a call to Ben.

38

Maggie's Place

Ben makes his way down the road, almost flying by a small sign partially blocked by a tree branch. He downshifts, slowing the car so he can read. "Maggie's Place," the sign states, with an arrow pointing down a small dirt road. Only one out of three bulbs on the top of the sign is lit. A zapping sound from the electricity comes in and out as one of the bulbs tries to come back to life.

Ben slows to a crawl and makes the right-hand turn down a narrow street. He hears the sound of the tires rolling over the sand, shooting the small rocks from underneath the tires. He imagines there's water on his left, but he can't see through the foliage. Both sides of the Charger are being brushed by the extended branches from the wooded area. He looks ahead and sees a small clearing. A rickety, old house with a porch light comes into view. The roof of the house gently slopes over the porch to give it some protection. A sign in front reads, "Rooms for rent." He pulls in and sees two cars parked. He looks at the house again and realizes this is the place. He wasn't expecting a five star resort but this place is struggling to have just one.

Maggie's Place looks like a flashback in time. It's surrounded by pine trees and looks as if nothing has been changed in years. Paint chips are peeling off the bowed boards from years of weather exposure. As Ben makes his way onto the first step of the porch, the board gives, letting out a loud creak. By the time he makes it to the second step, a light comes on inside the front door.

The door opens, and a woman puts her face to the screen and demands, "Who is it?"

Ben is startled. "Hi. My name is Ben. Lisa sent me, from—"

"Oh yeah, Lisa. We got two rooms open—the honeymoon suite or the single bed. Which one you want?" She pauses. "You look like a nice young man; if you don't have a woman with ya, I could sure make some time?" She smiles from behind the door with her jagged teeth. Her face is pressed against the screen, flattened against it. Ben makes out the white hair. She looks like a witch.

Ben feels dirty. "Uh. I'll take the single room." He pauses. "It's real tempting though." He decides to have fun with her.

She peers at him with her dirty eyes. "Oh." She giggles. "How many nights?"

"One for now. Don't know how many more."

"It'll be twenty-five dollars per night. Breakfast served at eight sharp."

Ben hands her cash. She points him down a small hallway and hands him a key. "Number thirteen," she says.

"Thank you. See you in the morning," he says.

"Not if you get lonely." She smiles and winks.

"Ewww," Ben manages to expel as he walks away, feeling dirty.

He turns quickly and heads down the hallway to the last room on the right. He puts the key in the door and enters the room. Feeling the wall to his left, he flips the switch. A light in the middle of the room buzzes and flickers. When it turns on, he sees one small window, a twin bed, and a dresser that barely fits in the room. The bed cover looks like it from the 1950s—some outdated floral designs. He puts his things on the bed, turns the switch to off, and passes out.

Ben falls into a deep sleep. Images of his friends playing on the streets of his South Jersey neighborhood appear into and fade out of his mind. He has a dream that he and Brian are locked up in jail. Slim Jimmy posts their bail. He takes them into the woods and tells Ben that he's a rat—that he shouldn't have told anyone about what he saw. Ben's on his knees. Before Jimmy pulls the trigger, Ben lets out his last scream. "Help me!"

He looks up at a person in the foliage. It's the man he saw get shot.

Ben awakes in a sweat.

His phone vibrates. It's a 305 area code. "Hello?"

"Hola, Ben."

"Why are you callin' me from a different number?" he asks Dianna.

"I'm calling from the hotel I work at," she tells him, frustrated, knowing he doesn't fully trust her. "I got the address for you. Listen; take this down. 1011 Cocoanut Path."

"Why should I believe you?"

"They do have my brother wrapped up in this somehow. I'm sorry for what I did to you guys! I had no choice. Please believe me," she pleads.

"I'll take this down. Dianna, if this is right . . ." He pauses, thinking about what this means. "Thank you. And let me know if you hear anything else," he tells her, simultaneously hanging up the phone.

He falls back asleep. Another dream comes into focus. He has a dream that this is all a Broadway play, where the characters of his life play themselves, their childhood, his neighborhood, the setting. The events of this weekend all come in and out of focus. He tosses and turns all night until the sun comes up.

An avalanche of dreams rages through his mind as Ben rocks throughout the night. One by one, the avalanches grow bigger and bigger, until the apex (and of course, the alarm clock) clang to a climax. His eyes open. It's seven a.m.

He sits up at the side of the bed and rubs the night from his eyes, wishing this was all a dream. He's facing the window. Sunlight peeks in from the side of the faded drapes. He walks to the sink and throws water on his face—not knowing what today may bring. He puts on his jeans and T-shirt and exits his room.

He walks down the hallway and hears music and smells the odor of marijuana. There's an exit sign and a door that leads outside. It's not until he closes the door to the back of the building that he sees a man sitting in a chair smoking reefer, the door blocking his view. He looks at the man and nods.

The man nods back and says, "How goes it?"

"Good, man. You?"

"Pretty good. Could be worse, ya know? Could be back in Vietnam."

Ben nods in agreement.

"You like Neil?" he asks as "Rockin' in the Free World" blasts through the transistor.

"Yeah, who doesn't?" Ben shrugs.

"I thought you were a little young to really appreciate it. Every Saturday morning, they got an hour of Neil. I like to smoke it up a little bit and really get into it. Know what I mean?"

"I can see that. I'm gonna go and get some breakfast. I'm sure I'll see you around," he says, turning back inside as the man nods.

Maggie's assistant is setting up the continental breakfast.

He sees Maggie, who has a plate of food for herself.

"Up early today?" the assistant asks.

"Yeah," Ben mumbles.

"Breakfast will be served in a few minutes," the man tells him.

"Eggs, bacon, ham, and toast. Help yourself, sweetie," Maggie tells him.

"Think I will." Making himself a plate, Ben heads onto the porch and plops down into a chair. He inhales his breakfast. A basset hound whimpers at his feet while looking up at him.

"I hear ya, buddy." Ben pets the dog.

Ben leaves the plate on the porch, jumps in his car, and crawls across the lot. He looks out the driver window and sees the man who works at Maggie's checking him out as he leaves. An eerie feeling gathers inside. Maybe it's just paranoia. After what has gone on recently, it's understandable. He makes his way out of the one-way street to drive around Big Pine Key to find the house. It looks like a small town and it shouldn't take too long.

39

CAFÉ VERSAILLES

Dianna is seated at a table. The Sunday morning *Miami Herald* lies next to her bread plate. Black Marc Jacob sunglasses hide her eyes. Her shiny brown hair flows down past her shoulders. The door to the café opens. The foot traffic on Washington Avenue passes as Patterson walks in with Stokes. Patterson sees it's a table for two.

"Go ahead and grab something to eat at the counter. I'll take care of this," he says to Stokes.

"Yeah. *Sure* you will." Stokes pokes some fun.

Patterson walks over to the table. "Hi, Dianna. Good morning."

"Hola. Good morning," she responds as she sits with her arms crossed.

"So we got some things to talk about today, huh?" He moves the napkin over as the forks clink against the glass plate.

"Yes. We do," she answers as she lets out a deep sigh.

"Well, let's start off with what you can help me with, and then I'll see if I can help you," Patterson says to her.

The waitress comes over to fill up Patterson's water, causing a pause in the conversation.

Dianna finally breaks the silence. "I know that Malo and his crew aren't in town."

"Really? Where are they?"

"They're in Big Pine Key—at one of their hideouts."

"What are they doing down there?"

"A couple of things. But the one you want to know about is the shipment they're picking up."

"Okay. I see. How do you know about this?"

"Pretty girls hear things," she states, not wanting to give up her friend, Tre.

"Yeah. I guess they do."

"They've been there for a few days. I think everything is gonna go down soon. I should find out later on today or tomorrow."

"Please let me know when you find out."

"No problema."

"Anything else?"

"Just something you can help me with."

"What is it?"

"Well, this is tough to talk about." She pauses, taking a sip of water. "My brother, Kelvin, got involved with Malo and owed him some money. He kept threatening him. Malo told him that he needed some help, from the both of us. My brother, you see, he's not bad—he's not like Malo—just a little misguided. My brother begged and pleaded with me. Malo had beaten him up, and I was worried about his safety. I'm very loyal to mi familia, my family," she corrects herself, "especially after my dad was killed. I couldn't handle it myself if something happened to Kelvin. My mom has no money and is in bad health. She wouldn't be able to take it. It would kill her. So I said yes—that I would help him."

"So what did you get into?" Patterson squints at her.

"Well, they had us set up some white boys from New Jersey. I feel terrible about it. I actually got to like one of them."

"Set up how?"

"Well, me and my girls were the decoys. The New Jersey boys were staying at the Catalina. We got them to hang out with us. Then we took them to a party where Castro's crew was. I didn't know what they were gonna do. I thought maybe they were drug dealers and Castro's boys were gonna rob them. But these guys were too nice and normal—too cool to be any of that. Now I find out they tried to kill one of them, except he ain't dead. And they took the other three to Big Pine Key to pick up their shipment."

"That's a pretty big story. How can I I can you help out?"

"Well, you see, they got my brother involved now too. I guess Malo didn't think we did enough. I'm worried what they're going to do to him when it's all over."

"I'll see what I can do. It's out of our jurisdiction, but maybe we can work with the department down there."

"That might be a problem. Castro might be in with them too. I got someone up here that gives me information and . . ." She trails off.

"And what?"

"The white boy that survived—I'm kind of in touch with him."

"Well, where is he? I need to talk to him."

"He went to Big Pine Key."

"What's his name?"

"Ben. Ben Jones."

"All right. Stay in touch with me. We gotta get moving on this." He stands up and grabs his jacket off the chair.

"Listen, try not to talk to anyone on this. Please. I even had to check you guys out."

"Check us out? You can trust us. Listen, the chief has us on this case because we are two guys *he* can trust. And me and Stokes over there go back fifteen years."

She nods. "I'm still worried. Castro's claws can dig deep."

"I know. Thank you for everything." He reaches across the table to shake her hand and heads out of the café.

"No problema."

"Stokes, we gotta go."

Stokes gets up quickly from the counter and follows Patterson onto Washington.

"Where's the fire? I was tryin' to order some food," Stokes complains as they race over to the unit.

"I just got word from our friend that Castro's crew is at another house in Big Pine Key. They kidnapped some guys from New Jersey and looks like they're gonna make them pick up the shipment somehow," says Patterson.

"How they gonna do that?"

"Not sure. Dianna also told me that her brother is involved. And she's worried that he's in way over his head."

"Okay. Guess we need to call the chief," Stokes says, processing what he's just heard.

"Yeah, but we might not be able to get any help from the department down there. Seems like they might be hooked in with Castro," he adds as he starts up the car and heads onto Washington.

"Aww shit. A lot of that goin' around these days," Stokes responds.

"Uh-huh."

"Well, it's got to come up here sometime right?" Stokes asks him.

"Exactly."

"And if we know where the shipment is being picked up or when, we might be able to follow the trail."

Patterson tells him, "You're smarter than I thought," and honks the horn, waiting for traffic.

"We just need to get down there or have someone be our eyes."

"I think I just might have our man, at least Dianna does. She's in touch with someone. You know those guys who Castro's crew got doin' their pickup for them?"

Stokes nods.

"Well they tried to off one of them, except he didn't die."

"*What!*" Stokes can't believe it. "Our white boy?"

"Yeah, that's what I'm thinking. And he must've found out where his boys were taken. Followed them down there. If she stays in touch with him, then we got eyes," Patterson replies.

Patterson and Stokes decide to relay their information to the chief.

"Chief?" Stokes asks through his cell.

"Yeah. What's up, Stokes?"

Stokes tells him about their new lead and information on the case.

The chief isn't as excited about the information as they expected. "I'm worried about cooperation between the other police force and logistics. Continue to work your contacts so that you can follow the shipment when it gets up here. Then we can nail those bastards, in our area. Go to the hotel where your white boy was staying and poke around."

40

THE HOUSE

Ben is driving through Big Pine Key when his phone rings—another 305 area code.

"Hola, Ben." It's Dianna.

"Hey."

"Did you find the house yet?" she asks him.

"No, still driving. Might ask for directions soon. This island is bigger than I thought."

"Well, listen. I was approached at work last night by some undercover officers."

"I'm listening. Go on," he demands.

"I had a friend check on them to make sure they were legit. They know something's goin' on. They know Castro has a shipment coming in. I talked to them about you guys and my brother too. I think they can help us. I trust them."

"I don't know if that's smart. What did you tell them about?"

"I told them everything. Including the part I played."

"What did they say?"

"They said that they were looking into it and they would be in touch with me." Ben doesn't respond. "Well? What do you think?"

"I think if I wait for the cops to help, it'll be too late for my boys and, from the sound of it, your brother too."

"So what will you do?"

"I'll figure something out. I always have."

"Listen, I know it's a lot to ask, but if there is any way that you can help out Kelvin . . . Please, Ben. I will help you out any way that I can!" she pleads.

"I won't promise anything."

"Please. I beg you!"

"I'll be in touch with you once I figure something out."

"Hold on. I also found out that it's going down Sunday night. I don't know exactly what time."

"You sure?"

"Yes. I told you; my friend is reliable. You should take this cop's number down, even if it's a last resort."

"Okay. What is it?" Ben asks her.

She gives him Patterson's number.

"Let me know if you hear anything else, like a time frame."

"I will, Ben. Good luck," she tells him with anxious faith and warning.

41

NO NAME PUB

Ben heads to No Name Pub and pulls into the dirt lot. He sees two locals in their pickup trucks, their boats in hitch. They've just pulled off the launch ramp. Water's still flowing out of the flow control valve, spilling onto the street. The transom on one of the boats reads, "Locals Only." Fishing is done for the day.

Ben steps out of the stolen car and heads into the establishment. A few more locals than last night are here. Looks like the lunch crowd. He scans around at the people seated inside. The man from last night is still on the left side of the bar minding his beer. At the table, three men wearing the typical fishing shirts—the ones with sport fish leaping out of the water—are seated. Khaki shorts and boat shoes with no socks finish the uniform. The men are a little boisterous after their day of fishing, sharing their tales of how the big one got away.

The mid afternoon sun shines down. Ben takes a seat where he sat the previous night. A young waitress makes her way over to him. She looks to be in her early twenties and easy on the eyes in a natural sort of way—no makeup, no jewelry or earrings, just lonely, wide, blue eyes.

"What can I get for ya?" she asks.

"Is Lisa workin' today?" Ben asks her.

"She only works nights."

"Okay. I'll take a water."

The fishermen at the table grow exceedingly louder as the beer and stories continue to flow. You name it, and it's told—stories about fishing, the weather, waterspouts, lightning, flying stingrays killing people in their boats as they cruise on the water. Ben hears, but he isn't listening.

Ben taps his foot and puts his hand on his head, pondering what to do next.

He sees one of the fishermen exiting the hallway from the restroom and head to the table. While speaking to the crew, the man gestures toward Ben. One of their crew turns his head and looks up at Ben. Another man turns around in his chair to get a view. Ben continues to stare forward out of the window while his hands tap nervously on the glass.

One of the men gets up from the table. He walks over, leans against the bar next to Ben, and puts down his drink.

"Can I get you something, sugar?" the waitress asks him.

"Yeah. You can get me a shot of that Don Julio stuff you got there."

"There you go." She pours the shot.

The man whips his head back and places the glass back on the bar.

"Ahhh." He wipes his mouth with the back of his arm. He turns toward Ben. "You see that guy over at the table?"

Ben looks over, nods, and answers, "Yeah. What about 'im?"

"Well, he wanted me to come talk to you. You see, he's my boss. We work on the boats you saw outside. He wanted to know if you were going to be around for a couple of days. We got some work. It pays well. We need the help—it being lobster season and all. The season ends the last day of March. The more hands on deck, the more lobster we can haul. Only seven allowed per person. You're young, and we just had to fire someone who was drunk and unreliable. You need some work over the next couple of days, son?"

"No. Actually I'm just stopping in town for a couple of days, and I'm really not looking for any."

"Okay. Well, if you change your mind, we'll be in here every day. My name is Buddy."

"All right, Buddy. My name is Ben. Thanks."

Ben hears the sound of car skidding to a stop in the parking lot outside.

Outside the No Name Pub, the driver's-side door of an Escalade swings open. Out steps a man who appears to be in his thirties. His boot heels touch down on the dry sandlot. He tries to use his cell phone but doesn't get any service. He looks over toward the bar and sees a sign for a pay phone. The man leans in the passenger window to speak with another man.

"Listen, cabrón, I need to make a call. I'll be right back, man."

The figure makes his way across the lot.

The locals barely notice as the shutters squeak open, but Ben shifts in his barstool and notices, out of the corner of his eye, a man walk in. He instantly recognizes the man from the Continuum, and his heart jumps in his throat. It's Jorge!

Ben holds his breath and lets it out slowly when Jorge heads toward the back of the pub, away from the bar and the stool he's occupying. Ben watches Jorge go to the pay phone in the back corner and make a quick call. Jorge drops the receiver back in its cradle, and Ben's mind races. As Jorge's attention moves toward the bar, Ben turns his head away and slithers over to the table full of fisherman.

"Hey, guys," he says, taking a seat at the fisherman's table with his back toward the bar praying that he'll go unnoticed, "can I get your number in case I change my mind?" Underneath the table, his hands are shaking.

"Sure. No problem," Buddy tells him.

"What can I get for you?" Ben hears the waitress ask, and he knows that Jorge is now directly behind him, standing right where he was seated only seconds ago.

"Two cokes." Jorge seems impatient. Ben hears shuffling noises, and he knows Jorge is now scanning the room. He can literally feel Jorge's eyes lock on the fishermen and himself; the man's steely eyes are almost burning a hole in his back.

More shuffling and a gruff, "Thanks," tell Ben Jorge has turned back toward the bar.

Ben watches as Jorge, drinks in hand, heads out of the door. As the door whips shut, he takes a deep sigh of relief, and his fluttering heart starts to slow.

"Thanks, guys," Ben says after he enters Buddy's cell number into his phone.

Ben walks away from the fishermen toward the shutters. Outside, one of the local men sitting in the parking lot gets up and enters the pub. Stepping out onto the dock and slipping behind a wooden beam, Ben watches Jorge go to his SUV and gas up. Jorge places the handle back on the gas pump and closes the gas tank on the truck.

A man walks by Ben on the dock and places a key on a hook. Ben glances over and sees a floating key with a chain that reads, "Buddy's."

The man turns around and yells, "Come on; it's quitting time!"

Ben turns in the direction the man was yelling and sees another man stepping off a boat with a transom that reads, "Buddy's."

Ben's attention turns back to Jorge, who gets in the vehicle and closes the door. As the SUV pulls out of the parking lot, Ben runs off the dock and jumps in his car. He makes the same turn out of the lot that the Escalade just made and falls in behind, keeping his distance and trying to remain as inconspicuous as possible. When the vehicle makes a left down a dirt road, he rolls by. Pulling off the road into the brush, he sits in the car for a few minutes, trying to figure out his next move. It's too light out right now to do anything. Castro's boys may be keeping an eye out over the property.

He decides to return at dusk and heads to a bait shop he passed in Spanish Harbor Key.

42

BAIT AND TACKLE

In the back of Eddie's Bait and Tackle Shop, Ben makes his way to the knife section and takes a look at a Bowie knife with serrated edges.

"Can I help you with somethin', son?"

"Yeah. I need a knife to work on the boat with. Which one you recommend?"

"Depends what you'll be doin' with it. But workin' on the boat, um, let me see." He pauses while searching his collection. "Most of the fishermen use this one." He holds up a small four-inch knife.

"That one looks a little small. I want one that's heavy-duty. Like this one." He points to the Bowie knife.

"Well, that sure is heavy-duty, son. You can use that one for more than fishing. Lot of hunters use that one too. Fourteen-inch knife; leather sheath; double brass guard here, of course; stainless steel, eight-inch blade," he says matter-of-factly.

"Yeah. I've seen it before," Ben says, thinking of his childhood days in South Jersey. "How much?"

"Thirty dollars flat."

"Okay. I'll take it. And these," he says, picking up a pole and net.

"Of course, if you're gonna carry that around, concealed and all, you'll need a concealed weapons permit. I guess you could keep it in plain view; there wouldn't be a problem. Of course that would be up to the officer. Know what I mean."

"Uh-huh. Thanks," he says, pretending to understand the local laws. "You got bait?"

43

THE HIDEOUT

Ben pulls across the street from where the Escalade is parked, stopping the car behind the brush. Grabbing his newly purchased pole, net, and bait, he heads toward the property. He finds a spot in the clearing, baits his pole, and casts it into the water. He's about three hundred feet from the house, hiding behind a tree. A light is on toward the back of the location. Two men are on an outside deck smoking cigarettes. Sliding glass doors open to the deck from the back of the residence. The deck leads to a dock that has two boats tied beside it. Ben wants to make sure this is the house.

He moves himself and his fishing equipment even closer now, slowly moving, gaining about fifty feet with each move. He focuses on keeping himself out of sight and trying to make as little noise as possible. It's almost-pitch black in this wooded area along the shore. Ben, now only about a hundred feet from the house, continues to crawl. Laying his equipment down, he hears a noise from the wooded area and whips around to see. It's too dark to tell what made the noise as he stares with wide open eyes into the blackness. His eyes scour the nothingness in front of him. He hopes it's an animal.

Ben can hear the men talking on the back porch. He tries to catch his breath as the sweat pours down his face. There's a light on the side of the house. The front is dark, and there's a clearing about twenty feet wide between the side of the house and where the wooded area begins.

Moving on all fours, he heads toward the front of the residence. Voices carry in the night air. He propels over the cracking sticks, twigs, and branches that cover the ground like a blanket. Now is his chance.

Ben quickly leaps up from the ground bolting from the blackness, through the light, and back into the blackness against the front of the house. His heart is pounding, and he's breathing very heavily. His eyes bulge out of their sockets, scanning the yard like radar. He hears the sounds of twigs breaking again from the brush. His body is on high alert.

Ben's always been frightened of sounds from the woods, ever since he was a child. The stories he heard about the New Jersey Devil—camping stories told around the campfire, courtesy of Mike—not to mention what he and Brian witnessed, always creep into the back of his mind.

Hearing *another* noise from the brush, he turns around to face it. As he watches something coming out from the darkness, his heart lumps up in his throat. Frozen, like cement, Ben can barely move or breathe. A figure steps into the light. He exhales deeply, letting the momentary fear flush out of his lungs. It's a deer, about the size of a large dog. The deer stops in its tracks, looks up at him silently, and darts back into the woods.

Ben turns his focus back toward the house and peers into the den. Not a soul. He moves to the front now, stepping onto the porch. It creaks as he steps on the wood. As he makes his last step, he sees headlights moving up the driveway toward the house. He jumps to the side of the porch, landing on the grass, and takes cover as the car rolls in. He thinks he's been spotted.

The car slowly comes to a stop. The headlights turn off. No one exits the car. Ben leans his back against the house as he tries to slow his breathing, his heart pounding out of his chest. He looks into the darkness, waiting. Finally, after a few minutes, a car door swings open. The driver exits and then another man follows. The passenger-side door opens, and the last of the three men are out. They walk up to the porch, speaking with each other. Ben doesn't recognize any of the voices. He's stuck to the building like a fly when he hears one of the men say, "I'm going smoke a cigarette, cabrón."

Ben knows if the man steps off the porch he will be done for. The door to the house closes. Ben's so close he can hear the smoker click his cigarette lighter. He hears his footsteps as he paces across the porch.

Ben sees the end of the lit cigarette appear from the side of the house. Something is moving in the brush. The small deer steps out, looking at the man on the porch before darting away. The cigarette is flung on the grass. He hears the footsteps head to the front door and move inside the house. Another close call.

Wiping the sweat from his face, Ben peers into the window. The man passes through the den. Ben makes his way toward the bedrooms to see if his friends could be in there. He looks in the first bedroom. Nothing. The next room is a bathroom. As he passes by, he hears someone enter.

He sees a man walking and, after a moment, follows to a smaller, hidden structure. Ben ducks for cover behind a shed. He makes his way closer to the structure and peers through a lighted window, hearing voices from inside.

Ben realizes the building is a pool house. His three friends are tied to wooden chairs. He tries to get a better look through the dilapidated window. Two men are keeping an eye on them inside and speaking with Jorge.

Ben turns around to survey the scene. Seeing no more movement from behind the houses or out on the docks, he heads into the brush between the pool house and the main house.

He races through the brush, running to the house by the front porch area. Someone inside is making his way up to the front. The front door opens and slams. Footsteps tap across the porch. There's a clicking sound of a lighter. The man steps off the porch to the car, opening the door, and sits there for a minute, not turning the engine.

Ben waits patiently. After a few minutes, the car turns on. Ben sees the headlights fading out of the driveway. He rushes across the front of the house and runs into the brush.

One of the men yells, "Yo!"

Grabbing a shotgun, the man races toward the brush at the side of the house where he's sure he saw something out of the corner of his eye. Another man is running behind with a handgun. They slow down at the side off the house. "What did you see, hombre?"

"Think I saw someone. Something moving into the woods. Just wait here a second."

For a moment, the two men continue to look into the blackness. To their right, they hear a noise. Their attention and guns focus on that point. Out of the brush steps a deer, who takes off into the night.

"Ha ha, cabrón!" chortles the second man. "Great job! You really did it this time. Ha ha!"

"Yeah. Whatever, hombre," the first man mumbles, realizing he screwed up.

They turn around, walking to the back of the house.

Cheo walks out to meet them. He's got everything set up to his satisfaction. "Me and Jorge are gonna head back to Miami. Make sure you don't fuck this up."

Oblivious to the fact he was spotted, Ben continues to make his way through the wooded area where he parked the Charger. He pulls away from the property. All he can do is think about his friends. He's the only one that can do something. Ben passes by a police cruiser and thinks about talking with the officers, but better judgment prevails. Castro's crew has friendlies in the Miami PD; he may have friends here too.

Ben's eyes are transfixed on the road ahead. He makes his way past the house where his friends are being held.

Ben's phone lights up. It's Dianna. She tells him that it's going down tomorrow night at midnight.

"Thanks, Dianna," he says to her before hanging up.

Ben's exhausted and contemplating his next move. He will do anything he can to help out the boys—anything. He pulls up to Maggie's Place. Maggie is on the porch, sitting in a rocking chair shooting the breeze with her cook.

"Dinner will be served early tonight at six," she says coquettishly. "Some fresh lobster for ya."

"Not hungry," he answers.

"Stayin' another night, sonny?" she asks.

"Tonight will be my last night."

"I'm going to miss you, Ben." She winks and smiles in her old, dirty way. "But I knew the time would be comin' soon."

"Yeah. Thanks," he says. But he has too much on his mind to be joking around with Maggie tonight. His friends and their situation—*his* situation—weigh too heavily.

Ben nods as he makes his way into the boarding house. He knows that he won't miss this place. He never wants to see it again as long as he lives. Entering his room, he lies down on the bed and stares at the ceiling, starting to figure out a plan.

"The boat!" He sits up as he expels the words.

The bait and tackle shop sold him a knife. He reaches down into his pocket and feels the metal.

44

THE POOL HOUSE

Rob opens his eyes as he's pulled out of the water. Everything is in slow motion. He sees Raul's face in front of his and can tell the man's yelling at him. But he can't hear a thing. As Rob's body reflexively jerks air into his lungs, his throat viciously gasping for air, Raul's snarling voice is the first thing he hears.

Raul's large, dark, open hand swipes at Rob and lands across his face. Robs hair and face fall back as the water sprays off of him. His hands and feet are still bound with duct tape. Raul holds him steady.

"Stay here!" Raul yells, as if he had another choice.

Rob sees bubbles from the pool making their way to the surface. It's Mike and Brian coming up for air. Rob has no idea what time it is. There's no clock on the wall. Rob sees the shriveled skin on his fingers. He leans his back against the wall of the pool to balance himself, completely drained of energy.

The boys have been in and out of the pool all day—a crash course with regulators and tanks. Raul's been doing what he was brought here for. The boys remain frightened and confused, and their morale is low.

"That's it. Finally you fucking gringos are listening," Raul expels.

One minute it seems like he wants to kill them; the next minute, he wants to reward them for finishing their task. "Now take off your regulators and get out of the pool."

Mike and Brian get out and are duct taped back to their chairs, water still dripping from their bodies. The two thugs exit the room. Raul makes his way over to Rob, who barely has the strength to stand. He lifts Rob out and plops him in a chair, taping him to it. Raul turns off the lights and exits the pool house.

45

THIS WILL BE THE DAY

Ben peels out of Maggie's lot and heads down the highway. He rolls into the dirt lot by the No Name Pub and parks the car. It reminds him of the unpaved street he grew up on in South Jersey. He thinks about the days in middle of the hot summer of his childhood when the men from the city department came down his street to lay asphalt and put curbs in. He and Brian were playing in the street. One of the men allowed them to put their names in the curb. It read, "Ben and Brian were here." The carving on Mockingbird Lane has faded along, with those memories.

He sees the fisherman, along with Buddy, leave for the day. It's time for him to make his move.

Ben makes his way over to the dock like he owns it. Three locals sit on the flatbed of an old Ford drinking their beer, paying no attention to him. They're seated about forty-five feet or so from the beginning of the dock. One of them made eye contact with Ben today while he was speaking with the fisherman and the man nodded to him. They won't be a problem. He steps across the rickety boards, which creak as he walks across them. Exposed nails poke up on both sides of the boards. Ben makes it to the fuel dock. The keys are in a metal box. He pulls the knife out of the leather case; the boat sits just a few feet away. He opens the unlocked door and sees the keys—the miniature palm tree on the key chain and "Buddy's" floating key—right in front of him. He can't believe it's still unlocked.

Ben's ready for the challenge, whatever it may bring. He steps out on the boat, untying it from the dock; puts the key in the ignition; and turns the engine. He looks over his left shoulder. No one is watching. Grabbing the wheel, he pushes the throttle down slowly and moves the boat away from the dock as quietly as possible.

He shuttles across the calm water with the sun setting just over the tree line. Turning east, he sees a Florida Sandhill Crane takes off into the air. The boat traverses through the current. There's a beautiful quiet that seems to yell, *Take in the scenery.* Other birds shoot out of the mangroves. Ben takes a look down off the boat into the water. It's clear. He can see the sandy bottom when there's no plant life blocking the view below to the ocean floor. He can't believe that, in the middle of all this darkness, there's so much light.

Everything is fine as he makes his way into the channel. He's just borrowing the boat for a little while—a simple joyride. A few boats are scattered throughout the channel. Most are sailboats that stay the nights on the water. This time of year during lobster season, which runs every year from August through March, a few more boats are wading.

Ben turns left underneath a small, fixed bridge that allows US 1 to continue south. After a few minutes of carefully making his way through the no-wake zone, he sees the lights of the house up ahead. He drops anchor a couple hundred yards away from the house. Throwing dive flags into the water to blend in with other boats, he waits for the moment as he checks his watch. He turns on the radio. There's call for some scattered storms from the local station. The horizon looks cloudy. In the distance, a cloud lights up with heat lightning.

The water is as flat as a lake. The night is dark, and the stars are starting to wake under the light of the moon. He sees the light on and grabs the binoculars to get some visual contact.

46

THE CATALINA

Patterson and Stokes pull up to the Catalina Hotel. They get out of the unit, and one of the doormen walks toward them. "Checkin' in?" he asks.

"No. Just here to see the manager." Stokes flashes his badge. "Is he here?"

"Yes. Let me get him," the doorman says and tells them to wait.

Patterson and Stokes wait where the lounge, check-in area, and bar converge. Guests flow in and out. A few ladies walk in with bags from the Lincoln Road Mall. A woman with a white cover-up leaves the hotel with her boyfriend, whose sandals flop with each step.

"Not as nice as the Lowes, but not bad," Patterson says.

"Yeah. And like I said, not as pricey," Stokes replies.

"I'm sure."

The manager steps out and approaches Patterson and Stokes. He extends his hand to introduce himself. "Hi. I'm Alex, the manager," he says in his strong Latin accent.

"Hi. I'm Officer Patterson. This is Officer Stokes. We just had a few quick questions for you about someone staying in the hotel."

"Of course. Whatever assistance the Catalina can offer to you gentlemen."

"We're looking for someone staying here. Unfortunately, we only have his first name," Patterson tells him.

"Sure. Again, whatever we can do. What is the name of the person?" the manager says.

"His name is Ben. He was with three other young men. Probably checked in a few days ago."

"Let me check on the computer. I will be right back."

"I'm gonna take a walk. I think you got this covered," Stokes tells Patterson.

Patterson nods in agreement.

After a few minutes, the manager emerges. Patterson sees Stokes speaking with someone outside. "Well, it looks like they were in room 324. His name is Ben Jones. I tried to speak with him the other day. We had some noise complaints from some of the rooms on the floor. He left in a hurry, and we haven't had any complaints since."

"When are they checking out?"

"Well, they're supposed to be checkin' out on Tuesday. Come to think of it, I haven't seen any of them since that day he left. I was lookin' for them so we could discuss the complaints, as I stated before. He must've been in some kind of fight or something. He had *some* bump on his face," the manager recalls.

"Well, thanks for all your help. If you see them around here, please give me a call." Patterson slips Alex his card.

"Sure, anything we can do to help you guys."

Patterson steps out of the front door, and Stokes gets up from the table he was seated at. There's a man at the table with his back to Patterson wearing a fedora.

"Who's that?" Patterson asks.

"Just some guy stayin' at the hotel. Figured I'd shoot the shit. You get anything?"

"Yeah. Our guy's name is Ben Jones."

"Great! We got his name now," says Stokes.

The man at the table pulls out a cigarette and lights it. The smoke flows up into the air.

As the officers step away from the Catalina toward their cruiser, Patterson takes one last look at the man at the table and continues to look him over as the car rolls away.

47

THE PLAN

Inside the pool house, the three boys are bound to their chairs while Castro's thugs keep watch. There's a knock at the door.

"Hola. Come in," Raul says.

It's approaching eleven o'clock in the Keys. As midnight nears, the thugs are set to leave to retrieve the packages. A man is ushered in by two of Castro's boys.

"Let me introduce you to these gringos," Raul says. He lets out a laugh, as do the two who ushered the new man into the room. "This is Mike, Brian, and Rob. This is Kelvin, the man who will be driving the boat and watching over you on your trip," he says while looking over at the boys. "Isn't that right, Kelvin?"

"Yes. But I was told there would be only two," Kelvin tells him.

"You must be a good listener. This little bitch right here," Raul says, referring to Rob, "he'll be staying with us as insurance."

Kelvin nods his head to show he understands.

"This will be a night you will always remember." Raul lets out an ominous laugh.

Raul exits the room while Kelvin takes a seat in a chair and waits. Two of the thugs wait in the room to watch over them.

Back in South Beach, Dianna is near the end of her night shift. She's had a rough day at work with only one thing on her mind—her brother. A few of Castro's boys in attendance at the bar do not make it possible to forget; nor does she want to. They keep their eyes on her from a distance. She decides to call her brother again, since he's not returned any messages from the last two days.

"Kelvin, please call me," she urgently demands. "I'm worried about you!"

She puts the phone back down and walks to the VIP table she must take care of for the night. Lil' Disgustin', a well-known, hot-selling rapper is sitting at the table with his crew.

After a few minutes of checking on the table, she makes her way back over to the bar and sees the red light flashing on her phone. She quickly picks it up. Her heart races while listening to the message.

"Hola, D. I'm a'ight. Talk to you soon."

She can't believe it. She's happy for the moment that he's okay, but she's dying inside about what she would tell her mother if something would happen to him.

The two thugs step outside the pool house to pull on a couple of stogies. Mike turns to Brian and Rob and whispers, "Listen, guys, even if we get back here with the stuff, they're gonna kill us. We need to make a plan," Mike states.

Silence follows for a moment while the boys, Mike and Brian sitting in their wet jeans, think.

"What if they're gonna let us go?" Rob hisses so Kelvin doesn't hear.

"They're not gonna do that. Mike is right," Brian responds as quietly as possible.

"Well, what are you gonna do? I'm gonna be tied to down here by myself. If you guys leave me, I'm dead. You heard them," Rob begs, whispering. He's pretty beat up. His left eye is swollen, and his face is bloody from some of Raul's punches.

"Well, we gotta get help," Mike states as Kelvin turns around, hearing the murmur of their voices.

Mike and Brian have had their heads pushed down and pulled up so many times their necks and the hair on their scalps is giving them pain.

"What's his deal?" Brian whispers back.

"I don't know. I've been wondering the same thing. Must owe them a favor or something," Mike mouths barely above a whisper.

"Think we could get 'im on our side?" Brian quietly asks.

"Don't know," Mike answers in a hushed tone. "Sounds like a long shot. If he knows who these guys are, I'm sure he's shitting his pants just like us. But we have to try to talk with him on the way out. Get friendly, see what his deal is. Once we get the stuff out of the water, he needs to be on our side or we will have to"—Mike looks at Brian and Rob—"we'll have to take care of him and throw him overboard. It's our only chance."

"Fuck," Brian says.

"Yeah, but it's got to be done. Once we have the stuff, we have something to negotiate with," Mike explains.

"Yeah, but remember," Rob warns, "we don't have any guns. They do."

"What if we grab the goods, take the GPS tracking device off it, and then dump some of it at a location on the way back. We'll only tell them the location if they agree to let Rob go. We tell 'em that we will allow one guy on the boat without a gun. They bring Rob and we show him the coordinates," Mike plans.

"These guys don't fuck around Mikey," Brian reminds him.

"I know. We'll dump the guy in the water with a lifejacket and take off," Mike relays.

"Who's to say that these dudes won't fire up another boat and come after us?" Brian asks.

"They probably will. But at least we got a chance then to speed off with a head start," Mike says, trying to be persuasive.

"So I'm just gonna have to sit tight and wait for you guys to get back? Then wait for these motherfuckers to agree to your plan? Fuck! Sounds a little too much A-Team B. A. Baracus." Rob is visibly upset. "You guys have to promise me that, if something goes down, you'll find a way, somehow, to let me know!"

"Yeah," Brian says. "If something starts to go down, we need to be able to send some kind of signal."

"What about the boat horn?" Mike says. "You think you can cut the duct tape with your belt?"

"I think I can take care of that. And I'm sure I'll hear the horn," Rob tells them. "I'll try to get out of here while all hell is breaking loose." He pauses. "Leave me with your phone. If I gotta get out of here on my own, maybe I can call the cops. They gotta have cops in this, wherever this place is, right?"

"The only thing though is, then, we're all on our own. You'll have to take off up the street and us by water. We can't turn around for you if they're coming after us by boat. Then we're all fucked," Mike says.

The two thugs hear the boys talking and step back inside the pool house. "Quiet, you fucking gringos!" One of them backhands Mike across the face. "Be a good gringo now," he says. He steps back out and closes the door.

The boys keep quiet. They'll go through with their plan. Mike and Brian will have to figure out their plan on the fly and make sure that, if something goes wrong, they blow the boat's horn.

"Kelvin," one of the man calls from outside.

Kelvin makes his way toward the exit.

Outside, Raul hands Kelvin a set of keys. "This if for the boat. You will take these little New Jersey bitches out there. They will dive down to pick up the goods. You make sure there is no funny shit. Got me?" asks Raul.

"Yeah. I got you," Kelvin responds.

"Good. If anyone stops you out there—Fish and Game, anyone—you are lobster diving. Got it?" Raul commands.

"Got it."

"You make it back here and everything will work out with you and Malo. I put some good words in for you with him and Castro. You will be taken care of."

"Thanks, Raul."

"Por nada."

"You can head back inside now, and we will come and get you when we're ready."

Kelvin steps back into the boathouse and takes a seat in the chair. He glances over at the boys and sees Mike looking him over. The other two pretend not to be paying him any attention. Kelvin's still thinking about his sister. He has his doubts about whether or not he will receive his share of the money from the job at the airport.

Kelvin remembers the stories of the gangsters from the older guys in the neighborhood. They always talked about how there used to be rules and order and how, these days, there are no rules. It has become every man for himself. Chaos. He knows that, if Malo has it his way, he will never see a dime. Kelvin squirms in his chair.

After Kelvin fades into the area of his memory where the room he's in disappears, he comes to the realization that he's a lost soul hung out to dry. With all of the things he has done in his life, everything has always gone wrong. Even with the heist that they were able to pull off so easily, so smoothly, all of his dreams of walking away are shattered. Those liquid dreams he has dreamt, just like the ones before, have evaporated through the South Florida air. All hope has been sucked out of his soul and replaced with despair. He's tired of the struggle of the slippery uphill slope he has had to climb, tired of gaining optimism when he feels he's moving forward and then losing it as his house of cards comes crashing down like a neutron bomb. Just like the roots of the newly planted South Florida palm sinking in quicksand, he can't get his feet planted firmly in the ground.

A half hour passes, and in come Castro's boys, including Raul and Malo.

"Hola. Nice to see you again," Malo says.

"Hola," Kelvin answers.

"So Raul has been saying some nice things about you. Says you have been, uh, let's say, cooperative. So I've been thinking that, if all goes well with these gringos and with the goods, we might be able to work something out."

"Sounds good, Malo," Kelvin replies.

"Yeah. Okay." Malo passes over Kelvin's response like he couldn't care less. "Now let's make it out to the boat with these fools and make sure you keep an eye on them."

A couple of the thugs make their way over to Mike and Brian to untie them from the chairs. As they're being escorted out of the pool house, Raul says, "Now remember to breathe through the regulator. Trust the equipment. You got no time to fuck around out there. Grab all three packages. Kelvin will take you to where you have to go. Just pick the stuff up and put it into the boat. Rapido!" he concludes more forcefully. "Got it?"

Mike and Brian nod their heads.

"Good."

They walk out onto the dock and step into the boat as Kelvin starts the engine.

"Here." Malo throws Kelvin a handgun. "You might need this. There'll be three packages; each contains five kilos. I don't have to remind you how important this is, do I?"

"No, Malo," Kelvin responds.

The thugs untie the ropes from the docks, and they're off into the black water in the night.

Ben notices movement from the boathouse and on the dock. He hears the boat engines fire up and sees the boat leave the dock. He starts to pull the dive flags in out of the water.

Swallowing the lump in his throat, he gets ready for the unknown. He turns the ignition and cruises slowly to follow the other boat into the canal.

Up ahead, the lead boat makes its way out into the main waterway. Ben keeps his distance and follows the lights ahead of him. The boat picks up speed. Ben waits a second and then hits the throttle. The hum of the engine puts him at ease for the moment. He's able to focus his thoughts on just himself, the boat, and the water. He can see the front of his boat carving through the calm evening waters, dancing across the surface like a water bug.

After roughly two miles, the lead boat starts to slow. Ben turns his boat to the south and slows as well. The lead boat seems to not be moving, almost drifting. Then after a few long seconds, it starts again, heading north.

⁕ ⁕

"Keep an eye on the green light. The faster it beeps, the quicker we pick up the shit and get out of here," Kelvin says.

After ten long minutes, the boat comes to a full stop.

"It must be here," Kelvin says, looking at the GPS, and throws the anchor overboard.

"Get out here?" Mike answers.

"Yeah, gringo. You heard me."

"You think they're gonna let us go after all this?" Mike asks him.

Kelvin doesn't answer. He looks Mike in the eye and turns away.

"They must owe you some kind of favor or something."

"What you mean?" Kelvin shoots back.

"I mean, you look scared shitless of them, but they take you down here, in the middle of nowhere, to do a job, and it seems like when this is over, you think you're going to be all right. Either they owe you some favor of some kind, or . . ." Mike trails off.

"Or what?"

"Or you're naive and dead meat. What's your deal with them, man?" Mike wants to know.

"Don't you worry 'bout it; just get your gear on, bitch." His response quiets the boys for the moment.

Mike and Brian continue to put their gear on. They help each other with the zippers on the backs of their wetsuits and then with the oxygen tanks on each other's backs.

"Now it should be right on the port side. Take this GPS with you. You should be able to see where it's at," Kelvin says.

"Time to go overboard, Bri. You ready?" Mike asks as they're seated on the side of the boat ready to dive in.

"I'm ready," Brian confirms and puts his breathing apparatus to his face.

"You think about what I said, Kelvin—unless you know something I don't," Mike warns him one last time.

Mike falls backward into the water like he's done this a thousand times before, just like everything else in his life. He comes up to the surface, making sure everything is on properly, and disappears below.

Up above on deck, Kelvin starts to pace in his mind and on his feet. Thoughts of Raul, Malo, and Castro flow through his head. "That gig was too good to be true. Would they really kill me instead of giving me my cut?"

Kelvin went around Castro to pull off the heist. Kelvin knows it would be easier for Malo to get someone to kill him than to pay him his share. It would only mean more money for Malo. All of the cards are stacked in Malo's favor. "I can't believe I didn't see this coming." But Kelvin knows his only shot at pulling off the heist was with the help of Malo. Now there's no ace up his sleeve and no leverage whatsoever.

Below the surface, all is calm. No boat, no Kelvin, no enemies, or worries. Just bubbles from the scuba gear, the flow of the current, the moonlight through the water to the reef and sandy bottom, and the blinking light of the GPS.

A couple hundred feet from the boys, Ben slips off of the back of his boat into the water. He slowly pulls himself around to the front and looks over in the direction he's heading, puts his foot on the bow, and kicks off into the darkness. He takes it slow so he won't be out of breath by the time he reaches the other boat. He's expecting to have to use his energy once he gets onboard. After a few strokes, he looks down into the water but can't see much. Thoughts enter his mind about what kind of animal life is lurking below.

He turns over to do the backstroke and looks into the sky, concentrating on the stars to help ease his worry about becoming shark bait. Not too many clouds. He's never seen stars that are so bright. The moon shines its light like a road on the water that leads into another existence. After some more backstrokes, he turns over and treads water to see where he's located. He's less than a hundred feet away. He grabs the knife from his pocket and fits it, still in the leather sheath, in between his teeth, continuing to make his way over to the boat and his boys.

Back on the dock, Malo checks his watch. He has a strict timeline. He wants to feel comfortable that everything is going as planned. If things do not fit within the timeframe, he'll know that something has gone wrong.

"Kelvin," he says over the radio.

"Yes, Malo?"

"Have you found the site?" Malo asks.

"Yes. The ducks are in the water."

"Make sure when they get back in the boat, you leave immediately. No talking. Just get back here!" Malo's paranoia is evident through his demands.

"Yes, Malo. Over."

An officer is in his patrol car when the radio picks up the frequency. "That sounds a little fishy," he thinks out loud. "Probably got too many lobsters per person out there." He places a call to the Florida Fish and Wildlife Conservation Commission.

48

A Fish Out of Water

Rob wiggles in his chair. The duct tape is starting to slice through his skin, and he can barely feel his cold fingers as the circulation is limited. He jerks his body again, this time more violently, but it's no use. This is not the first time that these thugs have bound someone to a chair. His hands are hanging behind him, taped together and connected to his feet. His feet are taped together and to the legs of the chair. His only chance is to rub the tape against the belt and try to break free. The options and time are running out. Rob realizes that he has to do this and do it on his own.

He thinks about his parents, his brother and sister. He thinks about the last time he spoke with each of them but can't even remember the last time he spoke with his sister. The conversations he had were routine and detached. Rob doesn't want it to be the last time he spoke with them, the last time he had a chance to better his relationships with each of them. But, as with a refugee in the eye of a hurricane, the outcomes and probabilities are against him.

Rob rocks the chair back and forth until each time he sways the chair is on two legs. Finally gathering enough momentum, the chair tips over, and he falls to his side, landing on his shoulder first. Then his face and head hit the cement, creating a simultaneous slap and thud from his skin and skull. There is some more wiggle room for his hands once he recovers, but the tape twists even harder, like a tourniquet, cutting the circulation even further. If he isn't able to slice through the tape in a matter of minutes, he fears that he will lose all feeling in his extremities. Pins and needles are setting in.

He starts to jerk violently on the floor, like a fish out of water, but it's no use. He's helpless. After tiring out, he catches his breath for a few moments, only to continue the futile effort over and over again. Rob's face is red and his shirt completely covered with sweat marks. It reminds him of his wrestling days and his resilience. If something goes wrong, he doesn't want to go down without a fight.

49

ON THE WATER

The GPS beeps faster until the green light flashes ferociously. Brian motions to Mike, and they spot the packaging on the floor of the ocean. Three different squares sit beside a reef. They take the canisters of oxygen attached to each package and break them one by one. The gas fills up inside each balloon, causing one package at a time to float to the surface.

Ben is being massaged by a slight chop. If he wants to get on the boat with no detection, he'll have to be very slow and very quiet. The problem is that, if he's too slow and gets noticed, he won't be able stand up to defend himself. Ben knows he would be in a very vulnerable position.

This is it! he thinks as he grabs the side of the boat to pull himself up. *One, two . . .*

A loud sound from the other side of the boat explodes in the night, startling him.

Hearing the pop that signifies his wait has come to an end, Kelvin stands up, making his way to the far side of the boat. He sees the first of the three packages floating on the surface and returns to the seat to grab a long hook so he can fish it out of the water.

Plunging the hook into the water, Kelvin leans over the side of the boat and pulls the package toward him. When it's close enough, he reaches over and starts to pull the package up slowly. He struggles with it for a few seconds before he's finally able to get it in the boat.

Ben hears another pop, which he now realizes is the second package breaking the water's surface. The figure Ben can make out on the boat moves back over to the side opposite his position, presumably positioning himself to haul in the package. Ben knows this is his chance.

He pulls himself over the side of the boat and is just a few feet away from the man by the time the man makes an attempt to grab the second package with the hook. On the first try, he misses and moves back to make another attempt. Just as he moves to send the hook back into the water, Ben delivers a hard blow to the back of the man's neck that knocks him to the ground and sends the gun tucked into his waist splaying on the boat deck.

Before Kelvin has time to figure out what has happened, a man is on top of him with a knife to his throat and the gun in his other hand. "Don't fuckin' move, bitch, or I'll slice your fuckin' throat!" the man demands. "What are you gonna do with my friends once they get you your shit and get out of the water? Answer me, motherfucker!"

Kelvin is extremely startled and trying to get his bearings. "I'm just out here with them," Kelvin pleads. "I got nothin' to do with it."

"Bullshit. You know what's gonna happen to them." Ben shakes the man with both hands clutched on the front of his shirt. With his right knee placed above the man's left thigh, he applies pressure and stares down at him like a rabid dog. "Don't you?" He asks like he's trying to pull the answer he wants out of the man.

"No. I don't even know what they're gonna do with *me*. Please!"

Ben lays a right hand into Kelvin's jaw. "Bullshit," Ben yells. "Tell me what's goin' on, or I'll kill you!"

Kelvin gathers himself. "Listen," he says in between catching deep breaths, "all I know is that I pulled a deal with Castro's boys." His chest is rising and falling violently. "They told me I needed to help them with this job or I wouldn't get paid on another gig we pulled. They drove me down here, and here I am, cabrón." Kelvin gets a good look at Ben in the moonlight and realizes who he is.

"What are they gonna do with my friends when they're done?!"

Kelvin doesn't answer.

"Answer me, motherfucker!"

"I don't know. They're bad dudes, man. What do you think?"

"So you were just going to let my friends get killed so you can get paid? I should kill you right now!" Ben threatens.

"Please, hombre! I had no choice. I think they might try to take care of me when this is all over too. They might do something to my sister. Oh Dianna!" He puts his hands on his head.

Ben tries not to react as a cool wave of realization washes over him. All is silent for a moment.

"Listen, your boys are in the water tryin' to finish this thing up."

The last of the packages rushes to the surface, making a loud washing sound as the water is turned up.

"See, hombre! And I *know* Malo. He's in charge of this shit down here! This whole thing is supposed to be on schedule—like clockwork. If it doesn't go down on time, he'll know something is up. Let me fish that shit out of the water, and when your boys come up, we'll talk."

"No funny shit or else!" Ben tells him.

"All right, hombre. Damn."

As Kelvin calmly puts his empty hands up, Ben allows him out from underneath him. Kelvin slowly rises and grabs the hook again. He snares the package and pulls it over into the boat. Ben keeps a close eye on him, just in case. As he leans in to grab the last package, Ben's boys poke up through the water's surface.

"Who's that?" Brian asks.

"It's Ben!" Mike answers.

They pull themselves into the boat and hug Ben.

"We thought you were dead! That's what they told us! What happened to you?" Mike asks.

Ben realizes there are only two of them. "We don't have time for that. Where's Rob?"

"They got him," Brian responds, "to make sure we make it back after this pickup. They're keeping him at a pool house."

"Yeah I know where it is. Shit. What are we gonna do?" Ben wonders aloud.

"How do you know where it is?" Brian asks him.

"I've been watchin' you guys since yesterday," Ben tells them, turning to Kelvin. "You're Kelvin, right?"

"Sí," he answers. "Yes," he stutters, realizing he's in the company of gringos. "How do you know?"

"I talked with Dianna yesterday," Ben responds.

"My sister?" Kelvin interrupts.

"Yeah, your sister," Bens says.

"You mean the girl that you were hooking up with the other night?" Mike snaps.

"Yeah," Ben answers.

"What did you say?" Kelvin demands.

"I mean the girl he met the other night. Yeah. Good friends," he sarcastically adds.

"What did she say?" Kelvin asks Ben.

"She felt she needed to help us out after she—and you—set us up."

"She and he"—Brian pauses—"set us up?" He's clearly trying to put the puzzle together in his weary mind.

"She wants me to help you get out of here. She thinks they're gonna hurt you," Ben informs Kelvin.

"We're not gonna help this motherfucker! Him and his sister got us in this mess? Let's fuckin' take care of him right now and save Castro the trouble." Mike lunges toward Kelvin before anyone can react and lands a right haymaker on the side of his head. Kelvin goes down in an instant, and Mike is on top of him, ready to pounce.

Ben and Brian are immediately there to pull him off.

"Let me at him!" Mike yells.

"We need to calm down!" Ben commands. "Listen. Dianna was able to tell me your location and when you guys would be making the pickup. I know they got us in this mess, but they didn't know what the deal was. I don't want to make excuses for them, but we need to pull this thing off now."

"Don't tell me you've gone soft on us, Ben. Is this because you want to hit that?" Mike accuses him.

"Yo, man!" Kelvin angrily looks at Mike and then Ben.

"No way. You *know* me. We've been through everything together, and none of us has ever sold anyone out," Ben says and then pauses while looking at Mike and Brian.

No answer from Mike is an acceptance of his last statement as the quietness calms things down.

"Listen, Kelvin here just told me that this thing needs to be on schedule. If it's not, the guy in charge is gonna get shifty. We need to figure this thing out now and get moving."

"We got something in place," Brian says.

"Well? What is it?" Ben asks.

"We were gonna see if Kelvin wanted in on it—when we got back on the boat. If not, we were gonna take care of him."

As they all turn to look in his direction, Kelvin can't believe his ears. The look of shock overtakes him. He had no idea that these boys were thinking about discarding him like an old tire.

"Since you're here and he's already in, well? On the way back to the dock, we're going to dump a package. When we get to the dock, we won't pull in; we'll just stay a few feet off. We can use the center console for some cover, just in case they wanna shoot. We'll tell them that we dumped a package and will allow one unarmed man on the boat. They need to bring Rob to us. We will deliver one of the packages and then we will take the unarmed man from the crew and bring him to the package we dumped."

"Why wouldn't they just kill you?" Ben asks.

"Then they wouldn't find the other package. These guys *want* their shit," Mike answers.

"What if they killed one of us and threatened to kill the rest if you didn't tell? What were you gonna do next? What if they start shooting, Einstein?" Bens asks him.

"We were gonna dump the guy in the water with the GPS, the lifesaver, and speed off. Then we figured that they would be after us on a boat, but at least we would have a fighting chance," Brian tells him. A look of confusion flows across Brian's face. "How did you get here?"

"I have a boat"—Ben pauses and points—"over there."

"Then we can split up, or we can take off on one boat," Brian tells him.

"What about Rob?" Ben asks.

"If something goes wrong, then we'll sound the boat horn to let him know to get out of there immediately," Mike replies.

"Is he tied down?" Ben asks them.

"Yeah." Mike and Brian nod.

"Well, how is he gonna cut loose?" Ben questions.

"He was gonna try anything. He's wearing that weird belt of his, you know, the one from Greenwich Village. Thinks he can slice through the duct tape in the back with it. He's got my phone too," Mike tells Ben.

"I should pull up near the house to see if I can get him out. If things go bad, he'll need to get out of there quick. And if things go good . . . he'll still need to get out of there quick," Ben tells them.

"Should we get them to bring Rob and one of their thugs on the boat?" Brian asks him.

"That's no good. They'll have all of us. What will stop them from killing us and forcing one of us to take them to the package? I'll take my boat up to the beach and try to get him. You guys keep Malo and those other guys busy. If something goes down in the meantime, we'll have a fighting chance." Ben pauses for a second. "I'll untie him and get out of there. It's our only option," he finishes.

"We'll keep them occupied as long as we can so you can get Rob out and then tell them to get Rob and the unarmed guy on the boat. It'll buy us a few more seconds while they walk back to the pool house," Brian suggests.

"You got your cell, Ben?" Mike asks.

"Yeah," Ben answers.

"You got the one I saw you in the pool house with, Kelvin?" Mike asks.

Kelvin nods.

"We'll run for as long as we have to. When we get on land, we'll call each other," Ben explains.

"Well let's get movin' then and keep this thing on schedule for a few minutes," Mike directs.

They troll over to Ben's boat. He scoops up one of the three packages his friends have just surfaced, climbs onboard his own boat, and says, turning to face the others, "I'm keeping this one for insurance." He stops and, looking into both of his friends' eyes, says, "Good luck."

They all know what's at stake.

Ben turns the boat around in the channel. He sees the boys up ahead and keeps his distance. As they near the house, slow the engines, and make their way to the dock, he stays to the left rear. Ben pulls over in the same area where he was before, throws in the anchor, and jumps into the water. This time, he knows there'll be no attention on him. He swims as fast as he can to shore while looking over at the boat. It's hard to see what is going on as he feels the rocky bottom and steps his way onto land.

Ben scurries along the wooded shoreline, weaving his way in and out of the brush toward the house. He has little time—only precious moments—with Rob's life hanging in the balance. The thugs are on full alert, but they're all focused on the boys, the boat, and the goods. There may be someone keeping an eye on Rob, but Ben knows can handle one man with his knife if he has to. He makes it to the clearing between the wooded area and the house.

Ben doesn't hesitate. He darts across the wooded area to the back of the house. He wants to see what's taking place on the dock, to make sure all of the crew is focused on the situation at hand. Putting his hand on the railing of the back porch, he peers over his shoulder to look at the dock. He sees the conversation going on between Mike, Brian, Kelvin, and Malo and his crew.

Ben runs through the woods to the front part of the house. He bolts across the yard to the pool house, opens the door, and runs in. Rob, who's still trying to untie himself with his belt, looks up. "What the fuck? What are you doin' here? I thought someone saw me trying to untie myself!"

"Don't worry about that. We need to get you out of here," Ben directs him.

"They told us you were dead."

"They tried." Ben pulls out his knife and cuts the tape from Rob's arms and legs. "Let's go," Ben demands.

Rob shakes and bends his arms and legs, trying to get some blood flow. Ben runs to the door and opens it, slowly peering around as Rob moves awkwardly behind. The feeling in his extremities is coming back.

Ben doesn't see anything. "Follow me!" Ben says.

As they run back across the yard again to the front of the house, he hears the front door open. Ben pulls Rob against the side of the house. It's one of the thugs who was smoking before. He's at it again on the porch.

"So I see you gringos made it in time. Good. That's real good. Now pull in so we can tie the boat," Malo commands.

One of Malo's men jumps onboard before the boat has even been tied to the dock and moves toward the packages.

But Mike steps in front of the packages, looking out at the shore eyes locked on Malo rather than at the man whose way he's just blocked. "No way, Malo," he says, using the toughest voice he can muster.

Malo's thug abruptly stops and turns his attention toward Mike.

"What do you mean 'no way'?" Malo asks and then turns around to his boys. They automatically raise their weapons and point them toward the boat. "Do you still feel the same way?"

"You're gonna do that no matter what we do. We want to make a deal."

"What could you possibly have that I want?" he says with a smile and all of the surety in the world.

Mike draws the gun Ben took from Kelvin, which he'd tucked into the back of his pants, and points it directly at the head of the thug standing in front of him.

Malo nods his head and bites his lip.

"We got one of your packages," Mike tells Malo. "We dropped it in the water at another location. If you take care of us right now, not only will you lose this guy, you'll assure yourself that you will never get it," Mike tells him.

"Who do you think you are fuckin' with?" Malo yells, and when he stops, he continues to breathe heavily. He realizes he needs to retrieve the other package. "Okay! Back off," Malo tells the men in his crew, who slowly lower their weapons.

"We want Rob brought out on the boat," Mike demands, silently praying he's given Ben enough time to get Rob out of the pool house.

"No. You take him to get the package now." Malo gestures to his man on board with the boys. "Then you bring the package back to the dock, and we'll give you your friend. You made your point. We'll let you go once the job is finished."

"No, Malo. We'll drop these two packages off here at the dock once you bring us Rob. Then one unarmed man can follow us in the other boat to the spot where we dropped the third package. From there, we'll take the boat out of here. We'll tie it to a dock up north when we feel safe. Me, my boys, and Kelvin will take off, and you will never see us again. You won't hear a word from us—not a peep."

"Ohhhh. So you got Kelvin on your side too. And here I thought these Jersey boys had whipped you and taken your gun, cabrón. Not a good move, Kelvin. What happens when we see you back in Miami, or even better, when we see your sister? Wait. Where does she work?

Oh, that's right," he jeers, getting a few laughs from his boys, "the Sagamore. Umm. What a pretty girl. I would hate to see some of these sharks get their hands on her."

As Castro's boys laugh, Kelvin winces, thoughts flowing through his head about what they'll try to do.

"I guess you don't want any part of that great deal we were gonna cut with you for taking care of this." Malo jabs. "You know, the cut from our deal at the aeropuerto?"

"I want you to bring Rob to the boat. Now!" Mike firmly demands.

"I didn't know you gringos got so heated." Malo turns to his boys. "Go get him and bring him out here." He turns back to Mike, thinking that he will still be able to take care of the New Jersey boys.

Ben looks back toward the water and sees two thugs heading back to the pool house. He has to do something. "Follow me!" he tells Rob. "We need to do this now!"

He moves up slowly to the front of the house. The man smoking the cigarette is making his way over to the side of the porch just like he did before. He leans around the side of the porch

"What the . . ." the man manages to expel when he's just inches away from Ben's face.

Ben lunges with his knife as the thug reaches for his gun. Ben's body is on heightened alert. His heart is racing. Ben beats the man to the punch and sticks the knife in his throat.

Ben notices that the two thugs heading back to the pool house have heard the commotion and are running toward them. He and Rob take off as fast as they can as one of the thugs takes aim.

Ben hears the boat horn and assumes Kelvin and the others have taken off.

Ben and Rob rush into the woods and make their way back toward the shoreline. They hear *pop pop, pop pop* and take cover by diving behind a large pine tree. Bullets rip into the tree trunk, and the bark explodes just over their heads. Fragments from the tree land on their bodies.

"Let's go!" Ben directs.

They get to their feet and sprint into the water. As they dive in, they hear the patter of gun shots once again, this time close enough they can hear the whizzing sound of the air as the bullets cut through the water around them. They make it back to the boat after a few strokes, and Ben hurriedly starts the engine. Bullets whiz by their bodies, and some penetrate the hull of the boat.

On the other boat, the boys keep a close eye on Malo's thug. "Sit down," Mike demands.

The man looks at him with a half grin. He's not frightened but sits in the seat anyway. Tattoos cover his forearms. A nasty scar crosses his cheek. By the looks of him, he's had way too many experiences to be afraid of these boys. He doesn't care about the boys taking off without waiting for the thugs to return with Rob. His only job is to get the package.

The boys pull into the area where they intend to tell their passenger they've dropped the third package. Kelvin slows the boat engines. He only has one thing on his mind, his sister. The boat coasts across the water.

"It's right around here. Here's your gear. Get in and get it." Mike hands the man the snorkel and fins. "It's not too deep. Here's the GPs. It will flash to green if you are within five yards."

The unarmed Latino looks at Mike, sneering, and unexcitedly grabs the gear. He puts on the flippers, his mask, and snorkel and slips overboard into the water, disappearing under the surface.

Rob drops one of the two remaining packages in the water and goes to grab the second.

"Forget about that. Keep it in case we need it later," Mike tells him.

On the dock, Malo's walkie-talkie crackles to life. "Malo?" says one of the men onboard the boat that has finally taken off to follow the boys.

"Yes, what is it?" Malo answers back.

"We have contact with the boat," the voice informs him. "Our man's diving, and it looks like they dropped one of the other packages in the water."

"Good. Stay on them," Malo tells them.

His phone rings. "Malo, is everything taken care of?" the voice on the phone asks.

"It's almost done, Cheo. But there's a problem."

"Well, what is it?" Cheo asks him as Castro sits beside him listening to their call.

"We have two of the packages right now. The New Jersey boys, and Kelvin, have used the last package as insurance, but we're handling that now."

"Do you have any kind of backup?" Cheo asks.

"Well, we have a boat in the water following them," Malo relays.

"Anything else I should know about?"

"Well. Homee is dead. He got knifed. I still haven't figured it out yet, but a few of the guys saw someone take off in a boat, and they shot at him."

"Shot at him? You need to get the packages and get out of there. Stay on the phone with me till this is over!" Cheo demands.

"Sí." Malo reluctantly agrees to follow orders as the vein pops from his forehead.

Over the walkie-talkie, another message comes through from the crew on the boat. "Malo. The boat's taking off. We're going to pursue them. It looks like they left our boy in the water to fish. We fired at them, but I don't think we hit anything."

Malo gets on the phone to tell Cheo what is happening.

"Call the dogs off. Get our package and get out of there! I want our guys up here in Miami as soon as possible," Castro whispers into Cheo's ear as he relays this information to Malo.

"Sí, Cheo," Malo replies. Then he gets on the walkie. "Don't follow the boat. Grab our guy and our lunch. We need to get out of here ASAP."

Ben heads off in another direction, trying to catch up with his friends under the light of the full moon. "Can't believe we made it out of there!" he says to Rob.

Up ahead, Kelvin has the boat on full throttle, and it bounces up and down over the water. Mike is looking out over the water while the motors hum. The night is beautiful, and the moon shines over them. After a few minutes of speeding, Ben catches up to the boys. Both boats slow as he pulls up next to them. Mike grabs the rail and pulls the boats closer. "Let's go," he demands. "Quickly!"

Ben kills the engine, grabs the package he kept, and jumps into the other boat. Rob follows.

The boys all hug each other and high-five—all except Brian. The others turn to look at their friend, who's seated on the floor at the back of the boat with his back against the bow.

Ben sees the look in his friend's eyes and immediately realizes something's going on. He feels a surge as Kelvin pushes the throttle down on the boat to continue their getaway.

"What's wrong with you?" Ben asks.

Brian is slumped forward, holding his hand over his stomach.

"Brian, it's all over now," he says. "You can relax."

Mike walks toward the back of the boat. Brian looks up at him with a tired look in his eye and mouths some words to him that Mike can't make out. He stands up to make his way over to him.

"What did you say?" Mike asks.

"I got shot." He holds up his hands, and Mike sees there's a significant amount of blood.

"Oh my God! We need to get to a hospital! Now!"

Ben steps to Mike's side, and through the dark, he can see the problem. He starts to breathe deeply and shake.

Brian slumps and begins to fall back down, and Mike and Ben catch him, easing him slowly back to the deck floor.

Mike shouts to Kelvin, "Do you know a hospital in the area?"

Kelvin answers, "No, but I'll get on the radio, say we have an injured diver."

"Hurry!" Mike demands.

Mike takes off his shirt and starts to apply pressure to Brian's back and stomach. "You're gonna be all right, Brian; just hang in there. We're gonna be at the hospital soon, and you'll be okay," he says, sounding like he's trying to convince himself more than Brian, who nods in agreement.

Brian's mouth is open as his body convulses.

Kelvin's waiting for a response. The radio lights up with sound from another boat in the area. The man on the radio tells him there's a hospital not too far from there—about a fifteen-to twenty-minute ride. It's located on the water in Marathon. The Fisherman's Hospital.

"Faster! Let's go!" Mike yells.

The boat speeds off in the cooler air of the night. The boys are huddled around their friend. None of them are talking. The shock is too much to take.

Ben's mind is flooded with moments he's shared with Brian over the years—the good times, the bad times. He thinks of all they've been through together. "Brian, you need to hang on for a little bit," he says, grabbing his friend's hand. "We'll be there soon!"

Mike and Rob have both taken off their shirts and are holding the cloth over the entry wound on his back and the exit wound on his stomach. They continue to hold pressure to the wounds, but even in the dark of night, they can tell that Brian is getting pale. He has lost a lot of blood and is in serious trouble.

"I want you guys to know that I love you. If anything . . . If I . . ." he says in a low volume as he gasps for breath.

"You're gonna be fine," Mike anxiously says.

"Let my family know that I love them." He looks Ben in the eye. "Get these motherfuckers."

"We will," Ben promises.

Kelvin has the boat on full throttle. Directions to the Fisherman's Hospital from the other boat crackle through the radio, and Kelvin points the boat in the right direction.

Each foot takes too long in the boys' anxious minds. Each light on the shoreline holds hopes of their destination. They blow by each one—each one crushing their hearts like an old car in an industrial shredder. The odds of Brian surviving are being erased and recalculated like a bookie's chalkboard before game time. It's the toughest fifteen minutes of their lives. They pull up to a boat ramp that leads to the hospital in Marathon. Brian is in and out of consciousness as they struggle to bring him inside.

In the black of night, he's pale white. The boys hold onto him to keep him warm, but it's not helping. Brian's body is cold. He continues to convulse. Their shirts are thick with his blood. With nothing left to sop up the blood, they put their hands over the wounds. Brian begins to shake at the sight of all of the blood. He's having a tough time keeping his head together. His lower jaw slowly slips toward the ground till his mouth's wide open. His dazed blue eyes try to reject the scene. Kelvin runs ahead to get the staff to come outside. One of the nurses bolts outside with a gurney.

"What happened?" the nurse demands.

"Some guys out on the water. They did it. They shot him!" Ben manages to expel.

They place Brian on the gurney, and the hospital workers begin to work on him. He's unconscious. The boys' emotions range from dejection to disbelief. Rob has his hands over his head and is walking in circles as they watch more of the hospital help bring the gurney inside the doors. The sheets are already covered in blood. They stand there watching as he's urgently ushered inside.

All of the commotion leaves with the nurses, the doctors, the gurney, and the intravenous bag. Everything was in fast forward. Now the world has come to a standstill.

Mike tries to console Ben by putting his arm on his shoulder. "Let's go in," he says.

Ben looks at him with tears streaming down his cheeks.

"He's gonna be all right," Rob tells them.

The boys solemnly walk into the waiting room and take a seat, expecting the worse. Mike's breathing deeply and staring in Kelvin's direction. Kelvin makes sure not to make eye contact. Ben sees the look on Mike's face and puts his head into his hands, preparing himself for what's coming. When Mike lurches toward Kelvin, Ben gets up and tries to keep his friend back, positioning himself in between the two as the veins bulge out of Mike's neck. Ben's face turns red from exertion, as he holds his stand. Rob is pacing around the waiting room.

After twenty minutes crawl by, the doctor walks out to give them the news.

"We did the best we could," he says. "I'm sorry for your loss. You will need to stick around here for a few minutes. One of the officers will have to ask you a couple of questions about what happened." In the flash of a muzzle on a February night in the Keys, Brian is gone forever. They'll never again see their friend alive.

"No, no, no." Ben starts to sob and shakes his head back and forth in disbelief.

Mike moves over to hug and help console him, but it's no use. He squeezes tighter and starts to cry himself.

Rob's lungs expand and contract violently as he continues to pace around the dimly lit room.

"Listen, I know you don't want to hear this right now, but you need to get a story together before the cop comes in," Kelvin says. "I'm sorry about your friend."

"Yeah, *you're* sorry? Fuck you!" Ben says to him as he starts to cry again.

Mike puts his hand on Ben's shoulder. "No. He's right. We need to get a story together." Mike pauses. "Listen, we can't say it was an accident. That's gonna make us look guilty."

"So what are we gonna say then?" Rob asks.

"First, we met Kelvin in Miami through his sister. Just like we did. What's your last name, Kelvin?"

"Castillo."

"You got that?" Mike says to Ben. "Castillo."

"Yeah. Got it."

"You met his sister at the club. We hung out with them a few days, and Kelvin told us he was gonna go diving at night for some lobster. We decided that we'd done enough partying and wanted to see the Keys, where we've never been before." Mike pauses to think about the rest of the story. "We were cruising across the channel and had been in the boat for a while. Kelvin was busy looking for the spot he goes to lobster dive—the same spot his father took him to ever since he was a kid. Well, we ran over a flagged spot of another diver and we slowed down to apologize to the man who was in the boat.

He said, 'No problem.' But the divers who floated to the surface were pissed. One of them said that he was just below the surface, and we were inches away from his head. As he was getting on the boat, he was shouting something in Spanish. Me, Rob, and Ben couldn't make it out. We looked at Kelvin, who we thought would understand. He looked nervous. Some of the guys on the other boat were trying to calm the man down, but before we knew it, he grabbed a gun, and we heard a pop. Kelvin started the engines, and we zipped off. We looked over at Brian and realized he'd been shot. And here we are."

"Why don't we just tell them about what happened?" Rob asks.

"They have cops on the take in Miami. Don't you think they have cops in the Keys too? You know how this shit goes," Kelvin responds.

"'These Cubans are tied into the drug thing even deeper. They're at the root of this," Ben says to him.

"I guess. You think they'll buy it?" Rob asks.

"You got the story together?" Mike asks them.

"Yeah," Ben answers.

"Got it," Rob responds.

"You, Kelvin?" Mike questions him.

"Sí. Yes. People die down here all the time during the lobster mini season. For a couple of days, all the amateurs think they're Jacques Cousteau."

As the group waits for the questioning, the Dead-End boys remember the last time they were questioned by police.

In walks the lone police officer on duty for the night in Marathon. "Howdy, fellas," he says. "I'm Officer Billy Curley. Heard you've been having a rough evening tonight."

"Yes, sir."

"Well. I'm gonna have to ask you some questions. Which one of you wants to go first?"

"I'll go," Ben tells the officer.

"Please come with me into the next room. Just procedure."

"Sure." Ben follows the officer into the room.

"Sit down and make yourself comfortable. You need any water?"

"No thanks. Had enough in the waiting room."

"Good. Let's get started." The officer pauses. "I'm sorry for your loss. How did you know the victim?"

Kelvin gets on his cell phone to call Dianna. There's no answer. He leaves a desperate message. "D! I need you to call me!"

50

THE LAST RUN

Dianna turns toward the bar after dealing with one of her VIP tables. Dodging vacationers and South Florida clubbers is something she's gotten used to; it's become a sixth sense. She makes it back without any collisions on a Sunday night holiday weekend. She sees the blinking red light on her cell phone showing her she has a voicemail.

Thinking it must be one of her friends who needs to get in the VIP area, she reaches for her phone. It vibrates in her hand. The caller ID reads, "Kelvin." She answers immediately. "Hola!" she says excitedly.

"D? D? I can barely hear you. Get out of there now!"

"What? Are you okay?" she asks him.

"Listen, I'm fine. But you need to get out of there now," Kelvin pleads. "Malo had me, but I got away. I think they're going to come after you. You need to take get out of there now, Mami!"

"Come after me? I'm in the middle of work right now. Kelvin, you can't do this to me!"

"D, trust me, this is bad. They will come after you. I think they were gonna kill me. We're gonna have to get out of town. You need to run!"

Dianna can't believe her ears. She looks up into the club, trying to gather her thoughts, and sees three members of Castro's crew enter. They're scanning the club. Kelvin continues to plead with her on the line, but she's not even listening.

"Listen to me," she says as she ducks behind the bar. "They're already here. I need to go. I'm sick of this shit. Always looking over my shoulder." She grabs her clutch from behind the bar. "I will call you in a few minutes, when I'm in the clear."

"Be careful!" he says as she hangs up in his ear.

Dianna slips out from behind the bar and down the hallway behind the club. A door leads to the street on the side of the hotel. If Dianna makes it there, she'll be outside. She'll have a chance. She opens the door and steps outside.

51

EL ULTIMO CHANCE

On the sidewalk, Dianna takes her first quick step toward escaping. The side metal door closes.

"Dianna," she hears from behind her and stops, her body stiffening. "Where are you going at this time? I thought you'd be working all night."

She turns around to see one of Castro's crew—one of the regulars who comes in with Malo.

"Yes, but my mom is having an emergency," she tells him as she continues to walk. "Gotta go." She walks as quickly as she can, but it's no use. She sees another one of the thugs heading in her direction from the back of the hotel and knows she has nowhere to go.

She stops, dropping her handbag in the street as her posture straightens up. Castro's boy grabs her by the hand as the Escalade pulls up, and they are whisked away. They sit her in the back in between two of the thugs. They drive north on A1A Collins Avenue. She begins to look around. They put a wrap around her eyes.

"Where are you taking me?" she tries to plead with them.

"Your brother is in a little bit of trouble. We need to see him again. And the only way we think we will see him again is if we use you," Castro's thug tells her.

"I thought you guys already used him!"

"Well, we did, but he didn't do everything the way we wanted. And he took off with some other people that we will eventually find to, say, finish the rest of the job."

"The New Jersey boys?"

"Maybe. Just sit tight and everything will be okay," he says.

Kelvin is finishing up his questioning with Officer Curley. They step out of the room together and meet Mike and Ben in the waiting room lobby.

"Well, I know that you boys have had a rough day, and I'm truly sorry for your loss. I have your contact information in Miami," he says to Kelvin. "And I have your information in New Jersey." The officer nods toward the other three. "I will be investigating this situation. Make sure that, if you guys are going out of town, you notify me. But I will be in touch with you every couple of days to update you on this ongoing investigation."

Kelvin's cell phone lights up. It's Malo. He tucks it back in his pocket.

"Thank you," Mike says and shakes the officer's hand.

Kelvin reaches his hand out and shakes the officer's hand and nods—something he has never done in his life. He hates police officers, especially ever since the useless detectives in Miami promised his family that they would solve his father's murder.

"You think they'll leave us alone now?" Rob asks.

"I don't know. What do you think?" Mike answers him, not really caring either way.

Kelvin's cell buzzes again. It's Malo. He answers this time to hear only, "We have your sister; we need to meet, and bring the other shit you owe us," followed by the silence of dead air as the caller hangs up.

"Fuck!" Kelvin says, looking at his cell phone in disbelief.

Ben and Mike look at him.

"They got my sister! Oh Dianna!" he says as he runs his fingers over his troubled face and through his hair.

"Where do they have her?" Ben asks.

He thinks for a minute. "They're gonna kill her if I don't go. I can't let her get killed for my fuckup! They're gonna take her to a place they had me at before they took me to the Keys, probably somewhere in Hollywood on the water. I need to go."

"Why? What if they kill you both?" Ben asks Kelvin.

"Then it's something I can die with. At least I will have tried to save her. I need to go there with a gun. I gotta get some way for her to get out. Then all hell is gonna break loose. I ain't gonna go down without a fight. I won't go down without taking Malo with me."

There is a moment of contemplation from Ben before he nods toward Kelvin and then finally unleashes his thoughts. "I can't let these bitches get away with killing Brian and doin' what they've done to us. And Brian wanted us to get those motherfuckers. I wanna go," Ben tells the others.

"What?" Rob says. "Are you crazy?"

"Listen, Dianna told me that I could trust someone if I needed some help. Maybe we can set something up. We got the goods that they want. Right, Mike?"

"Yeah. We got something," Mike reluctantly answers.

"Tell him you'll meet him but at a public place. Where could you meet?" Ben asks Kelvin.

"The Port of Miami. That's about the only place they don't control right now. It's too hot," Kelvin replies.

"Let 'im know we'll meet him there with the goods," Ben directs him.

Kelvin picks up his phone and dials. "The Port," he says into the phone after a moment. "We bring the goods. You bring my sister. Four a.m." He hangs up and then turns to the boys. "Listen, guys. I feel really bad about what happened to your friend. These guys are bad and had me by the nientes."

Ben nods. Mike just looks at him without any response. Rob looks off in the distance, thinking about the situation.

Kelvin turns the key in the ignition and backs away from the dock. It's after one, and they've all been through a lot. Kelvin sits in the chair and thinks about this mess, wondering how Castro's boys got to his sister so quickly. The last time he'd talked to her, he'd thought she'd be able to sneak out and get away. But that isn't the case. This is the reality—the real deal. He leans over to Ben and asks him to take the wheel for a few minutes.

"Sure. No problem," Ben tells him.

"I got us on track. Just continue to head straight," Kelvin directs him.

"How long before we get there?" Ben asks.

"At this speed, it will be about two hours."

Kelvin pulls out his phone and calls his friend Tre. "Meet me at Waterworld. Bring the Glock and extra clips."

"How many?" Tre asks.

"All of 'em," Kelvin directs.

Kelvin heads to the stern and takes a seat. He searches the console. Pulling out a piece of paper to write on and a pen, he starts to write a letter to his sister that he hopes with a miracle will not be his last.

Kelvin walks back to the front of the boat and takes the helm from Ben. A little over two hours to go and only one thing is on his mind—making sure his sister is safe. He couldn't go on otherwise.

52

EASY MONEY

"Malo! What the fuck happened down there?!" Cheo yells into the phone.

"Things did not go according to plan. That cabrón, Kelvin, fucked us over. The New Jersey boys got away. They took two of our packages. Kelvin's with them too."

"He was in on it?"

"Sí," Malo confirms with Cheo.

"I thought he was on our side. I hope I don't find out that they did anything to make him flip," Castro states to Cheo as he sits next to his associate and listens to the call.

"Listen, they got two of our packages. Kelvin saw easy money. That's all. The kid always wants to make a quick buck," Malo tries to explain to his boss.

"We'll see. But *this*"—Cheo pauses—"this is on you."

"Yeah, I know. Already got it under control. I got something he wants. We're meeting at the port at four a.m. We'll get the packages, and it'll be over."

"Sounds too easy. I heard some of our friends downtown already know about this meeting of ours."

"I'm not surprised. I already talked to one of our guys on the inside. It will be taken care of."

"Yes. It *will* be taken care of," Cheo warns ominously before cutting the conversation off.

53

WATERWORLD

The boat starts to slow, and the change in speed awakes Mike and Rob. They're seated back to back, holding each other up like each other's foundation. Ben hasn't even thought about sleeping. He's too riled up from everything that's occurred. Only thoughts of Brian stir in his tired mind. Snapshots of all the crazy times they've had flash in and out of his brain. His little brother is missing forever. The force from the constant breeze reduces until it stops colliding against his skin.

"Why are we slowing?" Ben asks.

"I gotta stop and get some protection from an hombre of mine," Kelvin tells him. "We need more than one gun."

Ben looks him over. The weight of the world appears on his shoulders, like the universe on Atlas.

"Don't worry. I'll be quick." A smile shoots across Kelvin's face.

Ben realizes it's the first time he's seen Kelvin smile.

Various vessels wade in the bay, holding their anchored positions. Multiple dinghies with ropes tying them to their motorized crafts allow their inhabitants to row to land. This place is known by the locals and police as Waterworld. It's an area where homeless people live on abandoned boats that have been discarded by their owners. It's cheaper for owners to abandon ship than to go through the process of decommissioning a vessel. They maneuver past the crafts and pull into a dock behind a small county park on Biscayne Bay. The sign reads "Dinner Key Marina."

As they slowly drift forward, the boys see a man smoking a cigarette on the dock. A few lights line the walkway behind him. The white quarter moon stares at them from above.

Kelvin steps off the boat, and embraces his friend, Tre. Rob and Ben's eyes are fixated on the men.

Mike discreetly moves toward the packages. He moves his hands inside and pulls the contents out, revealing five kilos. He breaks one of the kilos loose by biting the duct tape that holds the package together and places the kilo behind the scuba gear.

"Yo, hombre. Here it is." Tre pulls out a Glock nine millimeter. "This should help you out. Hollow points."

He hands him some extra clips.

"Thanks, amigo." Kelvin looks him in the eye.

"Listen," his friend adds, "If anything goes down, I want you to know that I'll keep in touch with your sister—you know, look out for her and make sure things is a'ight."

"Yeah. I know you will. That's why I called you, hombre. I gotta get her out of there."

"Be careful, cabrón."

They hug. Kelvin knows he has little chance of seeing his friend. His friend *knows* this is good-bye. Even if he somehow gets away, he will be hunted down like a dog. Kelvin steps off the dock and back onto the boat.

They're off swiftly on the water with the breeze touching their hair.

Downtown at the police department, Stokes walks into the chief's room. "Chief?"

"Yeah, what is it, Stokes?"

"We got some info. Something may be goin' down tonight. At the harbor. With Castro and his crew."

"How reliable is the info?" the chief asks him.

"Real reliable. Straight from Darius, one of my best informants. It's about a guy we've been lookin' for that may be involved with a car theft."

"Who's this guy?"

"Well, we think his name is Ben Jones. We don't even know who he really is or how he's connected. He was staying in a room at the Catalina. We just know that he may have shown up in Overtown on Thursday and later on that day may have stolen a car," Stokes informs the chief.

"That's a lot of maybes."

"Yeah, but you say it yourself. Where there's smoke, there's usually fire. And I've been smelling this guy's smoke for a few days now."

"Sure it's not the fire burning in the Everglades?"

"Funny chief, funny." He pauses. "I want to run this operation. Myself. I want to be in charge."

"Lookin' for some headlines, huh?" The chief pauses as he looks down at his desk full of paperwork and empty coffee cups. "All right. You *both* will get some recognition from the media though."

"Yeah. But I'll be one up on Patterson."

"You make sure he knows it's not about that. I have full confidence in either one of you to run this. You just asked me first."

"Thanks, Chief."

"Yeah, yeah, yeah," he states dismissively. "Just keep me updated. I'll be listening," he adds as Stokes makes his way out of the office, waving the walkie-talkie in his hand.

54

SOUTH FLORIDA SNOW

The clock at the Cuban café where Patterson's seated off Lincoln Road reads 2:15 a.m. Various characters are assembled at their tables. It's too early for the hungry party crowd that's just starting to pack these city clubs. Two men in their twenties who seem to know each other very well walk through the door. They let go of each other's hand and make their way to the counter. Patterson, who never sits with his back to the door—call it street smarts, whatever, especially at this time of night—always notices who walks into any place he's at.

"Hmm. Two more for their team," he jokes as he reads about the Marlins' futility in the previous night's preseason game. "The owner is an idiot."

His cell phone lights up. "Yellow?"

"Hey, Patterson, where you at?" Stokes asks.

"Catchin' the read on the Marlins at the café. You wouldn't believe . . ."

"Listen. No time for that." Stokes cuts him off midsentence. "I got word from Darius that something's goin' down tonight at the port. May involve our white ghost we've been lookin' for too."

"How reliable?"

"Very."

"Okay. So what's up?" Patterson asks.

"I told the chief, and since he thinks I'm the better officer of us two, he told me to run it."

"Get *out*! Chief musta had too much coffee tonight! Clearly he's not thinkin' straight."

"Well, looks like *I'll* be picking *you* up. I'll be there in about fifteen, depending on the taxi traffic down Lincoln," Stokes conveys.

"I'll be here," Patterson closes his phone. "Damn! I'll never hear the end of this from Stokes," he says out loud.

Patterson's waiting in front of the café, leaning against the *Miami Herald* newspaper machine when Stokes pulls up in the unmarked Ford. Stokes swings the car over toward the curb.

"Hop in so we don't have to wait for this traffic."

Patterson grabs the handle, lowering his body in. His kneecap hits the dashboard.

Stokes takes off before the car door is closed.

"What's the deal?" Patterson wants to know the plans.

"We've got a team of eight meeting us at the port. We're gonna take our positions and wait till somethin' goes down. We'll have four of us follow Castro's crew back to their location and the other four follow our white ghost's crew, if he has one."

"Well, looks like you've got everything covered 'cept one thing?"

"What's that?" Stokes replies.

"What am *I* gonna be doing?"

"We need some video evidence," Stokes says as he hands Patterson a mini video camera.

"Oh yeah. Think I used this with one of your ex-girlfriends." Patterson breaks into a mile-wide smile.

Stokes extends his favorite finger as they make a quick turn off of Lincoln. They head over the 395 causeway toward downtown to meet their fellow officers.

"What's that landing on the windshield? Bugs?" Patterson wonders.

"Nah. That's good old South Florida snow. Chief said something about a fire in the Everglades. Just a little ash. You know, like when you don't put lotion on your legs for a while," Stokes shoots back with a smile.

"You been thinkin' 'bout that one for a while huh."

They pull up to the gate at the container terminal where the cargo is loaded on and off the ships. The Miami Dade Police Department, US Customs and Border Protection, US Coast Guard, Florida Department of Law Enforcement, Florida Fish and Wildlife Commission, and Miami Dade Fire and Rescue Department all share the responsibility of keeping this port safe. Despite the black eye South Florida and its ports received during the 1980s with the cocaine wars, this is one of the safest, most secure, and most efficient of our time even though almost every kind of felon you could imagine works here. It's also one of the busiest.

"Can I see your badges please?" the security officer at the gate asks them as he yawns. The television sends flashes of light inside the checkpoint with every changing scene. The guard takes a look at their badges and IDs and looks up at them to verify.

"Where you guys going?" the guard asks them.

"To the shipping containment area. Meeting with some other officers," Stokes answers.

"Yeah. A couple of them are already here. Up ahead and stay to the right. Anything goin' on that I should know about tonight?"

"Not if you don't know already."

"I'll take that as a no then. Thanks." The guard lets them in. The arm of the security gate lifts up as the guard pushes the button inside the checkpoint. Stokes looks into the rearview to see him raising his arm up again to cover his mouth while yawning.

The phone rings in the security officer's booth.

"Hello?" the guard answers.

"Make sure the surveillance cameras are on and working. And don't respond to anything that happens." The Deputy Director catches the guard by surprise. "The Miami City Police Department is running a bust."

"Okay, sir. No problem."

Stokes and Patterson pass huge cargo containers of different colors. On the left side is the longshoreman dock. They see other enormous container cranes that lift those containers off of the ships and onto land. Stokes turns to the right and sees the eight officers waiting, a few of them brandishing AR-15 rifles and shotguns.

"Looks like they beat us here," Patterson acknowledges.

Stokes pulls up to the location, and he and Patterson exit the vehicle.

Stokes walks in the direction of the men and starts addressing them. "Thanks for coming tonight, fellas. I want you to know the chief personally requested you. I'm going to be in charge. We got word from one of my informants that something is going down. Sounds like a deal gone wrong. There will be an exchange. We'll take care of the perimeter and keep an eye on things. We'll have to take some video for evidence and must remain silent during this situation."

He throws two video cameras to different officers. "Officer Shalisi, you take your three guys here and set up on the south side. You," he says to one of the other officers, "take your three guys and spread out on the north side. Patterson will be roaming. Get pictures of them coming in and leaving. I'll give further instructions over the walkie-talkies." He pauses. "Everyone got that?"

A few yesses filter through the air as the men nod.

"All right then. Take your positions and sit tight. It may be a while. We got three hours till the sun comes up," Stokes commands.

55

THE PORT OF MIAMI

The officers get back into their cars and move toward their positions. Patterson's cell phone buzzes in his pocket.

"Yellow?" he answers softly.

"My name is Ben Jones. Dianna Castillo told me to talk to you if I have any problems. She said she spoke with you and that you were looking for me."

"Hi, Ben. I'm Sergeant Patterson. Yes, it's you that I'm looking for. What can I help you with?"

"I'm involved in a situation. Long story. My friends were kidnapped by some Cubans to pick up drugs. They tried to kill me. I helped get them away, but my best friend didn't make it." He swallows the lump in his throat. "We're meeting with them to swap some goods for Dianna. They took her."

Patterson's heart starts to beat heavily. "Where are you meeting them and when?" He waits anxiously for a response. The blood begins to pulse as his heart beats even faster.

"The port of Miami. Around four a.m."

"Oh my God!" Patterson mouths lightly, covering the phone as he exhales. He sees Stokes making his way over toward him from the darkness.

"Think we were set up by someone who works for these guys at the Catalina Hotel, where we were staying. There were a lot of people who had to be in on this beside these Cuban assholes," Ben explains.

Patterson thinks back to his visit to the Catalina and remembers Stokes talking to someone while he was asking around there.

"Okay. I'll be there and do the best I can," Patterson tells Ben. He has a sneaking suspicion that something is off but quite can't put his finger on it. He decides not to say anything to Stokes for the moment. His years of experience are taking over. Patterson knows that, most of the time, it's best to keep things to himself than to open his mouth.

"What's up? Is that anything?" Stokes asks, nodding to the phone in Patterson's hand.

"Nah. Nothin'." Patterson plays it cool. "Just my old lady wanting me to get some milk before I get home in the morning—if that'll ever happen." He pauses. "What time do you think this will be goin' down?"

"Don't know. Darius told me some time around four. But he wasn't so sure."

"Okay, cool. I love working Monday mornings," he sarcastically adds and then pauses. "I'm going to take a walk around, see if I can get a better view."

He heads off behind a container and calls Darius.

"Did you talk to Stokes tonight?"

56

NIERE

The lights of Miami grow brighter, reflecting off the water as the boat heads through Biscayne Bay. *This* is another city that never sleeps. Kelvin steadies the boat through as the high-rises reach up toward the sky just west of them in Brickell. To the right, South Beach glows like a fluorescent jellyfish. On the south side of the inlet sits Fisher Island. The port is located in between.

Kelvin slows the boat down. "Listen up, gringos. I'll take the package. I need to make sure my sister is gonna be safe."

"No complaints from us here," Rob says.

"This is the deal. I need one of you to grab my sister and bring her back—no matter what they do to me. You need to grab her and *drag* her back if you have to! Can you do that?" Kelvin asks, looking at Ben.

"I'll do it," Ben stands up to say.

"Fuck that! Let him handle it. He's the one who got us in this mess. I say we leave him to worry about his sister. *We* take the coke!

They killed *our* friend!" Mike yells. "We'll get something out of it. Fuck you and your sister!"

"Listen," Ben says, "he's gonna take the heat! We'll be able to get out of here." He turns to Kelvin, calming down. "I'll get your sister, make sure she gets back to the boat with me. I'll get her back safe." He turns back to Mike and Rob. "Get us *all* out of here safe."

Kelvin pulls a note out from his pocket. "Give this to her once you get back on the boat."

He returns to the console and pushes the throttle. Ben walks back to speak with Mike and Rob. "Listen, you know what it's like with these people. They're ruthless. There's nothing he could've done. I talked with his sister. He was in way over his head with these scumbags. And she helped me find you guys. She didn't know what was gonna go down."

"Still didn't need for us to be the ones to help him. I don't give a shit. So he's taking the heat now. He should be. And it's still not for us. It's for his sister. Fuck him!" Mike yells.

"I need you guys to keep the boat running and ready for takeoff when I get back here with Dianna. You got that?" Ben asks.

"I'm not gonna let you go out there alone," Rob says.

"Then walk out there a little ways and be my eyes from behind. Who knows what kind of setup this will be. If we're coming in on the water, guess we can always get out that way. We've had some luck with that so far," Ben tells him.

"Yeah. Unless you're Brian," Mike says.

"I got your back. I'll follow behind," Rob tells him.

"You know I got your back too. I'll keep the boat running," Mike says.

"I know you guys do," Ben responds.

"But this fucker"—Mike pauses and nods toward Kelvin—"that's a different story."

After a few minute's run through another channel, they see the container cranes at the port.

"That's it right there."

As Kelvin pulls up, the boys get to their feet. The boat pulls over to the side. "Grab the dock," Kelvin directs them.

The boys do as they're told.

"Give me the package."

Ben throws it up on the dock and pulls himself on the concrete slab.

"You can handle this thing, right, Mike?"

"Sure, but make it quick," Mike tells Ben.

"As quick as we can," Ben promises.

"Help me up," Rob says, extending his arm toward Ben's. He's hoisted up.

Mike looks over the console as the other three walk along the dock past blue and orange containers and the container cranes that reach higher in the sky than they ever realized.

"You think this is gonna be smooth?" Rob asks.

"Knowing Malo? Probly not." Kelvin pauses and turns to Rob. "This is the time when you wanna stay back," he tells him.

Rob looks at Ben and nods to him. "Okay. I'm your eyes from behind. Be careful," Rob says.

"I'll try." Kelvin pauses. "And thanks," he finishes with a sincere look as their eyes connect.

Ben and Rob walk a couple of hundred feet. Kelvin steps over to his right and looks up at one of the containers.

"What are you doing? Do you hear something?" Ben asks him.

"No. You think if I throw this bag up there I can get it on top?"

"Yeah. It's probably only twenty pounds. And that's about twenty feet. Why you wanna do that?" Ben asks again.

"I just want them to show me Dianna first. If we can get them to let her go, it'll give you guys time to get away."

Ben puts his hand on Kelvin's shoulder and looks him in the eye. "Thanks. I understand what you are doin' here."

"Yeah," he solemnly replies knowing full well he may be exchanging his life for his sister's safety. The ancillary effect is helping Ben and his friends get away. "Nothing's ever worked out for me anyway. What's the difference?"

"Your doin' *this*"—Ben pauses—"right?"

Kelvin puts the bag with the two packages of cocaine on the left side of his body and, with two hands, swings his body to the right and flings the bag in the air. It hits off the side of the top of the container and back down. Almost there. One more time. He flings it again, and, this time, it catches the top of the container. A part of the bag is still visible. They continue further up the dock and then walk back another hundred feet where there's an opening that's at the intersection of three docks.

"Let's hang here. This looks good—looks like we may have a shot," Kelvin tells him.

After a few minutes, a cool breeze sails through the air. The ashes from the fire start to fall to the ground.

"What is this?" Ben asks.

"Ashes. There's a fire out west, in the Everglades," Kelvin informs him.

"Oh. This happens a lot?"

"Normally you hear about something every year. Not this much though. But there's been a really bad drought. Must be a worse fire than normal. Niere. South Florida snow." Kelvin pauses. "The other kind."

They both crack a smile as the ashes flow through the air like snowflakes. The air smells like a chimney.

"Yeah. A lot like snow." Ben rolls his eyes.

Headlights come up in their direction. It looks like three vehicles. Kelvin has only one thing on his mind, his sister.

57

REDEMPTION

Patterson slowly puts his cell phone back in his pocket and is then quickly startled by a figure emerging from the shadows of one of the containers. It's Stokes.

"Looks like they're here. You ready with that camera?" He looks over Patterson from behind.

Patterson never turns around to look at him and lifts up the video camera.

"More ready than you know," he says ominously, wondering about the possibility of impeding betrayal.

From behind the camera, Patterson tries to steady his shaky hand. In the viewfinder, he sees two people standing. Waiting. He figures one is Ben. The other, who's male, probably Hispanic, he's not so sure of. Three cars pull up—two Escalades and one Cadillac CTS in between the two SUVs. The doors swing open. The driver steps out of the CTS and opens the back driver's-side door. Patterson recognizes him as Malo.

—✤ ✤—

Malo walks in front of his car to approach Kelvin. "Hola, cabrón. It's so nice to see you. Wish it was under a different set of circumstances."

"Cut to it, Malo. You got my sister?"

"Wooah. What's the hurry? I have *your* sister. *I* am the one running this show. You got the goods?"

"Yes," Kelvin answers.

"I don't see them."

"I want to see my sister first. You bring her out here. I'll tell you where the bag is. Don't worry. It is here, with us," Kelvin demands.

"You wanna see your sister, huh? Okay, we'll let you see your sister." His sarcastic voice ends. He turns to his driver. "Bring her out."

The driver walks to the back door and reaches in. He pulls out Dianna, who is crying. Her mouth is covered with duct tape, and her hands are behind her back.

"You see your sister. Now where is my fucking shit?" Malo yells, changing his tone.

"It's right back here—behind the container. You can send one of your guys to grab it."

Malo nods to one of his boys from the Escalade on the left. The thug takes a step forward.

"Without the piece!" Ben says as he steps up out of the shadow.

The thug stops and looks over at Malo. Malo recognizes Ben and nods to the man to take his gun out of the side holster. It's placed it on the ground.

"So I see you have some help from your New Jersey friend. I had a friend from the Catalina tell me you might be alive, but I did not believe him." Malo turns to Ben. "You white boys all look alike."

The man makes it back with the bag. "Looks good, Malo," the thug says, handing him the bag.

Malo looks inside. "It better all be there."

"Now my sister, Malo."

"Oh, your sister, that's right." Malo turns to his driver. "Let her go." The driver lets go of his hold, and Dianna runs to her brother and embraces him. He takes off the duct tape and hugs her some more. Then he nods for her to go to Ben. She walks over.

"Anything else, Malo?"

"Sure just one thing." As he raises his hand in the night air, a gunshot from a rifle on top of the container rips through Kelvin's chest. He is blown off his feet to the ground.

"No!" his sister screams.

Ben grabs her as she lunges toward Kelvin.

"It's too late! We gotta go!" Ben yells as he starts to drag her away.

She reluctantly picks up the pace but can't keep herself from looking back at Kelvin's body. A bullet ricochets on the ground at their feet, forcing them to run even faster.

Patterson drops the camera and fires a shot toward the container where he saw the shot come from. He runs toward the scene as Malo's boys scatter back to their vehicles after hearing his gunshot and then takes cover next to a container, ready to step out of the shadows and fire into the chaos. Footsteps slowly creep up from behind him and come to a stop.

"Stokes. I'm gonna take out Malo!"

"No. You're not," Stokes commands.

Patterson turns around to look at Stokes. Stokes points his gun at Patterson's body. Patterson's jaw drops, and his eyes open wide. A gunshot rips through his stomach. His body starts to fall in slow motion. His hands and arms flail through the air. He lands on his back on the pavement, staring at the clear South Florida night. Ashes float down from the sky onto his motionless body.

Stokes walks over to his partner as he lays there paralyzed in disbelief.

"Stokes!" Patterson gasps, the pain muffling his attempt at words.

Stokes leans down to him. "Sorry, man. We had good times. You just couldn't see the big picture." He moves Patterson's hands on top of his chest to cover the bullet wound. The blood has already soaked through the shirt where there's a gaping hole.

Patterson's eyes are wide open with fear—fear of what will be next. He takes his last few breaths.

Stokes takes his fingers and shuts the fearful eyes of a dead man.

Malo walks over to Kelvin. "It's too bad you had to do this to yourself. We pulled off that thing at the airport. I was thinking about making you a wealthy man." He sarcastically adds, "And don't worry. I'll take care of your sister for you." He pats him on the chest and turns to head back to the car.

"Malo?" Kelvin gasps.

Malo turns to see Kelvin's Glock pointed toward him.

"Don't worry," Kelvin says. "I'll take care of you."

The shot explodes through Malo's torso and into the headlights of the Escalade behind him. They shatter, and the glass explodes across the lot.

Kelvin's arms falls back to the ground from the recoil. He takes one more look at Malo to his left and smiles, knowing that he saved his sister.

He turns his head back to the sky as one of Malo's boys runs out of the Escalade to check on him. He fires one last round into Kelvin, finishing the job.

At the port entry, the chief and his backup barrel through the checkpoint. The security guard was watching everything go down on the surveillance monitor.

The chief pulls in and cuts off the cars as the police lights come on. The driver of one of the Escalades steps on the gas and rams into the police car. The chief gets out and pumps the shotgun into the driver's side through the windshield. The passenger pulls out his handgun to try to shoot through his window, but the chief pumps the shotgun again. Two thugs from the other Escalade try to make a run for it.

With the chief here now, Stokes knows the role he has to play. As the thugs run down an aisle in between containers, Stokes cuts them off in front. "Police! Stop or we'll shoot!"

The men stop and put their hands up, knowing their escape attempt is futile.

The chief steps up to the CTS with the shotgun. "I wanna see your hands!"

The driver puts his hands out of the window.

Ben races with Dianna and helps her onto the boat. Rob and Ben jump on as Mike pushes the throttle. They disappear into the channel.

Stokes walks the two thugs in handcuffs over to the chief.

"What the fuck happened?" the chief yells.

"Shit went bad!" Stokes responds.

"Where's Patterson?"

"Things got crazy! I couldn't watch out for him! He's back there." He shakes his head back and forth. "He got hit. He's gone." Stokes turns away and puts his face in his hands.

The chief runs to where Stokes motioned. He sees Patterson. He grabs Patterson's phone out of his pocket and, seeing the last number that called Patterson's phone, dials it.

Ben answers. "Thought you were gonna help me out."

"Listen, this is the chief. Who is this?"

"My name is Ben Jones. Where's Patterson?"

"Patterson is dead. It seems like he was trying to help you. We got a few men in custody so far. I heard about you from him. He said that you were staying at the Catalina with your friends."

"So what?"

"Well, I'd like to meet with you, find out what happened, see if we can help you get you some justice."

"How can I trust you? My friend is dead, and I think some of your men helped set me up!"

"Listen, you can trust me. I'm the chief of police. And you might be able to help me find out who helped set you up. And who killed one of my best officers."

"Well then, you come meet us. And come alone. I'll answer anything you want. A public place," Ben tells him.

"All right, we're in. You name the place."

"Café Versailles. I'll be wearing a Yankees hat. Eleven a.m."

58

THE MEETING

The chief walks in the front door to the cafe, swinging the door open. Ben is seated at the counter, watching the front door. Mike and Rob are scattered a few seats away, keeping an eye on things.

"Ben?" says Chief Gonzales.

Ben just nods.

"Listen, Patterson was one of my most trusted men. I know this thing got crazy. But I promise; you can trust me."

"How do I know that?"

"Well, I'm here now. Investigating. I want to see an end to this. Do some justice, even though it's not enough for Patterson—for his wife and kid."

Ben senses that he can trust the man sitting across from him and that the chief is speaking from his heart. He can see it in his face. "What do you need to know?"

"Everything."

Ben begins to relay their story. Their arrival at the airport. The cab ride. The Catalina. The beach. The party at the Continuum.

Overtown. Seeing Dianna at the hotel and the house in the Keys. The death of his friend."

"I'm sorry about your friend. You're lucky you're alive. You're one brave kid. Probably saved the lives of your friends." He pauses. "Where's the house in the Keys?" the chief asks.

"Big Pine Key."

"You got a location?"

"Here's the address; you find it. We're goin' home to bury our friend."

59

NICKELS AND DIMES

Chief Gonzales is seated at his desk when his phone rings.

"We checked on the owner of the house. It's a man we tracked to Venezuela. So far we haven't been able to track him down. Probably a fake ID."

"Okay. Let me know if you find anything on him," he says, not expecting much.

"Will do," the voice on the other end tells him.

The TV in his office is on Channel 7 WVSN—the local Miami station.

"This just in. A pot bust went down in Pembroke Pines. Police found the pot, but they also found $80,000 worth of nickels buried in the ground in a garage. The FBI has been called in to investigate. No word from the Fort Lauderdale police or the FBI on whether this is related to the airport heist. We'll keep you updated."

A knock on the chief's door interrupts the breaking news. Stokes walks in. "Chief?"

"Yeah?"

"You got a second?"

"Yeah, of course. Just got a DB we gotta take care of. Already been identified. Some guy name Tre—Tre Soriano. A local guy. Not much of a rap sheet." He pauses, realizing he's rambling. "Anyway, what you got? Did you speak with Dianna Castillo yet about her brother?"

"Yeah, I broke the news to her at her mother's house. They already knew. She said her brother was caught up with this Malo motherfucker."

"Yeah, well, he's on ice now." The chief pauses.

"Here's my report on what went down." Stokes throws a folder on the chief's desk.

"Don't worry about the report. How you holdin' up?"

"I don't know."

"Why don't you take a few days off? Go down to the Keys or something."

"Maybe I will." He looks out of the window. "After Patterson's funeral."

60

THE FUNERAL

The day of the funeral is overcast. It's a long service. The boys are seated next to each other in a pew at St. Jude Catholic Church. Rob is teary eyed the entire time, thinking about how he doesn't get along with his sisters and how he rarely talks to his parents.

Every once in a while, during comments about his deceased friend, Mike shakes his head. With no siblings and just his parents, he realizes how important his friends are, especially with one less member of his family now.

Ben breaks down every few minutes, his body shaking. Ben has had a family member die. It forces him to remember and hurt even more. Another brother gone.

The boys feel the worst for Brian's younger sister. She has tears running down her face when they see her walk into church. Her parents sit together, trying to give the illusion of a functioning family. The Dead-End Boys try to console her, but words only go so far. The guilt is ripping all of the boys apart on the inside.

Ben had a talk with Brian's father at the airport immediately after they landed. Ben didn't know if Brian's dad was going to beat him up right there or break down and cry. Ben's dad saw the shape that Ben's face was in and could see what he and the other boys had been through. But when Ben told him what he'd done—how he'd been left for dead; had stolen a car and driven to the Keys looking for a needle in a haystack; and how he'd found his friends, how they'd been so close; about the crooked cops and the people they were set up by, he knew that the boys had done the best they could.

An article in the *Atlantic City Times* told some details of what happened. The article made the boys look bad, painting them out to have been partying around the wrong crowd, insinuating that they were doing drugs and that Rob may have been in an altercation over a girl at a random house in the Keys. Talk around town suggested a more sinister reason for their trip—drug running being the most common theory.

So many people from over the years—former classmates, acquaintances, old girlfriends—come to give their condolences. Some of mourners don't say anything, just sending blank stares in the boys' direction. The boys feel what these people are thinking; they can see the blame in their eyes. Here's another situation where they feel isolated by the world and have only each other to lean on. The rules and the game are against them once again.

Through the crowd appears a familiar face. Ben's eyes dart toward the figure. But even before he sees who it was, his heart starts beating faster, fluttering—a natural reaction. It's Janet, his grade-school crush.

"Hi, Ben. I'm so sorry." She leans in to hug him. "I know how close you guys have always been."

"Yeah, thanks, Janet. Thanks for coming," he says, holding back the tears.

"Of course. It's great to see you. Sorry it has to be here like this."

"I know. You look great. It's good to see you."

"Take care, Ben," she tells him, her voice full of compassion. Then she meets his eyes with a steady gaze. "Call me if you need anything or if there's anything I can do."

"I will. Thanks."

Conversations like that come and go. Nobody knows what to say. Awkward silences are followed by, "I'm so sorry," or, "Stay strong." But again, none of it matters much to Ben. He's numb.

When Ben and the others get back to Brian's mother's house, Ben tries to eat but can't put anything down. Mike eats a sandwich, but most of his time is spent on the porch. Brian's mom just sits in the kitchen in a catatonic state. The boys can't tell whether or not she blames them.

Ben says his good-byes to a few people and nods to a few others on the way out, finally making his way outside. Mike is out on the front porch smoking a cigarette. Rob is next to him, staring down the street.

"I tried to stay for as long as I could. But I got to get out of here. I can't take seeing his family like this anymore," Ben tells Rob as the tears roll down his face. "I'm outta here."

"Okay. Me and Mike were thinking about leaving soon too," Rob says.

"We'll be outta here in a minute. I'm gonna finish my cigarette," Mike tells Ben. "We'll say our good-byes and then stop by your place?"

"I'll see you there," Ben tells them.

Ben is walking across the grass in the front yard in a daze. He steps into the street and glances back to see Mike and Brian going back into the house. Turning around he sees another familiar face. It's Chief Johnson. Ben has no idea what Johnson would be doing here, but his eyes catch Ben's and he heads directly toward him. All the years between today and their previous run-in are flooding back with each step he takes toward Ben.

"Hi, Ben. You remember me?" Johnson says with a half-smile.

"Of course, Chief Johnson." Ben wipes his eyes. "What brings you here today?"

"Well, it's been a long time. And even though you know I wasn't happy with you guys back then, well, I've had some years to think the whole thing over. And looking back, I hate to say it, but I think you did the right thing. You know, you had to protect yourself. You guys were up against something you never could win." He pauses.

"I may have looked down on you boys, assumed some things about you that I shouldn't have. You didn't have your father around." He pauses again and looks off in the distance. "Well, you were smart, way ahead of your young years. It's amazing how you boys got through that one."

"Thanks, Chief."

"And I'm sorry for your loss. I know it won't bring Brian back, but it's the least I can do."

"Thank you," he replies as he looks off in the distance.

"You know, I knew your father," he says, catching Ben off guard. Ben squints, focusing his attention on the chief's eyes. "That's right. He would talk about you to his prison guard buddies—more like brag I should say. He'd talk about how much talent you had—that you were a natural, how you'd make anything look easy. I'd see him at the jail every now and again. We had a friend in common. So I started to go to your games. I watched you guys for years, followed you in the papers during high school. You were a great player. You *and* Mike. You were a great receiver. And with Mike as the quarterback, well, you guys couldn't be *stopped* from scoring. The defensive side was another issue. I even remember them using you on both sides of the field. You were tough on that defensive side of the field too, even if you were undersized. I had one cop try to tell me that your friend Mike was the better athlete. I couldn't just let him get away telling me that. That boy didn't have the guts you had, the determination. And he would've never played on the defensive side. Probably be worried about messing up his hair. That was *your* team. They've never been the same without you two."

"Thanks, Chief," Ben says, almost cracking a smile while reminiscing.

"Anyway, I'll be retiring soon. Can't believe how fast it all went," Johnson says, reminiscing himself for a second as Ben nods in agreement.

"Well, good luck," the chief finishes.

"Yeah, you too."

Ben makes his way down the street with his head down, thinking about how many times in his life he made this walk through the lonely neighborhood streets. The ones where he and his friends, especially Brian now that he's gone, used to run around on in his youth. The same streets where their future that was laid out on the road ahead is now occupied with one less rider—a street where Ben can see less of the future up ahead but also now some of the tire tracks and wreckage left behind.

His neighbors are getting older, along with the homes they dwell in. The homes and the lives of the inhabitants inside of them no longer have the promise they used to have during his childhood. Now, that promise is fading like the paint, along with time.

The neighborhood seems different now. Not as many kids are running around. Some people try to maintain their dwellings, as if they're trying to hold on to or reclaim the past, while others let them slowly decay.

Some people have moved out of town, never to be seen again; others, like Brian, have left this world. Divorces, separations, the growing up of children, and their natural progression of moving out of their homes have changed the neighborhood landscape forever. The cycle of life spins round and round.

Tens of cars that carried people paying their respect are parked along the curbs on each side of the street leading around the corner to his street. Ben's head is down when he notices a man standing against a car smoking a cigarette. Ben doesn't recognize him but stops immediately when he sees the man's head lift; as the brim of his hat tilts upward, his face becomes clearer.

"Hey, kid."

Ben's mouth drops, and his eyes widen.

"I was just thinkin' about the last time you and me met on this street," the man relays.

"What are you doing here?" Ben manages to expel, feeling like his ten-year-old self.

Slim Jimmy lifts up the newspaper, revealing some sun spots covering his hand. Some wispy gray hairs blend in with the dark ones—some salt with his pepper. "We read this story yesterday. Figured I'd drop by and visit." He motions into the car where the driver sits, waiting. It's the other man Ben met with Slim Jimmy when he was a child. The man has a few more pounds on him than Ben remembers from their previous experience. His hairline has receded to the point of almost nonexistence.

"Yeah? We read a story about you too," Ben manages to answer.

"Yeah, well, I don't have to tell you not to believe everything you read in the papers. Do I, kid?"

"No." Ben shakes his head.

"So, is it true that these cops saved the day for you and your friends down there?"

"Don't believe everything you read in the papers."

Jimmy lets out a light chuckle. "I know a crooked story about crooked cops when I read one. I can smell it a mile away. You always were a smart kid—smart enough to keep your friends in line. And not to listen to that chief in there." Jimmy pauses. "I know what you think of me, who I am, what I do. But I was pulling for you back then. I knew you wouldn't rat. And I'm pulling for you today." He takes another drag on the cigarette. "I hope you know I threatened you and your mom for your own good."

"I understand."

"So how close *was* I to you that day?" Jimmy asks him.

"Let's put it this way. I know that you smoke Marlboro's. It almost landed on me."

Jimmy shakes his head and smiles while looking into the distance. "So anyway, I'm going away for a while. Maybe for good. You won't have to worry about running into me ever again—you or the Dead-End Boys." He winks.

"Some people walk in between the raindrops."

"Some do. Probably like some of those guys you ran into down there in Florida. Probably a couple of those cops too. Definitely not for boys like you from Absecon—not here on Mockingbird Lane. Most people have those raindrops fall square on their head. I wasn't put on this earth to be one of 'em." Jimmy pauses. "By the way, your mom won't be getting any cash in the mail around Christmas time anymore," he says to Ben.

"That was you all those years?" Ben asks him, and Jimmy nods.

When Ben got older, his mom had told him about this annual ritual. She'd never known who sent the money. Ben had always wanted to believe it was his father.

"Why did you do it, Jimmy?"

"Well I knew your dad wasn't around much. When you helped *us* out by not squealing, well, I thought I owed it to you, kid."

"All the dead ends in all the towns in all the world, and we were born in this one," Ben says out loud.

"Bogart, one of my favorites," Jimmy tells him.

Jimmy takes another drag, finishes his cigarette, and flicks it.

"Take care, kid."

"Good luck, Jimmy," Ben says to him as he gets in the car.

The driver salutes as he drives by. Ben hears the horn honk as the car turns the corner.

Mike and Rob are making their way back and turn to look at the car.

"Who was that?" Mike asks.

"Yeah. They waved like we were supposed to know them. I didn't recognize 'em," Rob follows up.

"It was an old friend. Come on. We'll sit down and have a talk."

Ben's mother comes to the door. "Ben, honey, why don't you boys come inside now? It's been a long day."

"Be right in. Give us a minute."

She closes the door.

"That was Jimmy." He tells them everything, relaying every detail of his final encounter with the gangster, even the last detail about the money.

"It's the only reason I had anything on those Christmases," he manages to let out before the tears well up in his eyes.

"We know," Rob says to him as he and Mike move closer to Ben on both sides.

"But there's another thing," Mike says, looking into his friend's eyes. "You still got us, and that ain't ever gonna change. We Dead-End Boys stick together—something those other people don't do. We stay together to the very end."

Rob starts to sob as they hug each other on the doorstep.

Ben looks down the street and sees two children playing baseball at the dead end, the same spot where he and Brian used to play.

A month later, an anonymous cash donation is made to the elementary school for $25,000 with one request—that the library will be called The Brian Robertson Library with a plaque that reads, "Shall we all walk between the raindrops."